# TOKYO SWINDLERS

# TOKYO SWINDLERS

## Ko Shinjo

Translated by Charles De Wolf

SHUEISHA

MD-*i*
Media Do International

*Distributed by*
Stone Bridge Press
P. O. Box 8208, Berkeley, CA 94707
sbp@stonebridge.com • www.stonebridge.com

Front-cover illustration and design by Keisuke Unosawa.

Netflix burst ©2024 Netflix. Used by permission.

p-ISBN 978-1-61172-084-6
e-ISBN 978-1-61172-968-9

Shueisha Inc.:
Shin'ichi Hirono, President & CEO
Naoya Higuchi, Publisher at Shueisha, Managing Director
Hiroshi Takahashi, Editor in Chief of MONTHLY NOVEL MAGAZINE "SHOSETSU-SUBARU"
Yuki Kishi, Editor of MONTHLY NOVEL MAGAZINE "SHOSETSU -SUBARU"
Keiichi Higashimoto, Editor of Shueisha Bunko
Kiyoto Tamura, Supervision

Media Do International, Inc.:
Daihei Shiohama, President and CEO
Beth Kawasaki, Executive Director, Content and Marketing

SHUEISHA

MD-*i*
Media Do International

# TOKYO
# SWINDLERS

Land and money are key to the art of the Tokyo swindler:

1 tsubo = 4 square yards

> 10,000 yen = $89*
> 1 million yen = $8,900
> 1 billion yen = $8,900,000

Gangsters have been known to cut off the tip of a finger to show contrition after an offense to the boss.

*In 2017, the year this story takes place, the conversion rate was US$1 = 112 yen.

# 1 ▬▬▬▬▬▬▬▬▬

"So what's your zodiac year?"

Gotō abruptly posed the question to Sasaki, who was sitting next to him.

"Eh?" Sasaki's face tensed up, his voice betraying confusion.

Takumi put his glass of iced tea back on the table.

"No no no!" exclaimed Gotō. "You've got to get yer act together now! Come on, we're about to go live! You've already had plenty of practice, so it's gotta be all there in yer head! Come on, man!"

Gotō sighed with exasperation and sat back down, his fat belly shaking, the blubber hanging over his belt.

In this coffee shop not far from the station, a woman in her late thirties, perhaps the same age as Takumi, sat with an open laptop, apparently about to set out for work; a middle-aged man in a rumpled suit was leisurely puffing on a cigarette, seemingly quite lost in thought. The seats were generously set apart, and perhaps because of the low background noise, no one was paying attention to the table facing the window.

Takumi put the straw of his iced tea into his mouth and looked inquiringly at Gotō. The sparse remains of his hair pomaded back, Gotō was dressed in a well-tailored suit, giving the initial impression that here in the café was a gentleman rather than a businessman. Yet now he was glowering at Sasaki.

"Sasaki-san … " Takumi tried to dispel the tension. "Look. When you meet the targets, you won't know just when you'll find questions flying at you or how they'll be paced. Get yourself mentally prepared to answer them. No need to get uptight. Just relax. Be totally natural. Above all, don't make anyone think you're trying too hard."

Responding to Takumi's calm and quiet tone, Sasaki gave a slight nod and looked at him imploringly.

"We need to have 'im recite it all over again from the start," Gotō muttered fretfully from the side. "This's got me rattled."

They had met Sasaki for the first time that day. All they had been told was that Harrison Yamanaka had been persuaded by the man's performance, that it was good enough, that it would pass muster when the time came.

"So then, what's your name?"

"Shi … Shimazaki Ken'ichi," Sasaki said slowly, bullied for a reply as Gotō nudged himself forward. Takumi continued to drink his tea, the ice now melted, as he listened to their exchange.

"Date of birth … "

"The 17th day of … February … in the 15th year of Shōwa."

Sasaki's eyes twitched nervously from side to side. The mustache he had grown for the occasion moved like a caterpillar as he spoke, glistening white in the July morning sunlight streaming in through the window.

"And what's the date according to the Western calendar?"

"Uh, that's February 17, 1940. The Year of the Dragon. I was born in Nagaoka, Niigata Prefecture … "

Gotō barked at him. "No, no no … Do not go beyond what you've been asked about. Once you start saying stuff you don't have to say, you'll be givin' it all away in an instant!"

Sasaki murmured an apology and stared down at the table.

Takumi promptly assumed a gentle expression and spoke

soothingly: "You need only give short replies to questions. If there's something you can't remember or a matter you don't know about, just say something vague and beat around the bush. We can always back you up."

"Yeah, well that back-you-up's got its limits," grumbled Gotō, his lips pouting. His concern was not unreasonable. One wrong utterance from Sasaki would bring the entire endeavor crashing down, including everything Takumi and his team had put together, the remaining 600 million yen snatched away as well.

As if to relieve his stress, Sasaki drank a glass of water and then resumed, reeling off a multitude of details, beginning with his name, date of birth, zodiac year, family makeup, the names and ages of his family members, the neighborhood setting, the name of the nearest supermarket, a description of the property and its exterior, and his reason for putting it up for sale. He appeared to have memorized the information quite flawlessly, despite being sometimes stymied for words.

The owner of the targeted property was a seventy-eight-year-old male named Shimazaki Ken'ichi, who since the death of his wife several years before had been living alone. The previous summer, he had settled into a senior citizens' residence.

Harrison Yamanaka and his staff had reportedly interviewed more candidates than usual in their search for the one to impersonate Shimazaki. Some were better actors than Sasaki, and some may have borne a closer resemblance to Shimazaki in height and overall appearance. There had been differences in opinion regarding the final selection, but Yamanaka's decision to hire Sasaki, with his superior memory, turned out to be the right one after all.

"So, Takumi-kun, are you sure about the paperwork?"

"Yes, I've gone over it again and again."

Three days earlier, after a final meeting of the team, including

Gotō, Takumi and Yamanaka had taken time to check the documents and certificates for errors and omissions.

"Here, could you take a look?"

As Takumi was removing some files from a brown leather Dulles bag at his feet, Gotō took out a small bottle of clear, quick-drying nail polish and placed it on the table.

"If you haven't already put some on, use this."

A close observer would have seen a faint sheen on Gotō's thick fingers. The varnish had dried completely, hardening and sticking to his skin as tenaciously as an insect shell.

"Thank you," came Takumi's polite reply, "but I've already done mine." He casually rubbed his thumb against his four fingers, conveying an ever so slight sense of the fakery involved.

There was a substance provided by a specialized supplier in the United States, an ultra-thin artificial film, applied to the ventral and dorsal sides of the fingers and palms and used by foreign intelligence agencies, the surface being textured with the contours of imaginary fingerprints and palm prints and coated with an oil containing the same sebum components as human skin. It could not be peeled off without using special chemicals and was durable enough to withstand hot water and minimal force.

Concealing fingerprints that could serve as physical evidence was indispensable for this line of work. Nevertheless, the use of nail polish had turned up with such frequency in fraud cases that the police detectives in the Second Division had recently come to suspect that when documents were quite devoid of prints, land swindlers were likely involved. Gotō's method was thus already outdated.

"Uh …"

As Takumi started to hand over the documents to Gotō, Sasaki spoke from across the table.

"What's the matter?" asked Takumi, turning to him.

"Shouldn't I be using this myself?" Sasaki asked, his gaze on the small bottle on the table.

"Hey no, you don't need it," barked Gotō, grimacing and waving his hand as though swatting away some winged bug. He went on in the tone of a parent scolding a child:

"Listen, you're elderly, so just sit there off to the side and, easy does it, answer a few questions, one by one. That's all you gotta worry about. Never mind the rest. That's our business. Once it's all over, you can just take yer share and head off to go soak in some hot spring."

Takumi, unlike Gotō, considered offering to give Sasaki the nail-polish treatment but quickly thought better of the idea. Sasaki was, as it were, the scapegoat, the nominal mastermind of the operation. He was the one most likely to take the fall for it. The severity of the crime and the nature of the case meant that his chances of evading the authorities' reach by fudging his fingerprints were virtually nil, the very idea providing no more than a false sense of security.

Takumi gave Sasaki a sidelong glance. Here was a man who was ever expressing his gratitude to Gotō and nodding assent to whatever he said; yet in his face were clear traces of long accumulated hardships, along with a faint hint of resignation and an acceptance of his fate. Now in his late seventies, he was working to pay off his debts, employed during the day as a part-time custodian in an underground parking garage in Tokyo and at night as a highway flagman, waving a red traffic wand. He had apparently once enjoyed a somewhat glamorous life, working his way up from waiter to manager in a high-class club in Nagoya. But it all slipped away when he tried to skim the establishment's profits, and now he was but a shadow of what he once had been.

"So you got some sort of hunch as to what you'll be doing when all this is over?" Gotō asked.

"Well, I've a friend of sorts way south in Nagasaki," replied Sasaki, his face downturned, "so I was thinking of staying with him for a while."

Sasaki was to receive exactly 3 million yen for playing the lead role in the operation and no more. Though not an insubstantial sum, it fell far short of what he needed to pay off his debts and likewise would not quite come up to the cost of fleeing Japan for Southeast Asia or elsewhere. Quietly going undercover in a provincial city here at home appeared to be the most realistic option.

Gotō rolled back his suit sleeve and glanced at the face of his Lange & Söhne watch, with its guilloche dial. The appointed time was approaching. He removed some documents from the files he had been handed by Takumi and began going over them one by one. Gotō had once been a respectable judicial scrivener—a kind of document preparation specialist—and even now had a most discerning eye. Seal registration certificate, certificate of registered matters, fixed asset valuation certificate, fixed asset tax assessment statement, driver's license, personal seal, property keys … Except for but a small portion of the materials, everything here was a forgery, prepared by a most meticulous craftsman.

"Make sure to hold on to the ID!" said Gotō, as he handed the personal seal and the driver's license to Sasaki. "You might be asked for it, so show 'em this. It'll seem more natural if you just keep it in yer wallet."

Sasaki stared with interest at Shimazaki Ken'ichi's driver's license, on which a photograph of his own face appeared, then tucked it away in his faded and frayed leather wallet. Along with the personal seal, he placed it in the inner pocket of the new flannel jacket Takumi had readied for him. Though he seemed somewhat unaccustomed to such attire, it allowed him to appear for the moment as a man of means.

"So, Takumi-kun, have you heard anything from the other party since?" asked Gotō, as he handed the document files back.

"No, nothing in particular. I was, I must say, a bit irritated at being pressured to wrap things up."

"And we're all right with the location?"

Takumi nodded, as he put the files back into his Dulles bag. The venues for such land transactions were most often bank reception rooms or conference rooms; if not, real estate agency offices were common. For this deal, however, Takumi and the others, being the supposed sellers, had designated a law firm in a quasi-third-party position. In addition to escaping direct confrontation with banks, which tended to evaluate people based on their professions, there was also the desire to avoid leaving any record on the security cameras inside.

"This one looks like it'll be a push-over."

Putting on a show of mock surprise, Gotō appeared pleased, the corners of his eyes crinkling with merriment.

Scrutinizing the many dark crannies in Gotō's expression brought to Takumi's mind old memories, and grim emotions steadily arose within him. He had the visceral sensation of a cracking sound, as though his heavily fortified and hardened heart had just burst open. Even as he became aware that he was involuntarily grinding his back teeth, his face began spontaneously to twitch, from his right cheek to the far corner of his eye.

"What's wrong?" asked Gotō, giving him a puzzled look.

"Nothing," came the reply.

Though the spasms continued, Takumi forced himself to smile, sipping water from his glass until they gradually subsided.

Sitting across from him, Sasaki was gazing out of the window with an unsettled expression.

"So now," Gotō continued, "how long you been hangin' out with Harrison?"

"About four years I'd say."

How many jobs had Takumi done with him? When the minor assignments were added in, they came to a substantial number.

"Really? So short a time? I've been at it much longer. With all yer gray hair, I would've thought you to be much more of a veteran, yer connection goin' way back."

Gotō sighed in apparent disappointment.

"So hey, how old are you anyway?"

Takumi's reply—he would be turning thirty-seven—had Gotō gaping in disbelief.

This was the second time the two men had worked together. Takumi had previously known next to nothing about the relationship between Gotō and Yamanaka.

"Not to stick my nose into it, but if you go on lettin' Harrison carry you 'round on his back, he's bound to toss you over. Don't be a sucker. Look out for Number One!"

"Thank you. I'll do just that."

Apparently displeased with Takumi's deft deflection of his preachy advice, Gotō abruptly gave him a sterner look.

"You know about that guy ... He was originally ... " Gotō started to elaborate but then fell silent.

A waiter appeared for water refills. Takumi, waving him off, looked down at the dial of his Garmin smart watch. His heart rate, according to the corner display, was normal, at 70. The digital hand said it was almost 9:20. The lawyer's office was just a short walk from the nearby subway station. It would be prudent to give themselves more than enough time to get there.

"OK, shall we be going then?" said Gotō, as he picked up the check and wiggled his hips to get free from the table.

. . .

As they were ushered into the reception room of the lawyers' office, representatives from Mike Home, the real estate agency, were already waiting. In addition to the president, who had met Takumi several times for preliminary negotiations and for concluding the sales contract, there were two of his subordinates, both wearing the same platinum company breast insignia, and a young man Takumi did not recognize, most likely the company's judicial scrivener.

After placing their bags on the seats before them, they immediately went about the ritual of exchanging business cards. Takumi was presenting himself with the name he was using for the project: "Inoue Hideo," of the real estate consulting agency "Sparkling Planning."

He went around the table with Gotō as they offered their formal greetings, which, in keeping with custom, meant few words exchanged, since they were now on the verge of a settlement, the climax of all real estate transactions, simultaneously involving both the payment of the balance and the transfer of ownership. In the room was a strange air of tension. The only voice that could be heard clearly was Gotō's, booming away in its relentless informality.

The business-card exchange was soon concluded, and now the full lineup of eight faces was apparent. On the buyer's side were the three representatives of Mike Home, along with the judicial scrivener they had engaged. On the seller's side were Takumi, ostensibly in charge of the transaction and acting as the seller's agent; Gotō, acting as the broker; and Sasaki, acting as the seller. At the end of the meeting table sat the witness, a lawyer in his early forties who customarily rented out space here in the Sakai Sōgō Law Office.

Takumi lightly nodded his head to break the ice, looked

around at each of the people from Mike Home lined up across the table, and began to speak.

"Thank you very much for taking the time for this meeting and for endeavoring so tirelessly to achieve our goal. Much has been demanded of you, but I am now ever so pleased that we have reached this day without mishap."

"The pleasure is all ours," replied the president, nodding his head in return. "Allow me to express our deep gratitude for making it possible for us to acquire this valuable property."

The president was a handsome man, and although already in his mid-forties, looked quite young for his age. In sharp contrast to his courteous tone was the rude look that he gave to Sasaki, seated with bowed head to Takumi's left.

This was the first time the Mike Home side had met him. Since the beginning of the negotiations, the president had more than once asked Takumi to arrange a meeting with the owner of the property. Of course, the more often he met the faux Shimazaki, the greater the likelihood that Sasaki would be exposed as an imposter. So Takumi had each time rebuffed the request, resorting to such excuses as "Shimazaki's" poor health or his difficult personality.

In real estate transactions, where large sums of money are exchanged, it is standard practice for buyers not only to verify all the relevant documents but also painstakingly to confirm— through personal encounter and a visit to the site—that the property in fact belongs to the alleged owner. The undisguised antipathy on the part of the real estate agency toward Sasaki, absent until today from every meeting, might thus be seen as only natural.

"As time is limited, may I suggest that we begin?" came Takumi's cheerful urging, with Gotō, sitting to his right, following suit:

"Right you are! I gotta say it's a strictly personal matter, but the fact is I gotta be goin' back to Osaka this afternoon."

Gotō gave a broad, self-deprecating smile, clearly intended to soothe his listeners. Their response was muted, and their hardened facial expressions remained unchanged. Takumi removed the documents from his Dulles bag and laid them out on the table, the judicial scrivener sitting across from him following his lead, with both sides confirming the documents necessary for settlement.

The property in question was a plot of land in southwest central Tokyo located near Ebisu Station. Its area was a little less than a tenth of an acre. The sale price of some 700 million yen had already been agreed upon with Mike Home. The price per tsubo was just under 7 million yen, quite a bargain when one considered the per-tsubo market price in the area was over 10 million yen.

The Shimazaki house was a two-story vacant building constructed more than fifty years before. The trees and plants in the garden were unkempt and overgrown. Despite its universally desirable prime location in the heart of the capital, there had been no complicated circumstances regarding rights, as the antiquated edifice, unmortgaged, had been inhabited by a lone elderly person. The owner's unwillingness to sell the land notwithstanding, the property was constantly on the radar of real estate agents specializing in this part of the city.

The news that Shimazaki Ken'ichi had moved into a senior citizens' home had not reached Takumi and his fellow swindlers until the end of the previous year, some six months later. Immediately they began scurrying about, making meticulous preparations and disseminating bogus information in every direction. Two months thereafter, they received word through a real estate broker that Mike Home was interested in buying the property.

Posing now as the seller's agent, Takumi had launched

negotiations, urging Mike Home to make the purchase, pointing to the substantial discount and hinting that there were many other potential buyers. Using a surreptitiously made duplicate key to show the property for inspection, Takumi was quickly able to conclude a sales contract and move toward settling the account that very day.

The judicial scrivener, who appeared to be the most steadfast of sorts, was going through the documents in the order he had received them from Takumi. Crossing his fingers in an attempt to maintain his composure, Takumi kept his eyes both on Gotō, who was examining and apparently assessing, one by one, the business cards they had received, and on Sasaki, who was sitting stiffly, looking nervously at those on the other side of the table. Before he knew it, Takumi began to sweat, as he again became acutely aware of the artificial film on his fingertips.

"Ah, you look so wonderfully young." Gotō suddenly turned to the judicial scrivener, who, at being so abruptly addressed, was now noticeably flustered. He wore rimless glasses and appeared to be in his early thirties.

"So how long you been registered?"

The judicial scrivener winced at Gotō's intrusive question. A little over five years came the reply.

"Then that'll mean you've taken the training renewal session only once. Professional ethics're important. Can you really handle such an important job now? I don't know, and you've got me a bit worried."

The room fell into an uneasy silence.

The younger man modestly bowed his head at Gotō's outburst, his face stiffening and showing dismay at what could only be a false accusation. Inspecting all of the documents by hand was an irksome chore. Did it seem he was going through the motions just to please Mike Home? With all eyes directed toward him, he nonetheless carried on. When he appeared to return to a document he had already checked, as though with a question about it, Gotō, who had been fretfully observing him, spoke up:

"Can't you hurry it up now!! We've not got the time for this! My train's not about to wait you know ... "

There was undisguised harshness in his voice.

"We're sorry," added Takumi politely, "but Shimazaki-san will be undergoing a routine health check in his nursing home this afternoon. So please ... "

The president, who himself had been watching the judicial scrivener with an air of impatience, nodded in acknowledgment. Takumi looked at him and remembered the president's pleading words at the very first meeting with the Mike Home staff:

"By all means allow us to make the purchase!"

The real estate company's major focus was on the development and sale of studio apartments intended for investment; launched seven years before, it had grown rapidly and now had more than sixty employees. Originally a real estate brokerage, it had evolved into a sales agency and exclusive wholesaler. This was the first time it was to develop its own properties.

The goal was to be listed on the first section of the Tokyo Stock Exchange, and undertaking in-house development was a stepping stone in that direction. With that in mind, Mike Home had for some time been looking in Tokyo for a suitable condominium site but had been unable to find one in the heart of the city, where competition was fierce and where there was already a surfeit of development. So when news got out that Shimazaki Ken'ichi's prime site in Ebisu was for sale, it was no wonder that Mike Home would be most eager to pursue the deal.

If, for example, one were to construct a condominium on the site—based on an 80% building-to-land ratio, a 400% floor-area ratio, a 45-foot frontage road, and a maximum-permitted

130-foot height—one would likely end up with 300-square-foot studios for single persons as well as some thirty larger units for families, all conforming to local ward regulations, even including the common areas. Here where the market rental price was over 20,000 yen per tsubo, an annual rental income of over 90 million yen could be expected when the property was fully occupied, and, after deducting expenses, the annual rental income would settle in at around 80 million yen. Assuming a yield of 3.5%, the condominium's appraised value would thus be more than 2 billion yen.

The president might well have been painfully aware of an either-or: all the various benefits that a signing of the contract would bring on the one hand vs., on the other, the losses the company would incur if the effort were to fail. The lack of any apparent sign of caution on his part concerning the confirmation of the documents' authenticity strongly suggested a desire to avoid upsetting the would-be seller in any way that might cause him to cancel the transaction.

The judicial scrivener, a thin and awkward smile on his face, turned to Sasaki:

"Well now, Shimazaki-san, please show us your photo ID so that we may verify who you are.

Sasaki, who had not said a word since entering the room, gave a slight, nervous nod. He reached for his wallet in the inside pocket of his jacket and took out the driver's license he had tucked within it, showing it to the scrivener.

"May I examine it myself?"

Taking "Shimazaki Ken'ichi's" license in hand, the scrivener checked its shape and appearance, ran his eyes over the name and address notations, and compared Sasaki's face with the photograph.

"Just to be quite thorough, allow me to pose a few simple questions."

Sasaki responded once more with a nod.

"Are you then indeed Shimazaki Ken'ichi? No mistake?"

"No mistake."

Sasaki's expression showed no sign of agitation. That he seemed to find it ever so slightly difficult to respond lent an air of authenticity to his performance.

"May I ask you to provide your date of birth?"

"The 17th of February in the 15th year of Shōwa."

Sasaki's reply did not falter. It was just as if he were replaying the exchange in the coffee shop. Takumi calmly listened.

"And your zodiac year ... " he continued in an indifferent tone, looking at the driver's license and a memo on the table.

"Uh, I was born on February 17, 1940, in the Year of the Dragon."

Sasaki answered with his eyes closed, as if trying to jog his memory. He had been so preoccupied with what he had memorized that he now provided superfluous information. Takumi felt himself grimacing at the false note.

"Which of these photos," asked the scrivener, now placing two sheets of photocopy paper on the table, "is of your house?"

On one was a color image of Shimazaki Ken'ichi's abode that appeared to have been taken from the front. The stone wall, long exposed to the elements, had turned black and was covered with moss. Beyond stood a house with a tiled roof, the sort of edifice now rarely seen in such a neighborhood. The other photo was of a house that appeared to have deteriorated over the same period of time. At first glance, the two houses seemed much alike, but they differed in the color of the tiles, the arrangement of the windows, and the construction of the walls.

Sasaki stared at the copy paper, his mouth closed, his Adam's apple moving wildly up and down.

It was an ingenious stratagem, not at all anticipated. Takumi had given Sasaki a glimpse of the Shimazaki residence by means of a photo, but he had not made him memorize the structural details. Perhaps Sasaki had forgotten, or perhaps he could not form a judgment based on these images alone.

Just as Takumi started to step to offer assistance, Sasaki, as though trying to make a lucky guess, pointed to the image of Shimazaki's house. The scrivener nodded, and just as he was about to pose yet another question, Gotō intervened in a voice that all could hear:

"Are ya still goin' on with it? The lawyer's already certified that Shimazaki-san's the genuine owner of the place. Is it right then for some scrivener who knows nothing about the case to go about doubtin' his judgment and that of a big-shot notary public?"

This he said as he glanced at the lawyer.

Before approaching Mike Home, Takumi and his team had singled out the attorney and sent Sasaki by himself to pose as Shimazaki Ken'ichi. Claiming that he had lost his title deed, he had requested a document that would serve in its place, one whose "personal identification information" would allow the sale to go forward. The lawyer had thus been brought in as a bona fide third party; at the same time, he would lend further authenticity to the project by using a venerable law firm, availing himself of the room he had been renting there.

The lawyer had at first been reluctant to prepare the document, perhaps because he feared undesirable contingencies or simply because he was suspicious. Even so, obliged by circumstances to be renting space in someone else's office, he had clearly not been bringing in much work. In the end, for a fee far beyond the going rate, he had accepted the case, together with the Kyoto-style practice of joint registration, and through a few questions and answers, such as date of birth, zodiac sign, and a forged driver's license, he had identified Sasaki as Shimazaki Ken'ichi.

Now suddenly under everyone's gaze, the lawyer was looking

down at his notebook, a hint of complacency in his expression, quite unaware, it seemed, that Takumi and his fellows had quite taken him in.

Gotō's words and support from the lawyer seemed to have had their effect. In any case, the matter of identification had been conveniently papered over.

"Well then," the scrivener began, addressing Sasaki. "Do you now intend to sell your house to the real estate company, Mike Home?" He presented a sheet of paper on which was printed an image of Shimazaki Ken'ichi's house. As everyone looked on, Sasaki, as though still in rehearsal, responded:

"Yes."

Following the scrivener's instructions, the president representing the buyer and Sasaki, the seller, signed and sealed the registration documents one by one.

"Please also put your personal seal here and here."

Though still looking ill at ease, Sasaki showed no hesitation as he filled out the signature with the familiar characters he had practiced writing so many times that it all seemed to him second nature. His action of stamping the official seal in accordance with instructions was likewise flawless.

The ambience in the room was subdued, the turning of pages and the scratching of pens the only sounds. Takumi observed Sasaki with a sense of relief. Seated beside him, Gotō looked on in silence, having ceased goading the scrivener, who, having examined the documents with their signatures and seals, looked around at the attendees and announced:

"All of the documents for registration are in order. You may proceed with the settlement."

Takumi, who had unknowingly been holding his breath, slowly exhaled through his nose. At this point, all that was left to be done was to transfer the remaining funds.

As per the contract, this was a bilateral transaction between the buyer and seller, the balance of nearly 600 million yen, the deposit and the interim payment having been deducted, was to be transferred from Mike Home's account to Shimazaki Ken'ichi. Of course, the money would not be transferred to the account of the real Shimazaki Ken'ichi, who was utterly unaware that his house was being sold. Through various tricks, including the forging of a driver's license, Takumi and his team had set up a fictitious bank account, with different Chinese characters representing Shimazaki's name. The down payment and interim payment had already been transferred to that account, all without arousing the slightest suspicion at Mike Home.

On hearing the scrivener's pronouncement, the president instructed a male subordinate to make the final payment. The employee then and there made a call to a colleague standing by at the bank, instructing him to execute the transfer. Voices were now subdued, before fading altogether, as a leaden atmosphere descended upon the silent room.

To Takumi, it seemed that considerable time had elapsed, but as he glanced at his Garmin, he realized that only three minutes had passed. His heart rate had jumped, exceeding 90. As he sorted the documents on the table, he was acutely aware of the sluggishness of the clock.

Once the remaining sum had been transferred to the fictitious account and confirmation of receipt had been obtained, notification was to come from Harrison Yamanaka, acting as Takumi's subordinate. After that almost everything would be settled. Normally, the process would be completed in less than an hour, but if the bank was hard-pressed with other business, it might take a bit longer.

For both the deceiver and the deceived, facing each other in a closed room with no verbal exchange and nothing to do but wait, the tedium was indeed odious. Gotō, too, seemed uncharacteristically tense. Perhaps tantalized by the endeavor's imminent success, he was staring down silently at his phone there on the table.

Now the president casually turned his smile toward Sasaki and spoke to him:

"Thank you for going to all of the trouble of coming here today. Might I ask: What is it like living in the senior citizens' home?"

Even though confirmation of the money transfer had not yet arrived, the president appeared to be in good spirits, no doubt because he had just concluded a transaction that was vital for the company. Excitement had spread across his face as though it were forcibly masking over some underlying anxiety.

In the case of individual sellers, it was sometimes the case that circumstances beyond their control had compelled the sale. Especially when it came to a rare property like this one, buyers might often resort to restricting their conversation to seasonal greetings, so as to ensure that sellers would not be upset over some trivial faux pas and back off. Thus, all unnecessary words were avoided. So for Takumi and his cohorts it was quite unexpected that the president of Mike Home should so actively engage with Sasaki.

"Yes, well, uh … hmm …"

Sasaki, who had seemed to have greatly relaxed upon completion of his task, was now thrown into confusion by this sudden question. Regarding the nursing home where Shimazaki Ken'ichi was then residing, Sasaki had been given only minimal information, such as its name and location and the fact that a considerable sum, exceeding 100 million yen, was required as a one-time residence fee. Were he to be asked about anything more, he would have no answer, and if he responded carelessly, they might all wind up unmasked.

"Ah, now let me tell ya, sir. That place where Shimazaki-san is stayin' is top-notch, far more comfortable than any second-rate hotel!"

Gotō, who had been concentrating on his phone, took over the response in his usual forceful manner. Even in his casual and borderline saucy tone, there was a hint of impatience.

"Yes, indeed. When it comes to luxury, it's one of the best in Tokyo. It's often featured in the media. Why, they even have a sushi restaurant."

"Yeah, right ya are. Sushi …"

Gotō, who strongly disliked fish, was flailing about on behalf of Sasaki. Neither he nor Takumi was at all knowledgeable about the nursing home.

Sensing the urgency of the situation, Takumi surreptitiously fiddled with his phone under the table, and now there came next to him a ringing. Sasaki, as they had practiced, reached in response for his own phone and pretended to speak to a non-existent caller.

"It's from the home," he said, covering the receiver with his hand, looking as if there were something of great importance to discuss. This had been a stratagem they had already mapped out for when they were in danger of raising the other party's suspicions. This time it had worked better than in their repeated coffee-shop rehearsals.

"Let's step out for a moment."

Takumi spoke so that everyone would hear and walked out of the room with Sasaki.

As he stood outside the lawyer's office, calming Sasaki, Takumi took his phone from out of an inner pocket and sent a message to Gotō, telling him to change the topic away from the nursing home. When some five minutes later he and Sasaki returned, the meeting room was filled with lively laughter. Gotō had done exactly as Takumi had suggested: He was concocting a mock comparative cultural theory, all about the differences in broth between western and eastern Japan, as observed in the stand-up noodle shops in the railway stations. By exaggerating the contrasts, he had everyone guffawing. The crisis now past, Takumi sat calmly listening to Gotō's eloquent yarn.

"I remember now!"

This was the abrupt voice of the young woman on the Mike Home team, an apparent novice employee who had until now said not a word. Interrupting Gotō, she turned to Sasaki. Her eyes, rimmed with false lashes, were open wide with delight as she clasped her hands in front of her prominent breasts, which the men did not fail to notice, even through her suit. She was exclaiming, as though having just had a sudden revelation:

"Isn't that the nursing home where Izumi Sushi's second-best chef goes to do his thing? That's right. I'm sure of it. I've been going to Izumi Sushi forever. My parents are huge fans of the guy."

The woman, who obviously felt a strong connection to the sushi restaurant, was laughing and chattering on uncontrollably, oblivious to the subtle admonition of the president, who was sitting with a forced smile on his face.

Gotō had broken out in a greasy sweat, his efforts to deflect the conversation only serving to encourage her.

"The sushi there is really, really good," she went on. "And the tumblers they use are so cool, all made of Edo-style faceted glass. Are you a frequent customer too?"

Again to Gotō's chagrin, she had turned to Sasaki. Confusion was apparent on his face; he could reply only in a mumbled whisper.

"Ah, mmm, well ... "

"I really envy you being able to enjoy such delicious sushi at your home every week. The owner's is really, really good all right, but I'm also totally wild about what this other chef produces. The red vinegar with that indescribable airiness is fantastic. I think he comes in once a week. What day is it then?"

His head drooping, Sasaki stared at her without a word, as though in a daze, as she peppered him with questions for which he lacked even fake answers. Looking on, frozen to his seat, Gotō also seemed to be at a loss for words.

Takumi felt his head suddenly burning. He wanted to gesture to call for another meeting outside, but somehow his body would not move. As desperate as he was to save the situation, he found himself tight-lipped, with only a smoldering impatience growing within him. The members of the Mike Home staff had all begun to look doubtful when he abruptly exclaimed:

"Wasn't it Tuesday? Or Wednesday?"

He folded his arms and looked thoughtfully but fretfully at the ceiling. Seeing that he had everyone's attention, he smiled awkwardly and then, as though coming up with an excuse, exclaimed:

"Oh, please excuse me. Actually, I did go for sushi the other day. It wasn't such a fancy place, just one of those conveyor-belt joints. And when I asked for salmon roe, they piled it up so high that it spilled onto my plate. Now I've suddenly remembered what day it was. Sorry about that … "

It was incoherent, meaningless blather, no more than static buzz, and yet it was clear that the attention that had been focused on Sasaki had shifted.

"No, it was Wednesday. After that I went to that mama-san's place, and there was this college girl cozying up to me. Ya know, Miki, the one who says she works on Wednesdays when she's got no classes."

As though having regained his senses, Gotō now immediately

joined in the conversation. There was no longer any hint of irritation in his voice.

"I was too sozzled to remember. But it was Wednesday, wasn't it now?"

"Where, sir, do you usually go for drinks?"

Takumi, who also had regained his usual calm, turned to speak to the president so as to prevent Mike Home from having any further control of the conversation. Though the worst of the danger was now behind them, he went on with idle chit-chat to avoid further questions being posed to Sasaki.

Takumi's phone now rang. The call was from Harrison Yamanaka, who confirmed that the payment had been received. Clutching the phone, Takumi nodded proudly at Gotō. Sitting at the other end of the room, the lawyer, having put on an air of indifference, suppressed a yawn. The tension in the room had eased, the atmosphere now relaxed.

The scrivener, having completed the transfer of fees and bank records and holding copies of the receipts and confirmation of the transaction's conclusion, headed off to the legal affairs bureau to complete the transfer of ownership. Observing all of this, Takumi raised his voice so that that everyone present could hear: "The business has now come to a successful end. Thank you all for your strenuous efforts!"

■ ■ ■

The private room rang out with cheerful voices.

As Takumi and the others were chatting and looking down at the menu, the sliding door at the entrance opened.

"Grilled meat again? I thought it would be Robuchon this time, and I was really looking forward to it."

Reiko, a shocking-pink Haut à Courroies bag in her hand,

entered the restaurant and stood there, her lips pursed with dissatisfaction.

From beneath her short, sleeveless black dress her legs angled slightly inward and her brightly colored hair with curled tips hung over her full breasts. Her face, which had been treated with hyaluronic acid and injected with Botox, had an unnaturally stiff appearance, and there was indeed a faint hint of her true age. Even so, at least from behind, she did not look at all like a woman nearing fifty, and she was often approached while strolling down the street.

"What are you saying, Reiko-chan?" asked Gotō, looking up from the menu. "Celebratin' a successful conclusion to an operation means goin' for meat. All that Frenchy stuff smacks of foreigners anyway. A real downer!"

Takeshita was sitting next to Gotō, smiling dryly, his all-ceramic white front teeth peeking out.

"Reiko shouldn't be going to such a fancy joint with us. We'd just get the boot when Gotō starts spouting nonsense again."

"So ya say … Takeshita-san, but ya wouldn't be bounced, 'cause they wouldn't let ya in the door in the first place!"

Gotō gave Takeshita a mischievously joshing look.

A thrice-weekly visitor to a sauna with a tanning salon, Takeshita had an unusually dark complexion, made all the more striking by his all-white attire, including high-priced shirts and sneakers. He was to turn fifty-four this year, but though he boasted of looking nearly half his age, there was something unmistakably old and sleazy about him.

With his own network and organization, Takeshita had been in the forefront as a "land scout." The success of the project had been due in large part to his having been able to learn early on that Shimazaki Ken'ichi had moved into a nursing home.

Harrison Yamanaka, the oldest of the group, was sitting to

the right of Takumi and had been observing the conversation. He now spoke in a low but beneficent voice:

"Reiko-san, I'm sorry for not having been more attentive. But I preferred a place where we could talk freely. Let's do Robuchon next time."

His double-breasted suit, custom-made from high-grade English fabric at a top-class tailor in Ginza, harmonized with a hand-rolled, gorgeously crimson silk tie. His dark hair and goatee were elegantly trimmed to give him an air of dignity and respectability, as was befitting a wealthy man, while at the same time helping to conceal his true face and age—both that of a criminal with two convictions to his name.

"Reiko-chan, stop yer prattlin' and come on over here," exclaimed Gotō, putting his arm around a lounge chair to his right.

"Gotō-san talks too loud, and he smells of pomade, so Takumi-chan, may I sit next to you?"

Reiko took a seat next to Takumi. A mixed scent, sweet and floral, permeated the air.

"Takumi-kun, call a waiter for me, will ya? Let's order sake. Sake. But we'll be startin' off with beer. For five."

"I don't want beer. I'll have Dom Pérignon Rosé."

Takumi called the waiter and passed on the requests of Gotō and Reiko. An order for the most expensive course had already been placed at the time of the reservation.

A bottle of Dom Pérignon was soon brought in, uncorked, and poured. With his right hand, a prosthesis fitted to his pinky finger, Harrison Yamanaka raised his glass, and everyone followed suit.

"Well done, well done … I am greatly pleased that yet another project has met with success. I would like to thank you all once again for your endeavors. I am confident that you will continue to aid us in the future. But for now, let us forget about work and enjoy ourselves this evening. Cheers!"

Harrison Yamanaka's prim voice, somehow incongruent with his nearly six-foot frame, had everyone cheering in unison and sipping from their glasses.

The meal began with hors d'oeuvres that included yukhoe and namul, followed by grilled abalone. Then finely sliced wagyu was placed on the grill net, portion by portion. There was the sizzling sound of meat, lean and fat, cooking on the gas roaster, as a savory scent wafted across the table. Glasses of sake were drained one after another, as amiability filled the room, together with gentle laughter.

"Nah, Takeshita-san, it was terrible the way Takumi-kun froze in the middle of it all, but, ya know, a sushi restaurant in a nursing home? That's too much. And that girl—did you see her tits?—got ta blabberin' on and on. She even got herself tangled up with old man Sasaki. What a real pile of it, it was, all right!"

Gotō, who was on his second or third glass of makgeolli, squinted his eyes in amusement, as he recounted to the others the whole story of the settlement. He had consumed quite a bit of drink. His large face was completely flushed, and his balding head was covered with sebum, reflecting the ceiling light.

Takumi listened with a wry smile to Gotō's story but then, feeling the call of nature, stood up from his seat. As he left the room he asked a passing waiter for the location of the restroom and was given a courteous answer, without the slightest hint of disdain. He wondered how he might appear to the man, who no doubt had to deal with many a customer in this high-priced establishment. Despite Takumi's neat coiffure and his skin tone, together with the single-breasted suit he had purchased at a large-scale retail store, his gray hair was that of an old man and perhaps suggested an indeterminate age.

When he came out of the restroom, Takumi saw Harrison Yamanaka standing in the corridor. He gave him a perfunctory greeting of appreciation and started to walk back to the room when Yamanaka in a low voice remarked to him as he passed: "Don't let them catch you off guard."

Takumi had no need to be told. No matter how much alcohol he might consume, no matter how momentarily carried away he might be, he had no intention of losing track of himself.

As he returned, everyone was still reveling in the food and drink. Gotō was imbibing makgeolli and going after Takeshita with apparent gusto.

"So are ya gonna be puttin' yer share of the reward into that cult of yers?"

"Of course. As the number of students is growing, we're going to have to boost the number of yoga classes. And we've got to come up with scriptural texts, booklets, and other goods for the believers."

Takeshita responded to the question in a tone of pride.

Takumi had heard that Takeshita had acquired an independent religious corporation and been actively engaged in missionary work, even as he continued as a land scout. Takumi had initially been skeptical that such a dubious enterprise would succeed, but the number of believers had been steadily increasing, along with donations and offerings.

"How could such a coal-black cockroach of a guru like you possibly attract any followers?"

Reiko stifled a laugh as she stole a look at Takeshita's face.

"Well, I don't go public, and I don't have to. Most everybody who goes in for celebrity status is an idiot. If you don't do anything wild and carry on normally, people will naturally come to you."

"What do you mean by 'normally'?" asked Takumi, struck by the word.

"Ah. What it all comes down to is that everyone seeks salvation. Everyone's more or less anxious about illness, poverty, the afterlife, the pain of living without a reason, and so on. We claim to benefit people in this life, but we also tell them they will be saved both in the here and now and in the next world if they are generous in their offerings and diligent in their faith. Ripping off a whole clan, kit and caboodle, until it's flat broke or promising that some illness will be cured? That's just not the way to go."

"So, Takeshita-san, is money the reason you're doing this religion thing?"

Takumi was well aware that religious organizations, unlike ordinary corporate bodies, are favored with tax exemptions and thus a ready vehicle for accumulating all sorts of assets, tangible and otherwise.

"Of course. It's not that I want to be any sort of guru, but once you've got a certain amount of money, you can relax. Besides, I don't want to keep going on crossing dangerous bridges."

Takeshita was talking big, but was neither entirely mocking nor entirely serious.

Although Gotō had made light of Takeshita's pronouncement, he was now, as of two years before, married to a woman with a child of her own and had been keeping his new family entirely in the dark about his business as a land swindler. He too could not go on with risky ventures.

Both Gotō and Takeshita, whose father was a gangster, had once been honest men. Both had had their reasons for going over to the dark side and had now joined forces strictly for the sake of money. Both had criminal records, and mindful that at any moment they might wind up on the wrong side of the prison wall, they had surely given thought to making a break somewhere along the line. Harrison Yamanaka never seemed to have had enough of conning people, but the likes of such a man, the essence of the swindler having seeped into the very marrow of their bones, were surely few and far between.

"By the way, has old man Sasaki already headed off to Nagasaki?"

Takeshita had turned his attention to Reiko as, tongs in hand, he placed chateaubriand on the grill.

"This morning," she replied, as she reached out with her chopsticks toward a plate of kkakdugi.

It had been Reiko's job to arrange for the impersonator. Sasaki, whom she had hired, had apparently been found through one of her collaborators' contacts. She had first met Harrison Yamanaka while working as a manager in a dating club and then began helping him with his endeavors. As with her cohorts, her background was murky.

"Oh, yes, Harry. Before I forget … "

Reiko set down her chopsticks and handed Yamanaka a stack of receipts she had been carrying in her Haut à Courroies bag.

Yamanaka was responsible for all of the project's overhead, including the expenses for Sasaki and the lawyer and the cost of preparing the forged documents. So his share was naturally larger than that of the others. In this case, out of the 700 million yen that was swindled from Mike Home, 300 million was to go to Yamanaka, the ringleader; 100 million each to Takumi and Gotō, the negotiators with the highest risk of arrest; 150 million to Takeshita, the backroom operator who set up the support team; and 50 million to Reiko, who had laundered the money and transferred it to the various fictitious accounts.

"I know about Sasaki-san's airfare to Nagasaki, but this bill for food, drink, and lodging is close to … a million."

Harrison Yamanaka looked at the receipts, then turned to Reiko.

"There were a lot of adjustments to make this time. I don't think that it's a lot to ask for."

"It *is* a lot."

Gotō's face darkened: "It's none o' yer business, so shut it!"

Reiko took her glass by the stem with her red manicured fingertips and sipped her champagne, a prim look on her face.

"All right. If that's how it is, I understand. I'll be transferring the money to your account later," said Yamanaka in a relaxed voice.

They had devoured the astonishingly tender slices of chateaubriand, so that the row of blue flames on the slightly flickering grill had nothing left to cook. Gripping his glass, Takumi stared blankly into the fire, then coming out of his daze, twisted a knob under the table to turn off the roaster.

The waiter appeared to place bowls of cold noodles and gukbap in front of everyone.

"By the way," remarked Takeshita, as he gulped down his bowl of rice soup, "the president of Mike Home has been outed. It's all in today's issue of *Face*."

"Eh? What's he been caught up in?" asked Takumi. His impression of the president was that he was a man who appealed to women, and it seemed he had been out fooling around. Still, he was not a celebrity. It would not have occurred to Takumi that a weekly photo magazine might be on his tail.

"Mind you, I don't know exactly," Takeshita continued. "But it seems he's been hanging out with what's-her-name, that TV announcer. They got snapped as they were leaving some apartment together."

As though to emphasize his cynical remark, Takeshita pulled back a corner of his mouth, again revealing his ceramic teeth. "That's a riot. He's feelin' so top o' the world, thinkin' he's pulled off a deal that, in fact, has got him snookered, that he goes off for a tryst with some chick and gets caught on camera. Now there's a real piece o' work!"

As Gotō flamboyantly clapped his hands and laughed, Reiko, who had passed on the carbohydrates and was eating melon for dessert, burst out with a laugh of her own, apparently much amused.

Harrison Yamanaka looked at Takumi.

"The Legal Affairs Bureau may reject the application for the property transfer as early as next week."

The forged documents had been most adroitly concocted, but the driver's license number and the information recorded on the IC chip were those of a person other than Shimazaki Ken'ichi. If checked, they would be exposed as bogus, and soon Mike Home would be notified that its application had been rejected.

Takumi returned Harrison Yamanaka's look and nodded.

"In any case," Yamanaka continued, "we can't afford to dilly-dally. I'm leaving for Cancún tomorrow morning."

Yamanaka looked around at the others and determined that they too were all leaving the country that week and would be keeping their distance from Japan until the dust had settled. Reiko was going to a condominium in Hawai'i to meet her lover there. Gotō would tell his family that he was taking a business trip but then head for Singapore and Macau to blow money at the casinos. Takeshita would be relaxing at a villa in Monaco.

"What about you, Takumi-chan?" Reiko inquired, as she scooped up the last of the melon with her spoon.

"So it's again off to the mountains, are ya? Phooey! Makes

no sense, gettin' yerself worn out for nothin'!" remarked Gotō with a frown as he ate Reiko's portion of cold noodles.

Takumi's response was only a vague smile. His plan was to head north from Tokyo by car the next morning, stay the night at an inn in Minamiaizu in Fukushima, and then traverse the Maruyama slopes for five days and four nights.

This was the second time for him to undertake such an excursion. In the mountains, the roads and trails were not maintained because there were none to begin with. The only way to climb was to follow the narrow streams during the season of lingering snow or thereafter, once it had all melted. The previous time he had made the journey the landscape was still blanketed in white. The scenery was quite different when there is no snow, and this time he wanted to allow himself as much leisure as possible, luxuriating in nature's grand inundation of green.

There was a knock on the door, and the waiter came in to bring after-dinner coffee.

"So what's next?"

Gotō sipped from his cup and looked at Yamanaka.

"Depending on what Takeshita-san can provide us, I'm thinking of aiming at higher peaks."

He was twirling a double ring on his right pinky, a tick of his that he often displayed when contemplating a promising idea.

"What do you mean by 'higher'?" Takeshita asked.

"So high that it wouldn't be odd if the dead descended."

His reply came without hesitation. Reiko, who had been fiddling with her phone, looked up in surprise.

"What do you mean by 'the dead'?"

Takeshita raised an eyebrow.

"The higher the mountain, the easier it is to lose your footing and fall."

There was no further comment, as all fell silent. The sound

of other customers leaving the restaurant passed through the door.

Harrison Yamanaka guffawed.

"Just joking. Sorry to startle you. I was merely speaking in general terms. It has nothing to do with us. Forget it!"

Takumi wordlessly sipped his coffee. Yamanaka's laugh seemed to hint that he was not exactly joking.

"At least I don't intend to take on the dangers that the last project entailed. If we succeed, the returns will be substantial. But it's nonetheless high risk, high reward. If any of you want to back out, do so while you still can. I won't force you. I can look for others."

He then smiled his usual smile.

"Let's meet up again in three and a half months. I'll be contacting you with more details."

And with that he called for the bill.

. . .

Tatsu looked downcast as he listened to the chief of Investigation Section II. He stood as if trying to straighten his slightly bent back, his wrinkled and gnarled hands folded in front of his small frame.

"As for the matter of reinstating and keeping you on, the application has run into some flak … We really went all out for it, but I'm afraid … "

The younger man spoke awkwardly from his seat behind his desk. Despite his elite position in the agency, he did not appear terribly full of himself, and in his words could be discerned a modicum of genuine sympathy for elders on the verge of retirement. Tatsu had braced himself for this outcome and now felt even somewhat relieved, thinking of it as somehow involving someone other than himself.

Behind the supervisor rich sunlight streamed through a window. At the edge of his field of vision, Tatsu glimpsed the green of the trees along the road fluttering against the pale blue sky. Standing upright and immobile, he replied:

"I understand. Thank you for taking the trouble. I shall now be able to take leave of you all without any regrets."

"How are you feeling?" asked the chief, looking into Tatsu's deeply lined face.

"Thank you for your concern. I'm fine now."

Some six months had elapsed since Tatsu's collapse from kidney and liver failure, forcing him into the hospital for two weeks. His doctors had attributed it to alcohol and stress. After years of work as a detective under intense pressure to solve major cases—sometimes keeping him from returning home for months at a time—it was no wonder he had incurred health problems. It was not simple misfortune.

"Relieved to hear that. I hope you will continue your investigations, even as you pass on the wisdom of your experience to the upcoming generations."

Tatsu silently listened to his superior, who now seemed a bit more at ease.

"I'm also looking forward to your assistance in apprehending the land swindlers."

Whatever he said, the section assigned to white-collar crime had in fact traditionally focused more on corruption. In recent years it had dealt with, among other challenges, bank transfer fraud, which targeted ordinary citizens and resulted in annual losses amounting to several tens of billions of yen, with the number of cases in excess of ten thousand

By way of contrast, classic fraud cases, such as land scamming, which involved a mixed bag of real estate brokers and other professionals, genuine and counterfeit, had a negligible number of victims. Apparently the second division could not afford or was unwilling to allocate any more manpower to such cases. It could, however, be the sort of niche in which an over-the-hill detective with only a high-school education might quietly end his investigative career.

"I shall do my best," said Tatsu, giving a slight bow and then exiting the room.

Returning to his seat, he sank all the way down and leaned back. The air he was unconsciously holding in his lungs seeped out through his nose with a faint rasping sound.

His colleagues were out on an investigation, and there were only a few others around. Except for the sound of an occasional telephone call, all was quiet in the office.

Tatsu, set to retire at the end of the fiscal year, was no longer called upon as an investigative team asset in major cases, those requiring large-scale, long-term endeavors. He was at most asked to provide logistical support, acting as a glorified gofer. Even so, he could not help feeling grateful for the benevolence from above: He had been kept on thanks to no particular merit of his own beyond stick-to-itiveness and steadfast honesty.

After staring upward for some moments, Tatsu slowly sat up, took a worn file from a drawer, and spread out the contents on his desk. As he was flipping through the pages, his hand stopped at one particular spot.

It was a record of the personal history of a man. His real name was "Yamanaka Harrison," though he had used several aliases. Among his associates, his name was apparently rendered in Western order: Harrison Yamanaka. Born in Shimane Prefecture in 1955, the son of shopkeepers, he had joined a criminal gang after graduating from high school. For some sort of misstep he had been expelled at the age of thirty. Thereafter, leveraging the prowess he had acquired in land swindling while still in the gang, he had orchestrated a series of scams, gaining notoriety in the real estate racket. Following the bubble economy's collapse, he had been arrested and prosecuted as the ringleader in a fraud case involving multitenant buildings in Tokyo. He was convicted and given a five-year prison sentence. He had remained quiet for a time after his release, but soon finding himself in financial straits, he had resumed his criminal activities. He was currently a suspect in several large-scale fraud cases.

Tatsu turned a file page and directed his gaze at a case mentioned in a corner of the document, one that had occurred more than ten years before. The mastermind was Harrison Yamanaka, and Tatsu had been called in as a member of the investigatory team. A thorough two-year search operation had led to the discovery of Yamanaka's whereabouts and his apprehension. Continuous day-and-night interrogations were carried out. Then, much to Tatsu's surprise and amazement, the evidence was found insufficient, and no indictment was brought. Though Yamanaka had denied the allegations and remained silent throughout, the investigators had worked beforehand in perfect sync with the prosecutors, and the evidence presented by the team, including Tatsu, had been more than enough to demonstrate the suspect's guilt. Rumor had it among them that some most peculiar interference had come from a retired but still influential prosecutor, one in cahoots with Yamanaka. Even now, the truth remained obscure.

On the day Yamanaka was released, Tatsu, standing at the entrance of the prosecutor's office, heard the man who had uttered not a word during all the time he had spent in the interrogation room now gloating in triumph. On seeing Tatsu, he momentarily scowled, then flashed a provocative grin. Since then, as with all of his fellow detectives involved in the investigation, the very existence of Harrison Yamanaka had continued to smolder in Tatsu like lingering embers.

As he was returning the file to the desk drawer, a colleague who had been carrying out questioning in another room returned. Still in his thirties, he had recently been assigned to Investigation Section II. He wore a grim expression.

"What's wrong?" Tatsu inquired.

"It's that guy who's come from the Shibuya station."

Tatsu had heard that a case apparently involving land scamming had been sent over to headquarters.

"How did it go?"

"Yeah, well the victim was all red in the face, screaming bloody murder about having been conned. I dunno. I saw the *Face* piece on that flashy dude and his announcer cutie pie."

The young man's disdain was typical of some careerist types. He spat out his words in an offhand manner.

Fraud cases involving land swindlers were difficult to investigate. In the already murky real estate business, where people of unknown background roam freely, there were many stakeholders, and transactions were complex. With everyone claiming to be a victim, it was difficult to discern who the real victims were. In this case as well, the president of Mike Home, though claiming to be among the harmed, might also be seen as the perpetrator. The possibility that he had himself engaged in fraud in dealing with financial institutions could not be overlooked. Tatsu could somewhat understand his fellow detective's skepticism.

Tatsu asked if he could look at some of the investigation data compiled at the Shibuya station.

"Ah … an impersonation?"

The documents indicated the all too typical pattern.

The impersonator had already made himself scarce. The president of Mike Home, who had come in to report his victimization, and the lawyer who had identified the identity of the impersonator had both been interviewed on a voluntary basis.

"Is the victim still here?"

"Why no. They sent him on his way," came the perplexed reply.

"I'm sorry, but I'm going to have to ask you to call him back," said Tatsu, his eyes still on the document.

"But ..."

Tatsu noiselessly flapped his tongue and looked up.

"I won't cause any trouble."

Tatsu's gaze was devoid of emotion, and his colleague awkwardly fell silent.

# 2

The stream was flowing sluggishly, the water level low. Gingerly taking one step at a time, he felt the chill of the water on his ankles as it permeated his spats and the soles of his rubber-boot-clad feet sensed the jagged stones scattered along the bottom.

Takumi, a fifty-liter rucksack on his back, stopped and wiped the sweat from his brow. As he rehydrated himself with a portable bottle-shaped water purifier, he turned his eyes to the surrounding landscape.

The dense, old-growth beech forest on both sides of the river was a brilliant green. On the surface of the water, out of which sharp rocks arose, the midsummer sunlight breaking through the interlocking leaves was dazzlingly reflected. A choral shrill of cicadas poured down as though driven by the heat that enveloped the ravine.

Breathing deeply, he drew in the thick scent of the forest, as if the entire scene before him had been crushed and wafted into his nostrils, filling with clean air his lungs deadened by the dust of the city.

He had entered the Kurotani River water system early in the morning from the forest road and ascended the Oyu River at a leisurely pace, taking periodic breaks. To reach the summit of Maruyama, nearly six thousand feet in elevation, he still had a long way to go. He had planned his ascent with more than enough time to spare and had no intention of hurrying.

As he moved upstream, the rivulet grew ever narrower. In no time, the beech forest ended.

The sun had already passed its zenith as he moved beyond Higashinosawa Junction, and his shadow shimmering on the surface of the water now fell toward the east.

In a level area among the trees, slightly above the stream, he found a suitable camping spot and removed his backpack. Having gathered fallen branches, he lit a fire, then took his fishing rod and headed toward a deep pool he had been eyeing along the way. Carefully casting the fly to avoid alerting his prey, he landed it in the rocky shadows. Reading the flow of the water, he repeatedly swung his rod, but the fish were not biting. Shifting to a spot upstream, he at last caught a good-sized char.

He returned to his campsite, cleaned his catch, and cooked it in a pot of rice. Once he had finished his simple but sumptuous meal, his tasks for the day were at an end.

He could see and feel that it had begun to rain. Cold air was creeping in as darkness fell, the only light now coming from the fire. He wrapped himself in a synthetic-fiber jacket designed for sleeping and into a titanium mug poured some Islay malt. While sipping on the whiskey, he tossed a branch into the fire to keep it burning. The heat gradually spread to envelop his cold limbs, warming him to the core. The glow of the firelight, constantly flashing orange, illuminated his slightly intoxicated face as the coals crackled, sending sparks into the night sky. He watched the flames battling each other as he rolled the mellow, peat-scented Scotch around in his mouth. The skin on his face began to twitch. The roar of the all-consuming fire pierced the silence of the night and clung relentlessly to his ears.

It had been late in the evening six years before, when a fire broke out in his parents' home in Yokohama, not far from the sea. At the time he had been living in a nearby town. Rushing home, he saw the familiar two-story wooden house engulfed in flames as men in fireproof clothing did battle, armed with water cannons. Endless clouds of smoke billowed up, the smell of burning embers filling the air. The firefighters' frantic, rage-filled voices resounded; the scene was as bright as day.

Takumi, who for some time had been staying up all night at work, stood silently behind the onlookers and stared at the burning house as if watching fireworks. When he overheard someone say there were still people left inside, his attention leapt to his parents and to his wife and child, who happened to be staying at the house at the time. Everything seemed so unreal that he felt strangely serene.

Some six months before the fire, the family-owned business had gone bankrupt. A trading company specializing in medical equipment and supplies, it had some fifty employees. Takumi's uncle, who had taken over from the previous generation, was the company's spokesman; his father was managing director. After graduating from university, Takumi started work there in sales. Until the bankruptcy, the company had somehow managed to maintain profits and withstand all the changes in the marketplace, and there were none of the power struggles common in family-run businesses. On weekends and vacations, Takumi's father would take his employees and their families to the coastal town of Zushi, where the uncle had a vacation home, to enjoy some relaxation by the sea.

The bankruptcy had obliged his father, as joint guarantor, together with the uncle, to shoulder a debt burden in the hundreds of millions. He had spearheaded the transactions that triggered the debacle and now apparently felt solely responsible for it. Utterly abandoned by his relatives, he grew emaciated, and his eyes became sunken. He had been struggling mightily to salvage the business, with Takumi tirelessly working beside him day and night. The fire had occurred in the midst of those efforts.

The remains of Takumi's mother, wife, and son had been found in the ashes and were so completely charred that, when he saw them in the police inspection room, they were all but unrecognizable, coal-like clumps. According to the firefighters on scene, the wife appeared to have been holding her son as if trying to shield him from the flames.

The evidence suggested that this was likely no mere accident, and so the investigation proceeded with the working hypothesis of family suicide and/or homicide as the cause. The father then confessed that, in utter despair, he had sought to save his family from suffering. Handed a twenty-three-year sentence for murder and arson of a domestic residence, he was currently incarcerated in Chiba Prison.

Takumi had not once gone to visit his father. He had had a mother, a wife, and a child; his father had caused their deaths. Crushed by that reality, he had shut himself up in his room and remained there …

Something was moving on the flat of his right hand, which was still clutching the mug. The small dark body of a leech, about the size of a fingertip, was, like an inchworm, forming a bridge with its body as it made its way to the base of Takumi's thumb.

From the fire he took a twig, its tip aglow, and gazed at it for a moment before, as though remembering his purpose, he brought it to bear. A faint sizzling sound was heard, the leech peeling off and falling to the ground. A spot on Takumi's palm was wet with dark blood. He repeatedly jabbed the red tip of the twig into the leech lying there in the darkness at his feet.

All the next day was drearily cloudy, but on the following morning, when Takumi intended to make his ascent, the sky was unexpectedly clear, as if the previous day's weather had been a lie.

The sunlight was mercilessly intense; sweat was pouring out of his entire body. He was already at an altitude of over 3,600 feet, and the upward path marked by the stream was now as steep as any staircase. His smart watch showed that his heart rate was approaching the 130s, and breathing was difficult. His backpack, though slightly lighter due to the provisions he had consumed, dug into his shoulders. He climbed, placing his hands on the rocks, as he struggled his way upward. The stream showed ever less water and soon was gone.

His advance continued up the ridge. A dense thicket, with trees about the height of a man, stood in the way. To reach the summit there was no alternative to going through it, and he was determined to push forward. Yet no matter where he turned, his view was blocked by dense bamboo grass and twisted bamboo roots, and here and there his feet could not find their way to the ground. The branches and leaves of the bushes that he forced aside came recoiling back at him, bouncing off his face as though deliberately aiming for his eyes. Again and again his legs were caught in the undergrowth; already unsteady on his feet, he nearly fell over. With uneven breaths he plowed his way through, cursing all the while.

Yet now suddenly there was a break in the thicket, and his field of vision widened.

"Ah!" he involuntarily exclaimed.

Spreading out before him was a meadow. A yellowish undergrowth covered the entire area, the ponds that dotted the landscape reflecting the clear, pale blue sky. Momentarily Takumi forgot he was indeed on the mountaintop. A sea of green crept along the gently sloping ridge to another summit to the northwest, enveloping the graceful form of the bimodal peak.

He set down his backpack and ambled through the meadow following some faint footprints. But no matter where he gazed, the only other sign of human life and activity was that same backpack. In the distance he could see the majestic peaks of Minamiaizu, including Asahidake and Bontendake, the thick mountain haze extending endlessly. The soft touch of the grass was soothing to his tired feet.

He sat down and slowly leaned his upper body back. All that he now beheld was the vast firmament, as he raised a forearm to shield himself from the glittering sunlight that played in the corner of his eye. A gentle breeze brushed his sweaty cheeks as he caught the scent of vegetation. Listening to the whispering of the birds in the meadow, he drifted off to sleep. Contrary to his fears, the weather held steady, allowing him to set up camp there at the foot of the meadow.

He scooped some water from the snowy mountain ravine and cooked up the alpine leeks he had plucked along the way. All around him darkness had already fallen.

The stars hung scattered across the heavens, each one a radiance but all shining together. The flickering of stardust that had traveled unimaginable lengths of time to arrive here held him enthralled for as long as he gazed.

How many overlapping coincidences had brought him to this place?

If it had been raining, he might not have camped like this here on the mountaintop. If the Ebisu project had failed, he might now be searching for new targets on behalf of Harrison Yamanaka. Had it not been for his family's business bankruptcy and his father's unspeakable cruelty, he might never have given any thought to leaving the sea and climbing mountains.

The house fire had made him a solitary man, and he had remained barricaded in his trash-littered room. Exhausted by a bottomless sense of loss, he had given his mind over to a profound sense of resignation. He would stare at the stained ceiling, perhaps hoping that his life would quietly draw to a close. In the end, however, thinking he was too young give up on life, he had decided to go on, with hope in nothing and trust in no one.

Grazing his ears, so long accustomed to din and bustle, were the fading chattering of the crickets and the murmuring of a gentle breeze.

A moment now came when he lost his focus, as he stared at celestial shadows consuming all the light, his mind eroded by memories of years ago, when all he could see was a dirty windshield …

■　■　■

Bridge piers on the Metropolitan Expressway overhead were dully reflected in that windshield.

He had parked his car on the shoulder of the road and for a long while been reclined in the driver's seat. His languid eyes caught traces of headlights, appearing and vanishing, in tandem with the sound of the traffic.

It had been less than six months since he had taken out an impossible loan to buy this old Suzuki Jimny. His face was faintly reflected on the border of the grime-encrusted windowpane. Only his hair, which had recently and abruptly turned white, seemed to be floating in the darkness of the night.

Stirred by the sound of an emergency brake, Takumi half-raised his head and saw a taxicab stopped just ahead of him. The back door opened and a middle-aged man in a suit, apparently the passenger, emerged.

"That's because you'll always be a bottom-feeding loser. I'm going to file a complaint with the Taxi Center. Remember that, you piece of shit!"

Perhaps he had been displeased with the route taken to his destination; perhaps it was due to the driver's manner. The man was holding the door with one hand and yelling abuse into the taxi with such intensity that Takumi could hear it all.

The cab was partially blocking the four-lane street, forcing vehicles coming from behind on their way to Roppongi to swerve right. Takumi looked at the driver, who was holding his head down, his hands clenched around the steering wheel. He appeared to be in his thirties and thus of the same generation as Takumi.

The driver's expression, as seen in the cab's interior light, combined vexation with a disagreeable passenger and trepidation at the prospect of being penalized as a consequence of a bad report. His career as a driver, it seemed, might well be short-lived.

It had been about four months since Takumi had himself been laid off from a taxi company.

He had felt no attachment to the work; nor had he been attracted by the recruitment ad he had seen: "Fully furnished dormitory! All-expense paid second-class driver's license!" As someone who for a long while had hermited himself away, he had few options. His only motive in this particular job was negative: It would keep his contact with other people to a minimum.

As the days went by he learned his way around the city and became accustomed to taxi driving. He was, however, repeatedly taken to task for being brusque and sullen toward his passengers, and when his attitude did not improve, he was fired. He was left only with some modest savings and the faint realization that the service industry would never be for him. In the end, he did not seek out another company but turned his back on the cab business entirely.

Although the line of work he had now undertaken was of

a different sort, it was the same in this respect: that here too he lacked motivation. The job provided the resources that allowed him to scrape by but otherwise meant nothing to him. He was floating through the shadows of the world, half-hoping that he, like some lost kite, still dangling a severed piece of string, would be torn apart by a gust of wind.

The phone lying on the passenger seat rang. Takumi reached for it without stopping to verify the caller and hastily tapped the icon.

"Where the hell *are* you?"

The haughty voice of the young manager reverberated throughout the small car.

Ever since starting this job, Takumi had kept his phone on speaker mode while on duty. It was not a habit carried over from his days as a cab driver. He instead felt that this way he could pass off any offending words as somehow having nothing to do with him.

He could hear in the background the incessant ringing of phones. On this night too, it seemed, there was no end to the number of men looking for women.

"I'm in Akasaka, waiting for Saki-san."

It had been nearly forty minutes since Takumi had been languishing on the street in front of a hotel. Saki, still in her room, had informed him ten minutes before that she had completed her assignment, but she had yet to make an appearance at the entrance.

The arrangement was for 120 minutes, and in keeping with the club's high-end reputation, the price was close to 100,000 yen, even though the service did not include intercourse. The customer had paid a hefty fee for an extra sixty minutes. Perhaps he had taken quite a liking to Saki, who claimed on the website to be a "working model."

The customer was a man named Uchida, who had recently

been making frequent use of the club. Like almost all the others, the name he gave was most likely a randomly chosen alias. "Uchida" always specified this hotel. At the club, the staff remembered him well.

The rule was for the driver to go the customer's room to collect the fee in advance of the escort's service. This particular time a different driver had been given that task, but Takumi had seen Uchida on several occasions. He was a tall, soft-spoken man around sixty years of age. He always wore a bathrobe, and when he paid, he invariably displayed an impressively long billfold, brimming with cash.

"Are you still waiting?" asked the manager in a hectoring tone. "Tell her to hurry up! We're all backed up! When Saki shows up, you're to take her to a condo in Tamachi. I've sent you the address."

Through the windshield he could see the taxi from before flashing its hazard lights. The driver, at last rid of his passenger, pulled the lever at the side of his seat and closed the rear door. The moment the interior lights went out, he shouted something. The sound of traffic drowned out his voice, but from the movement of his lips, he seemed to be saying, "Hey, don't mess with me! Who d'ya think you are?"

Now it was Takumi's manager, exclaiming in a harsh voice: "Hey, you got it? You could at least answer me, you idiot!"

"Yes, I understand ..."

Takumi reached for his phone, his eyes still on the road ahead, and ended the call.

Frustrations that had condensed within him now spilled out with a sigh. As he leaned back in his seat, he sensed the presence of another. Saki, devoid of makeup, was standing at the window on the passenger side.

"What the ... It's you again!"

Saki slid into the front seat, her slender hips encased in a tight skirt. Crossing her legs, she raised her feet, still shod in high heels, and set them on the dashboard.

"I told 'em I really can't put up with this car. It's shabby, dirty, and cramped. What if there's an accident and I get hurt? ... Oh, and let me tell ya: If you try to peek up my skirt even for a second, I'll be takin' a fee!"

Takumi ignored her and started the car.

Saki was calling someone, perhaps a friend or another escort. She was using a dirty windowpane as a mirror, her fingertips fiddling with her hair, as she spouted her litany of woes.

"Listen! Listen! That client just now really made me sick," she exclaimed. "What d'ya think it was? Nah, it wasn't anything like *that* at all! He wanted to lick my face. For the whole hour. Just my face. He says he gets off on any stuff that I find gross. Right? Isn't that the worst? Yeah, I know. OK. I let him do it. But isn't it normal to do whatever if someone's gonna fork over 30,000?"

Takumi was steering with one hand, his attention focused on the road ahead.

The taillights of cabs wandering the streets in the dead of night in search of customers were pulsating, reminding him of red sea-fireflies. As long as he stared at that cluster of lights, perhaps he could escape all the world's cacophony.

He finished work with the coming of the dawn.

He bought a bento, serving as neither dinner nor breakfast, along with a beer, and returned to his apartment. The sun, shining through a gap between the love hotels across a narrow alley, created a small bright spot, seemingly avoiding there on a shelf the electric kettle that had once been a part of his life with his wife and child.

Sitting on the futon in his six-tatami-mat room, Takumi drank his beer while glancing at the mail. Among the sales and restaurant advertisements meant for the previous occupant, there was a long, white envelope. It had been forwarded from a Yokohama address. On the front, Takumi's name was penned in neat but wavy letters; on the back the address and name were written more perfunctorily: Chiba Prefecture, Chiba City, Wakaba-ku, Kaizuka-chō 192, Tsujimoto Masami. Takumi had involuntarily memorized the address, having seen it so many times. As he continued to sip his beer, he took the envelope, leaving it unopened, and crumpled it with all his strength before tossing it into the cardboard box that served as his trash receptacle.

His routine the next day was the same as before: dealing as best he could with complaints from the manager and escorts.

Two weeks later, he was parked in front of the hotel in Akasaka, absent-mindedly staring at the dirt on the windshield, when his phone rang. It was Saki, calling from her hotel room, more than thirty minutes before the scheduled end of service.

"Come here right away!" came her voice through the speaker.

Had there been some sort of trouble? The customer was again Uchida.

He left the car on the shoulder of the road and made his way up to the room to find Saki standing in the entrance, wearing only a bath towel. She had been licked on the face, the same as two weeks before. Her makeup was quite ruined, and her eyeliner and lipstick were smudged. One might well have taken her for a badly made-up clown.

"What's happened?"

Saki responded with an intense look of hatred in her eyes. Uchida, she said, without so much as resorting to a prophylactic, had forced her to have penetrative sex.

Dressed in a bathrobe, Uchida was sitting in a club chair by the window, staring out at the lights of Tokyo Tower and nursing a glass of whiskey, a nonchalant expression on his face. Noting Takumi's gaze, he smiled wanly and stood up.

"Well now, I'll give you the whole story. She was so filled with desire and so enraptured by my technique that she was begging me to leave her with my superior genes. I had no desire to do it, but I went ahead and entered her vile organ. Again, it was not what I wanted. It was what this nymphomaniac herself insisted on."

Uchida spoke with astonishing eloquence and without the slightest sign of anxiety or concern, as though he were calmly championing a righteous cause.

"Cut the crap!" Saki screamed. "Why would I do or say anything like that?"

Uchida's expression remained one of complete serenity.

"You mustn't lie, you know … She was like a doggie on all fours, pointing her ass at me, her pussy dripping wet. Maybe she got so excited she's forgotten all about it, but she greedily stuck that toy up her anus. And even then she couldn't get enough, so she was waving her little butt and begging me for my penis."

"No way I did that!"

Saki was shouting, her words and intonation reflecting the shame she felt, conscious as she was of Takumi's gaze.

Takumi's eyes turned to one of the twin beds. The midsection of the sheet was wet and sticking to the mattress. A purple sex toy in the shape of a phallus and a string of black marbles lay on the floor.

"You're not being honest," said Uchida, shaking his head in disappointment.

From the pocket of his gown he took out a stick-shaped mini recorder and pressed the switch. The sound of Saki's feverish groans and heavy breathing issued forth. Her voice could be heard quivering, as she pleaded with Uchida, echoing almost precisely what he had just asserted.

"Stop it!"

"Fine, right away, as soon as you come clean."

Saki was bawling and squalling, and Uchida watched her out of the corner of his eye as, in obvious pleasure, he kept his ear to the recorder.

"It wasn't like that! I didn't mean that. That's not what I was doing!"

Saki crumpled to the floor, her clownish face twisting and turning, tears covering her lipstick-stained cheeks.

"Well now, there you have it …" said Uchida, as he turned off the recorder and walked over to Takumi, a thick wallet in his hand. Taking out three 10,000-yen bills, he counted them one by one and held them out:

"Here, something in the way of a nuisance fee."

Takumi stared at the money, then responded: "No thanks."

Uchida's face took on an expression of disbelief.

"I won't accept it. I'm not going to tell the club anything about this one way or the other."

"Oh …" murmured Uchida in surprise.

"I'm not interested," said Takumi quietly.

"What are you saying? You're a man from the club, right? You've got to back up a client."

Takumi saw Saki glaring at him as she sobbed.

"I'm not taking anyone's side in this," he said quietly. "If you want to pursue the matter yourself, go ahead. Do as you like."

Takumi's cheek muscles began to contract violently, catching him unawares.

Uchida, who had been calmly looking on with interest, took a business card from his wallet and handed it over with a smile, as if to say, "Just in case you find yourself in a jam …"

The Uchida incident that evening became, as a matter of course, an issue for the club. The manager grilled Takumi and reprimanded him for his allegedly negligent handling of the situation. He was then fired, without being given the slightest opportunity to defend himself.

Now once again out of a job, Takumi returned to spending many a day staring at the stains on the apartment ceiling. What, he thought, mumbling to himself on the tatami mats, was he to do? He had no desire to do much of anything, but he lacked the savings needed to carry on in this manner indefinitely.

Through sheer inertia he ended up looking for a driver's job with another escort service. He applied to several companies but from each received the same brusque response.

He rolled over in his futon amidst the empty lunch boxes and plastic bottles that littered the floor. Almost buried therein was a crumpled white snippet of something. He recognized it as Uchida's business card. After staring at it for a moment, he picked up the phone.

Takumi heard a familiar voice on the other end but his at first was not recognized. Recounting the trouble with Saki at the hotel in Akasaka seemed immediately to trigger the memory of his listener, who, sounding vaguely suspicious, asked him what he wanted.

Might he have any work for him, Takumi asked, adding that he could at least be a driver and that he would very much like to be in Uchida's employ.

"I doubt that," came his instant reply. "I don't think you have the slightest interest in working for me."

He spoke quite firmly. It was clear that Uchida was not a man to whom one could simply toady up.

"You're absolutely right," Takumi replied, "but I really need a job."

Uchida laughed in apparent amusement.

"Well, unfortunately, we're already managing with enough drivers."

Takumi, who had not had high hopes to begin with, gave perfunctory thanks and ended the call.

So, he told himself, it seemed it would be another attempt at landing a gig with a call-girl service.

Feeling hungry, he had gotten up, intending to go out to buy a bento, when his phone, left lying on the tatami mat, rang. It was Uchida, who asked expectantly:

"About what we were just talking about … Is the only work you'd be willing to do driving?"

"No. I'll do any job, as long as you pay me … "

He had replied in a puzzled voice, as he could clearly sense the person on the other end of the line begin to chortle.

And thus began Takumi's relationship with Uchida—or, rather one should say, Harrison Yamanaka.

■ ■ ■

It was in the following week that he was asked to carry out his first job for Yamanaka. It was, just as he was told, a task that anyone could carry out. He was to go to a factory at a given time on a given date and pick up goods in exchange for payment.

"Is that all there is to it?"

Harrison Yamanaka nodded as he took a sip from his teacup. The payment would be 30,000 yen, which included transportation and other expenses.

"There are, however, a few precautions."

These proved to amount to a long list, which Takumi noted before leaving the coffee shop in the late afternoon.

The factory was about an hour's bumpy train trip and a short bus ride from the center of the city. Not far from the station, a residential area appeared, and now from the bus he saw the heavily congested main highway franchise restaurants along with business offices, their sales vehicles parked by the side. Takumi felt a stirring in his chest as he continued to gaze at the humdrum suburban landscape, his hand clutching a paper bag containing a bottle of liquor. He got out at the closest bus stop and, consulting a map, walked for about five minutes until he saw, across from a used-car dealership, the target building. It was not a large factory employing hundreds of workers, but rather a small-scale operation, with no more than twenty or thirty. From the outside, it looked more like a warehouse.

Following Harrison Yamanaka's "precautions," he went past the factory and began circling the site. It was dotted with an auto body shop, a rental storage facility with several small containers stacked atop each other, plus a spot for construction materials, with houses densely packing the gaps.

Takumi nonchalantly took notice of his surroundings. There was an elderly man with a bent back, out walking his dog, but he could see no one else, and likewise no sign of suspicious vehicles. He had been instructed, should there be anything unusual, namely the presence of police personnel, to turn around immediately and leave.

He stepped onto the factory premises and peeked in through the open entrance. The on-again-off-again sound of machinery filled the air, along with the odor of ink mingled with some sort of chemical. Unopened stacks of paper were piled up at the entrance, and along the walls large, aged printing presses stood in a row; in front of each one employees in blue work uniforms were laboring under fluorescent lights dangling from the ceiling.

Takumi approached a nearby male worker, who was checking the finished printouts.

"Excuse me. Where is the president?"

The man turned a tired face to him.

"Second floor," he replied curtly, turning back to his work.

Upstairs was the office. The staff appeared to be out. In the back, alone at a desk, sat an old man in work clothes whom Takumi took to be the president. He was on the phone, speaking in a weak voice, his completely bald head glimmering.

"Yes, sir. I'm sorry, sir. Didn't I tell you? The money's coming in today. Can you wait just a little longer? Please. I'm asking you ever so humbly. Please."

Seeing Takumi, he pulled the receiver away from his mouth.

"Hey!" he said. "Are you here from Uchida's place?"

Takumi nodded, conscious of being somewhat agitated himself.

"The money's arrived," the president said over the phone before setting it down.

"First, give it to me," he said in a low but resounding voice.

Takumi handed over the thick envelope that Yamanaka had given him. The president snatched it up. Wearing rubber fingertips, he fumbled ineffectively with the flap as he hurriedly sought to pull out the bills.

Takumi silently observed the older man's ever so slightly trembling hands. It was clear why Yamanaka had advised him to buy a bottle on his way. Without a word of thanks, the president grabbed the gift of whiskey, opened it, put his mouth directly on the tip of the bottle, and sent the amber liquid down to his stomach, a gurgling sound emanating from his throat. It was a Chichibu single malt that Takumi had quite expressly stopped at a department store to buy. The desperate look on the man's face suggested he would have been happy with any type or brand of alcohol.

The president wiped his wet mouth on his loose shirt sleeve and once more counted the bills in the envelope. The hands that had been shaking were now wondrously steady.

"Exactly right," he remarked, then bent the envelope to fit into the pocket of his slacks, took out an A4-size envelope from his desk drawer, and tossed it toward Takumi, as if it were the most foul sort of substance.

Takumi went over to a neighboring desk and looked through the contents. Inside were utility bills for gas and water, property tax notices, and watermarked residence certificates. There were enough for altogether seven people. Had these been forged at this factory or with a subcontractor? Of this, Takumi had not been informed.

Putting on the vinyl gloves he had brought with him, he perused the documents, checking each and every one for such information as name, date, monetary amount, and address. Everything seemed in order.

"Hey, kid!"

The president, who as he drank had been keeping an eye on him, now put the bottle on his desk.

"Why do we have to deal with scoundrels like you bastards? Why do we, who have been working so hard, have to deal with the dregs of society such as you?"

His sunken eyes were a cloudy yellow.

"Hey, don't fuck around. Answer me, asshole!"

Takumi's face moved not a muscle, and he said nothing.

"Listen to me," the other continued. "I've come up all this way from nothing, doing without all kinds of things, gritting my teeth."

His bitterness and resentment poured out. For him, it was apparently an old grievance.

"Why do I have to be scavenging for garbage like you after all this time? Hey, garbage. It's you, garbage. Are you listening to me, asshole? Can't you even speak, you piece of shit?"

"Excuse me. Good day to you," said Takumi, nodding.

He left the factory, the bellowing of the president and the pounding of the printing presses echoing behind him. It had indeed been an "easy job"; he nonetheless felt burdened.

By the time he was back in Tokyo, arriving at Shinjuku Station, the sun was already setting. The streets were crowded with people, and the flashing lights and signs were jarringly intense. His appointment was in twenty minutes. Following Harrison Yamanaka's instructions, Takumi hurriedly made his way to a major electronics store nearby to do some shopping and then headed for the entertainment district with its densely packed restaurants.

The stand-up eatery to which he had been told to go was open wide and drafty. Even the drum tables set up in front were full of customers. Before entering, Takumi looked nonchalantly behind him but saw no sign of anyone on his tail.

"Come in! Come in!"

Waitresses dressed in indigo-dyed half coats were shouting boisterous encouragement at each and every customer.

Takumi positioned himself at the counter by the wall and placed the paper bag containing the forged documents at his feet. First pretending to look at the menu, he glanced around.

The U-shaped counter, able to accommodate some twenty people, went all around the sides of the restaurant; in the middle was a grill with skewers of various pork entrails, emitting fragrant smoke. The place was nearing full capacity. As he looked at the bustling crowd, he was reminded of Harrison Yamanaka's precautions.

"Don't let your guard down even if you don't see anyone following you. You never know if there are plainclothes detectives, passing themselves off as ordinary customers. And they may not all be men. Pay attention to their feet. Plainclothes detectives don't wear leather shoes or hard-soled, heavy sneakers but rather running shoes, so that they can sprint. And those running shoes don't at all go along with their overall attire, which is quite square. So if you're paying attention, you can spot them. If you can't see their feet, take a look at their eyes. That'll give them away too. They're not relaxing or enjoying their drinks and snacks. They aren't caught up in half-inebriated chatter. They aren't lost in thought, licking their bitter cups of brew as they reflect on their failures at work. They aren't incessantly seeking out someone to talk to after losing in love. No matter how much they seem to be staring at the glass or plate in front of them, their eyes will always be sharply focused outward."

If there were such a person, Takumi was immediately to leave. Yet none of the customers here seemed to fall into any of those types. Takumi ordered beer and grilled skewers, removed his watch from his wrist, placed it on the counter, and waited for the arrival of the person he was to meet.

He had not been told anything of who it might be: old or young, male or female? He had no idea. Harrison Yamanaka said the other party was to identify him by the paper bag from the electronics store at his feet and the watch on the counter.

He had finished most of his skewers, but no likely person had yet appeared. Takumi looked at his watch: If there was still no one after twenty minutes, he was to assume something had gone wrong and should promptly leave the restaurant.

"Oh, come in! Come in!"

An upbeat voice of welcome resounded.

Takumi turned slightly and stole a look at the entrance. Someone was standing there, a bespectacled man in his fifties, dressed in a suit. He was carrying both a nylon business satchel and a paper bag with red-backgrounded logos of various electronics manufacturers. It was the same design as the paper bag Takumi had at his feet.

The man was shown to the corner of the counter. After taking a sip of the oolong tea that was served to him, he motioned to the waiter and moved to stand next to Takumi, who reached for his mug and brought it to his lips.

Who was he, Takumi wondered. Unable to resist, he stole a glance at him. The man was perusing the menu while calmly munching on stew and drinking his tea. No doubt aware of Takumi's presence, he seemed quite absorbed in a time dimension of his own. Again, was this the man he was to meet? *Harrison Yamanaka told me there was no need to speak to whoever it was.* Takumi keenly felt the discomfort of his uncertainty.

The man finished his stew and downed the rest of his drink. After paying his bill, he left, as if he had some other establishment to visit.

Takumi glanced down at his feet. Though how and when he could only guess, he saw that his bag had been switched. The envelope containing the forged documents was gone, as were the discount-bin headphones he had purchased earlier. In their place were a few DVDs, each with a title printed on the back.

"Can I get you another drink?" came the voice of a young headbanded waitress from off to the side.

"No, thank you … Everything was fine. The check please."

He sipped his now lukewarm beer and turned his attention to the alley intermittently visible beyond the entryway's flapping curtains. Their day's work complete, workers were strolling past in twos and threes, shoulder to shoulder, all in apparent harmony, of various ages, male and female, raising cheerful voices. Takumi found himself ruminating over the curses hurled by the president of the printing factory.

■ ■ ■

This was the beginning of a succession of assignments

TOKYO SWINDLERS | *67*

Takumi received from Harrison Yamanaka. The tasks were "easy" and significantly more lucrative than the part-time job he was doing at the same time.

He paid numerous more trips to see the liquor-besotted president. He also visited another printing plant and someone on the inside at a major printing company, nicknamed "the tool-maker," who was a source of forged seals. Looking back, Takumi surmised that he had been subjected to tests, those detailed "precautions" being part of it all.

He never complained about his remuneration and never turned down a job. Perhaps it was because of this, along with his success at avoiding blatant mistakes, that one day Harrison Yamanaka summoned him to a coffee shop in a back alley of Kabukichō in Shinjuku. He thought it would be the usual request for work, but this time there was a twist.

"Soon it won't do to be dealing with driver's licenses without an IC chip."

Harrison Yamanaka was stroking his beard and looked unusually thoughtful.

Takumi knew that for several years now people's licenses were gradually being replaced by IC-compatible versions. Unlike the previous plastic cards that had personal information simply printed on them, these new licenses were not only printed and watermarked but also included an embedded IC chip that contained additional encrypted and more detailed personal data. Special equipment was used to read the information and verify authenticity. These new cards were reportedly already being distributed to license holders; not only the police but also banks and other private companies had adapted to the system.

Takumi may have been little more than a gofer, but he knew that Harrison Yamanaka was surely involved in some sort of fraud involving various forged documents. The introduction of the IC chip in driver's licenses was presumably making it difficult for him to carry out his usual line of work.

"Perhaps he's the only one for the job ... "

Harrison Yamanaka was muttering to himself. He had been staring out of the window at the sunlight in the alley, but he now turned his gaze back to Takumi:

"Might I ask you for a favor?"

A few days later, as though the rainy season had returned, it had been drizzling all morning. After waiting for nightfall, Takumi took the train to an industrial area on the seaside.

From the station, he boarded a local bus and headed for his distant destination, which seemed to draw no closer even as the number of his fellow passengers steadily diminished. Residential houses too were now fewer. Factories, warehouses, and parking lots with trucks and commercial vehicles lined the industrial road running parallel to the route. A convenience store appeared from out of the darkness, its empty interior making the fluorescent lights seem dazzlingly bright.

Takumi leaned back in his seat at the rear. Traces of light from the streetlamps shone through the raindrop-stained window before fading away.

With few conveniences, this area was neither close to any entertainment district nor charmingly picturesque. What was it like to live alone in such a place?

The man he was to meet, Nagai, was a bit younger than Takumi. According to Harrison Yamanaka, Nagai possessed an extraordinarily lucid mind and outstanding skills. He had won a medal at the International Mathematical Olympiad when he was a high-school boy and been invited every year to attend overseas technical conferences sponsored by world-class software companies. Despite his promising future in Japan and abroad, Nagai had somehow disappeared from the public eye and was now, apparently, doing Internet work only when the mood struck him and otherwise living as a virtual hermit.

Harrison Yamanaka plan was to enlist Nagai's help in forging a driver's license. The scheme could not be carried out with watermarking or other printing techniques alone; it was also essential to skim and duplicate the chip.

Nagai was a complete and total night owl and would engage in meetings only after dark. As indication of the young man's difficult personality, Harrison Yamanaka had worked with him only one time and subsequently been refused. He had informed Nagai that Takumi would be visiting him that evening, but from past experience he was not getting his hopes up.

Hearing his stop announced, Takumi put his hand to the edge of the bus window and pressed the red button.

The quiet factory area where he got off was about a ten-minute walk from Nagai's apartment house. The small building was a three-story reinforced-concrete structure with white walls, seemingly quite old, the exterior noticeably deteriorated. Each floor was a single dwelling; the first two looked unoccupied, and Nagai's was on the third.

Takumi pressed the doorbell, but there was no answer. He had refrained from contacting Nagai by phone beforehand, but now he called the number, the ring going unanswered. Takumi wondered whether he might have stepped out.

Just to be sure, he tugged on the doorknob; the door, lacking a U-lock or a chain, opened without resistance. Feeling a bit guilty, he peeked inside. The light above the entrance was off, so the only illumination was from a streetlight over his shoulder.

The house may originally have been used as an office and later remodeled for residential use. There was no place to take off one's shoes, the concrete entryway flowing directly onto the earthen floor of the kitchen, some six tatami mats in size. There was also no place to step, just a huge heap of empty lunch boxes and plastic bottles overflowing from strewn-about bags of garbage.

Across the kitchen was a room. The door was slightly ajar, but darkness obscured the view.

"Excuse me!" he called out in a loud voice.

There was no answer. He was on the verge of concluding that Nagai was, after all, not at home, when he heard a popping sound like the lid of an empty plastic box being crunched in. He could make out a dark shadow creeping toward him from the other side of the room.

He braced himself to deal with this unknown presence, but then saw that it was nothing more than a rather small black cat. Wearing a red collar and showing no sign of alarm, it innocently rubbed its soft head against Takumi's leg. Without hesitating he bent down to stroke its back. It seemed to have been well cared for, plump, with a fine coat of fur.

While Takumi was engaged with the cat, the door he had been holding ajar with his back slammed shut. He now noticed a faint white glow in the corner of the room to the rear. It looked like backlight from a television or computer screen rather than from some electrical fixture.

He stood up and after some hesitation turned on the front-door light. The lunchbox containers and plastic bottles were indeed in disarray, but they also seemed to have been cleaned and simply left undiscarded. There was no smell of rot.

Cautiously, so as not to tread on those containers, he stepped further into the interior; the cat came from behind, nimbly passing him and disappearing into the back room.

Takumi walked to the room's entrance, pulled wide the half-open door, and then nearly let out a scream. Standing in front of him was a man.

He was thin, but taller than Takumi, who was slightly less than five foot eight. His appearance was decidedly odd. The hood of his parka was pulled far over his head; his chest-length hair extended down between the headphones hanging around his neck. Covering his face was a white surgical mask such as those sold in drug stores, and, though he was indoors, he had on large black sunglasses, through which Takumi could not see his eyes.

"Are you Nagai-san?"

It was a foolish question, but Takumi could not bear to remain silent.

"Who are you?"

Through the mask the voice was muffled and difficult to hear. Just like his face, the tone revealed no emotions. Behind Nagai was a room measuring about ten tatami mats. Two computer monitors glowed on a desk by the wall.

Takumi identified himself as a messenger from Harrison Yamanaka. He asked curtly whether Nagai could help in the forging of an IC chip for a driver's license.

"I'm not working for anyone right now."

That sounded like a hard no. Nagai's response was so blunt that Takumi could hardly bring himself to employ all the wheedling phrases he had thought up beforehand. Still, he pressed on and told him, according to Harrison Yamanaka's instructions, the exact amount of substantial compensation he would receive. And would he reconsider?

Nagai replied quickly, standing as motionless as a statue: "Get out!"

Takumi could sense that any further attempt at negotiation would only make Nagai angrier. All he had been asked to do was deliver the message of a job offer; he was not responsible for the outcome of that mission.

Takumi was about to give up and turn on his heels to leave when a sound came from a nearby shelf. A black shadow crossed in front of him: It was the cat, leaping toward its master.

Nagai reflexively caught the cat with both hands, but not before the impact of its front paws had knocked his sunglasses to the floor. Out of the darkness came the dry clattering sound of plastic.

Takumi gasped as he saw Nagai's bare face now illuminated in the bright light from the front door. The skin was scarred, with countless large and small wrinkles forming a bumpy keloid surface like an astringent fruit rind. His unnaturally large nose, which could not be concealed by the mask, was misshapen; it appeared to be the artificial result of some surgery. Particularly wretched was the left side of the face. The eyebrow was completely gone, and where it had been had collapsed, almost completely blocking the eye below and perhaps even blinding it to light. A cloudy lens appeared to be peeking out from the small opening.

Nagai instantly covered his face with his left hand.

"Don't look at me!"

Startled at this angry outburst, the cat jumped down from Nagai's right arm.

Not unaware of the wrong he was committing by ignoring Nagai's wishes, Takumi nonetheless could not remove his unreserved gaze from that face. He had seen scars like that before.

For his court appearance on the day his father was finally sentenced for murder and arson of the family home, the bandage that had been wrapped around his right hand was removed. The burns he had sustained as he set fire to his house were so severe that he had had to undergo multiple skin grafts. The keloids made it look as if melted red wax had been smeared all over the back of his hand and up as far as his elbow. The skin on the fingers of his left hand was a mass of fused scars. Though they differed in color,

Nagai's wounds were of the same type that Takumi remembered seeing.

"Burns?"

If not, he thought, it must have been some strong acidic chemical that had caused such damage.

"I told you not to look!"

Nagai bent over, his voice choking. His frustrated scream reverberated through the once silent room, the volume limited only by the slurring of his words.

Takumi looked into Nagai's vacant left eye.

"It must have hurt ... " he said. His words spilled out involuntarily. Whatever he may have been thinking, what he was saying was not motivated by pity.

Nagai turned around, a look of rage on his face: "I'm going to kill you, you bastard!"

Takumi felt a dull pain near his cheekbone, and now all was a blur as he clawed the air with both hands. Losing his balance, he fell backwards into the clutter on the floor. He heard the dull thud of plastic being crushed against his back and hips.

Grimacing, he sat up and saw Nagai's two eyes—the one full of emotion, the other quite devoid of it—both staring down on him.

"Don't act like you have any idea what you're talking about!"

Through the mask came a furious, unbridled voice, the words trailing off at the end.

Takumi was leaning on one elbow and rubbing his cheek. Slowly getting up, he stood atop the crushed bento boxes and turned toward Nagai:

"My wife ... and my three-year-old son ... and my mother."

He felt what seemed to be a cut inside his mouth. He could taste the blood as he gazed at Nagai, whose right eye looked back at him doubtfully.

"All of them were lost in the fire," he continued. "There was nothing left. I've got my hands full just dealing with that. There's no way I've got the space to try to understand *you*, man!"

He had intended to be forceful, but the tone of his words could only come across instead as self-deprecating.

"My father was in debt and in desperation set our house on fire. Everything was all coal black. They were all burnt to cinders. They had been so soft. Now they were cold and crumbling, falling apart when I touched them."

This was the first time for him to tell anyone about what had happened. If it had not been Nagai, if it were not for his horribly disfigured face, and if it had not been caused by burning, he might not have been able to so honestly express the feelings deeply buried in his heart.

Nagai stood there, his right eye turned toward the void. He seemed to be at a loss.

The cat emerged from between Nagai's legs and calmly stalked about the kitchen; with each footstep came the faint rustling sound of plastic.

"I'm going," said Takumi and turned to leave. From behind him he heard no reply. As he passed through the doorway, through its narrow gap he thought he heard muffled sobs paired with deep, constant, and painful breaths. He closed the door.

In the afterglow of the streetlamps, he could barely make out the rain. It was coming down harder than when he arrived.

If he hurried he could still catch the last bus to the station. The spray hitting his umbrella was cold, and his feet grew heavy as he walked on. A fence stretched along the road to his left, a road that had seemed so ordinary on the way here but that now seemed to go on endlessly.

Through the wire fence he could see five or six freight cars with dark green tanks parked at the rail yard, looking quite abandoned standing in the rain. He felt the urge to tear down the wire mesh and knock them all over.

On the other side of the canal, perpendicular to the railroad tracks, he could see an industrial complex. From its intricate structure of pipes and steel frames emanated a relentlessly harsh light, turning the surface of the water, covered in tiny ripples, to a pallid, ashen color.

■ ■ ■

The following week, he again paid Nagai a nocturnal visit, not at Harrison Yamanaka's request but rather on his own initiative. After he reported that persuading Nagai to take on the job appeared to be as difficult as ever. Yamanaka had nodded and said he would seek another gambit.

Nagai looked quite surprised at seeing Takumi again. When asked whether he might like to share the Shōkadō bento Takumi had bought at a delicatessen in front of the station, he consented with surprising candor.

Nagai sat cross-legged on the floor, as he ate, removing his mask but still wearing his sunglasses. As with his left eye, the skin around his mouth was pulled tight, so his lips did not move freely, and it was with admirable dexterity that he brought the rice and side dishes into his mouth.

In the darkness, as he ate his own portion, Takumi talked about how he had lost his family in the fire and gone on living since then. Nagai in turn spoke freely of his sudden accident at the age of twenty, of the severe burns he had suffered from the flames ignited by gasoline spewed by the motorcycle he had been riding, and of how he had thereafter come to shun all human interaction. He said that it had been a long time since he had been able to talk with anyone at length. Perhaps, despite avoiding such, he had yearned for conversation.

As he spoke, he became more talkative, struggling to convey his pent-up, unexpressed feelings as fully and honestly as possible. Takumi continued to listen in silence, occasionally injecting a word or two.

Nagai returned from the kitchen with a coffee mug in each hand.

"Do you have fish in there?" Takumi asked, his eyes on a corner of the room.

Atop a waist-high cabinet stood a large aquarium tank, measuring more than three feet across. As the room was dark and the aquarium unlit, there was no way to know what lay within. The only sounds emanating from it were the hum of the motor and a vague intimation of water.

"Just a few," said Nagai as he handed Takumi a steaming mug before turning on the fluorescent light installed in the ceiling of the tank.

Before their eyes now appeared a dazzling waterscape.

Takumi stared in surprise and wonder.

A frameless glass box formed a rectangle out of a mass of clear water, creating a microcosm within. Gentle undulations spread from the moss-covered rocks on the front left to the bottom. Several kinds of aquatic plants in vivid green covered the entire area like a meadow; a school of tropical fish of sapphire blue was gliding by in a majestic procession.

"Did you do all of this … by yourself?"

Nagai nodded, somewhat shyly. He picked up a pair of long-handled trimming scissors specially designed for this task and removed the tank lid. Realizing that Takumi did not know what he was doing, he offered an explanation as he went about tending to the plants.

Filled with freshwater, the aquarium, Nagai said, is a pseudo-ecosystem, with various external aids such as lighting and filtration systems. The strictly controlled water quality is based on a delicate balance, and if the balance is even slightly disturbed, the organisms within, including the bacteria, will be unable to survive.

Nagai was calmly and carefully pruning the plants. His devotion was something Takumi could well understand.

"Have you been doing this for a long time?" he casually inquired.

"No, it's only been since the accident—or rather since my marriage plans fell apart." Nagai's tone was flat.

"Marriage?"

Before the accident, Nagai explained, he had been engaged. After, the relationship continued, his fiancée being devoted to his treatment and rehabilitation. Yet at some point a look of fear appeared in her eyes. Though somehow trying to be accepting, she was, he concluded, unconsciously avoiding him. For her sake, he had then on his own ended the engagement.

Takumi was in no mood to offer words of comfort. Reminded of his own dead family, he did not want to hear anything from others who might presume to understand.

It was suddenly time for the last bus. Nagai appeared to have more to say, but Takumi stood up, promising to come for another visit.

"Are you in a hurry?" asked Nagai, calling him back.

"I have to catch my bus."

"You want me to skim a driver's license, don't you?"

The abrupt remark momentarily had him at a loss for words. It was quite unexpected.

"Yes, but are you sure you want to?"

Rather than reply, Nagai exposed a row of teeth. His tight skin made it awkward, but now for the first time he was offering Takumi a gentle smile.

It was a few days later that Takumi met Harrison Yamanaka in the Kabukichō coffee shop to tell him that Nagai had agreed to take on the job.

"How did you persuade him?"

"I suppose it was the cat …"

In response to this seemingly facetious reply, Harrison Yamanaka gave Takumi a puzzled look.

By modifying an off-the-shelf commercial product, Nagai was able to produce an IC card reader/writer that perfectly met Yamanaka's expectations. When a driver's license with an IC chip was skimmed with Nagai's terminal they could capture not just what was printed on the face of the card, such as the date of birth and facial image, but also data such as the legal domicile and PIN number that, due to the introduction of the chip, were no longer visible. This extracted information could then be transcribed onto another IC card that, even if run through a dedicated license checker, would not be detected as a forgery. The only task remaining in order to produce an elaborate counterfeit driver's license was to print a watermark along with the printed information from the original copied card.

Takumi went around to racetracks and pachinko parlors with the modified terminal and searched for would-be "customers" who matched the age and gender of Harrison Yamanaka's target. He lent them small sums of money and ran their driver's licenses through the terminal, one after another, under the guise of identity verification.

• • •

It had come as something of a surprise to Harrison Yamanaka that Takumi had succeeded in persuading the recluse Nagai to change his mind. Takumi may have benefited from coincidence, but Yamanaka's view of him was in any case altered. Simply put, from this one incident Yamanaka had come to have far greater confidence in him. He had then approached Takumi with the idea of making him a full-fledged participant in his operations, and it was just about this same time that Takumi was beginning to hear how Yamanaka had quite a reputation in the demi-monde as a land swindler.

"Well now, Takumi-san," he had asked him, "how about giving it a try?"

Takumi had hitherto found no purpose in life, each dull and dreary day idly spent in monotonous drudgery. Whether or not he became a swindler, he did not care who or what he was, as long as he had enough money in his pocket.

Once Takumi agreed, Harrison began to teach him the knowledge and skills required for the occupation. He went so far as to provide what he called "practical" training: the opportunity to learn about sales and transactions at a real estate company he had a relationship with.

Takumi absorbed the teachings voraciously, even attempting to boost confidence in his skills by acquiring agency certification using another person's name. However impure his motives, the experience of learning the unknown and doing what he had once been unable to do gave him a fleeting sense of fulfillment.

It was only after his "land master training" was completed that it became clear to Takumi that Harrison Yamanaka was more than a mere fraudster. He was well versed in Real Estate Transaction Law, Real Estate Registration Law, Land and House Lease Law, Urban Planning Law, National Land Use Planning Law, and Condominium Unit Ownership Law, as well as local government ordinances. He could easily recite articles and precedents of the Criminal Law and Criminal Procedure Law. He could even quote passages from such classical works as those of Aristotle, Hegel, and Marx.

In the presence of someone with such a memory and range of knowledge, one could not completely dismiss as mere boastful blarney his claim to have been a University of Tokyo dropout. By the same token, while working as a brothel driver, Takumi had witnessed sides of Yamanaka so lacking in empathy as to suggest he had been a psychopath from birth.

As Takumi acquired expertise backed by a wealth of experience, he gradually began to put it all into practice, initially involving simple projects like deposit fraud related to real estate transactions. Growing steadily more accustomed to the work, he found himself becoming ever more absorbed in it.

One particular day, he was attending the settlement of a transaction in the reception room of a brokerage firm. The plan was to use a faux seller to defraud a would-be buyer out of nearly 200 million yen. All that was left was to wait for the remaining funds to be transferred. Takumi, who was part of the operation, watched as the plan smoothly proceeded, maintaining the poker face that had become second nature to him.

The would-be buyer was a man in his thirties living in western Honshu. Circumstances had led him to resign from his company job and take over the family business. Quite nervous in the presence of strangers, he noted, his cheeks reddening, that this was his first time to invest in real estate. He was not at all like the overbearing, quirky types Takumi had been encountering. The buyer's sincere personality was evident in his every word and action, and he did not appear to harbor the slightest suspicion toward Takumi and his cohorts. As they all waited for confirmation of the money transfer, the buyer offered up suitable topics of conversation and was constantly endeavoring, with his clumsy manner of speaking, to be attentive to everyone.

"My mother used to run the company," he said. "But some years ago, she was diagnosed with an incurable disease. As you may know, it is quite a dreadful ailment: You gradually lose control of your body and eventually you're even unable to breathe. Worst of all, there is no specific treatment for it."

The room fell silent.

"She is now still able, with the help of my father, somehow though barely, to take care of herself, but that can only go on for so long. I'm ashamed to admit I've been selling tofu-making equipment for some time, even though I don't know the first thing about business management, investment, or real estate. I am, however, so very fortunate and happy to have had you all come to the rescue!"

Takumi nodded in response. Just from being touched by some stale kindness, a buyer comes to trust someone he has only just met, knowing nothing about the person, and thus blithely exposes himself. Takumi was reminded of having once been much the same as this would-be buyer …

Back in the days when he was still selling medical equipment as a sales representative for his family's company, he had met a man introducing himself as a medical doctor. They happened to be sitting next to each other at the counter of a bar in a hotel not far from Yokohama's Yamashita Park and ended up chatting a bit.

Appearing around fifty years of age, the man said he was working independently, unaffiliated with any hospital but instead traveling from one to another on call. He was quiet and had a good-natured air about him. Just when he seemed on the verge of some declaration, he would only mutter without a trace of irony or ostentation that he was prepared to give up everything if it meant saving others. Touched by the man's evident kindness, Takumi felt that a load had been lifted from his chest. Aided by the alcohol, he found himself speaking more freely than usual.

By now Takumi was weary of constantly entertaining clients and equally of putting up with the arrogance and outrageous demands of the physicians he was doing business with. He had no one with whom he could speak or consult, and out of a sense of duty and responsibility toward his family and relatives, he dared not consider turning his back on the job. It was only this man now who, while offering not a word of either encouragement or criticism, silently listened as Takumi confided his troubles.

They bade each other farewell at the bar but remained in contact, the man offering Takumi personal advice and even introducing him to the hospital where he had professional ties. About a year later, a cryptic expression on his face, he asked Takumi whether he might meet his company's staff. Feeling much indebted to him, Takumi had no intention of refusing the man's request and so introduced him to his father, then the managing director. After first talking him into carrying out a small business deal, the man used the trust this had gained him to lure the utterly unsuspecting father into a much larger endeavor, the one that then led to the company's bankruptcy.

Thereafter the man disappeared, and it was only some time after the company went bottom up that it became apparent that he had no medical qualifications and had been going to hospitals under the guise of being a "medical consultant."

Takumi's mind was still lost in the past as the current transaction was winding up.

The would-be buyer, no older than Takumi, went around shaking the hand of each person involved, quite unaware that he had been hoodwinked. He finally reached Takumi, who on extending his right hand found it then clasped in both hands by the other. There was in the man's grasp a softness mingled with the warmth of his body.

If Takumi had, long ago, seen through to the true identity of the man posing as a physician, he and his family might have been spared catastrophe. If this man today had smelled a rat somewhere along the way and possessed the clarity of mind not to be deceived, he might have saved himself from great financial loss.

Yet Takumi had no sympathy for him: Strong lads laugh; weaklings weep. It all came down to that, neither more nor less. Just as he had once been the beast's prey, there were now new victims to be fully devoured.

"Thank you so very much. Yes, thank you, thank you. With this I think that I may at last have shown myself to be a devoted son."

As he was shaking hands the man was bowing in a most exaggerated manner. When he slowly raised his head, there was not a cloud of doubt in his eyes.

Takumi felt goose bumps of excitement; it was as though all his lifeblood were seething with excitement, as though he were enraptured by the perverse and visceral awareness that he had crushed the last remnant of whatever youthful conscience he may once have had.

But cheating others out of their money did not fill the emptiness in his soul. Even in succumbing to evil, he could not remake the past. Whatever thrill came from exploiting the goodwill or conscience of others, that too gradually came to sink into a mindless abyss. Before he knew it, Takumi had become as devoted to his line of work as any addict to his drug. Only when immersed in acts of fraud did he feel transparent, free-floating, and utterly detached from the cares of the world.

He gave little thought to ever turning his back on it all, and so, not surprisingly, that opportunity never came. And thus it was that four years had passed since Takumi had become a swindler.

# 3

After climbing the Maruyama slopes that summer, Takumi had, to escape the heat, rented a cottage in Furano, Hokkaido, and spent his leisure fishing and driving around wherever the urge took him. By the time he returned to Tokyo the trees lining the streets had begun to take on autumnal tints, and on some days there was a chill in the air.

One day he slipped into a suit for the first time in quite a while and made his way to a private lounge in a long-established Hibiya hotel. There he met Harrison Yamanaka and his cohorts.

"Takeshita-san is late."

Gotō opened his mouth wide and took a bite of his hamburger steak sandwich. He had apparently won quite a sum in the casinos of Macau and was looking quite relaxed.

It was unusual for the time-conscious Takeshita to be late. He was not answering his phone.

"Hasn't he at least called to say that he's been delayed?" whined Reiko as she reached for a scone on the three-tiered tea stand. During her stay in Hawai'i she had apparently quarreled with her lover.

"Not yet."

Harrison Yamanaka glanced at his watch and drew his teacup to his mouth. His companions were seeing his face for the first time in three and a half months. It was tanned golden brown from exposure to the Caribbean sun. He had kept his youthful appearance, his dark hair and goatee as meticulously groomed as ever.

"Maybe his mind's still stuck in Monaco, or maybe some white chick there has quite deboned 'im."

No one laughed at Gotō's bit of nonsense. The meeting was being held to discuss the next project. Takeshita was in charge of compiling materials for it, so without him they could not proceed.

"He's the sort of person who never misses work, so I don't think we have anything to worry about."

The lingering look of concern on Yamanaka's face belied his reassuring words. Just as Takumi had picked up his phone to call Takeshita once more, the door behind him opened.

Preceded by a member of the hotel staff, Takeshita entered the room, a Louis Vuitton attaché case in hand, and sat down in a neighboring seat, letting the full weight of his body sink in. He looked like a different person: His darkly tanned cheeks had hollowed, and his double-lidded eyes seemed all the larger. Leaning back in his seat and silently staring at the table, he resembled an invalid forced to fast for many days.

"What's wrong?" Yamanaka asked, abruptly speaking up. Takeshita slowly turned his head and replied, his gaunt face flashing a smile.

"Ah, well I was constantly up all night thanks to this job, so I was off and on taking a bit of speed. I fed it to the broad I hooked up with at Narita, and then she got so wired that we kept goin' at it gangbusters. I'm worn to a frazzle!"

A hearty laugh erupted in the room.

"Takeshita-san, can I now have what I asked you for?"

Takeshita met Yamanaka's request with a somber look and extracted a bundle of documents from his attaché case, a summary of the research that he and his subordinates had conducted.

Takumi took the sheets and began to turn them over, one by one. They contained information about potential targets, including maps of demarcated plots attached to a land register, maps of their surrounding areas, certificates of registered matters, photographs of current conditions, market prices, property outlines such as zoning and building-to-land ratios, and personal information on the owners' backgrounds and family relationships. To the best of Takumi's knowledge, Takeshita had never before prepared such a large volume of detailed information when selecting target properties. Such was a measure of the enormous commitment that Harrison Yamanaka, both as client and creator, had put into the risky endeavor.

As Takumi was examining the materials, Takeshita, now looking a bit pale, pulled out a pen-type e-cigarette from his attaché case.

"Takeshita-san, have you started smoking?" asked Gotō, looking up from the materials.

"No, this isn't a cigarette. It actually gives you a bigger kick than nicotine."

He was about to vaporize a solution of methamphetamine using an e-cigarette device and then inhale it.

"Don't do that here!" exclaimed Reiko nervously.

"Not to worry! Not to worry! It's all right to smoke here, and my dear alveoli will come through for me and absorb all the active ingredients."

Takeshita put the e-cigarette in his mouth, pressed the button, inhaled the vapor, and then held his breath for a moment before exhaling. The gloomy shadow that had covered his face just a few moments ago was swept away, his vitality quickly restored.

"I've been resurrected!" he declared with relief. His eyes were dilated, a hazy light within them glimmering.

"Now that I'm feeling myself again, let's get started."

With that authoritative pronouncement, Takeshita turned his attention to the documents in his hand.

"So, I've marked the head of each entry with my own tentative evaluation, ranking them A, B, C. A indicates 'recommended,' B 'unproblematic'; the rest are in the C category, but they're tricky, and there are too many of them, so I've left them out."

In the papers, a handwritten alphabet letter was at the beginning of each listed property. Two of the properties were A-rated. Seeming to slur his words, Takeshita noted that these were basically the only ones that needed to be considered.

"First, on page 1, the property in Akasaka. As you can see from the map, it is near Tameike and is currently a parking lot. The registration is all in order, and there is no mortgage. I think the location makes it a good buy, and with current market conditions, it ought to fetch a solid 2.1 to 2.2 billion."

"Takeshita-san, when ya say this is an A-rated property, are ya goin' by the land alone?"

To Gotō's question, Takeshita replied with a knowing smirk: "That's one thing, but not the only thing. The owner of the place is a rich old man of about seventy. A while back he got himself a second wife, a Filipina about twenty, and now he's become a papa. It's a crazy story, but the kid is his first, so naturally it's his darling baby. He wanted to be able to leave some money for the little one, so he moved to Singapore for tax purposes."

To get the tax break, Takeshita went on to explain, basically meant having to spend the entire year there. So setting up an impersonator or proxy during his absence would have a real chance of success.

Reiko was looking at Takeshita, as she spiked a strawberry with her fork and put it into her mouth.

"You mean he's about the same age as Sasaki-san from before?"

"Yeah, I suppose so."

"Well then," she asked with a studied expression of dissatis-faction, "we should've asked him again. It's so much trouble find-ing people!"

"There're no shortcuts on this!" snorted Takeshita. "To begin with, the man's completely different in height. He's been doing karate all his life, and I hear he's a strapping old dude."

Harrison Yamanaka glanced at Takeshita and without a word looked down at the documents again.

Takumi flipped through the pages and pointed out some-thing that had been on his mind: "The other one with an A rating, in Nishi-Shinjuku … You considered it before, am I right? At the time, as I remember it, the conclusion was that it would be a hard nut to crack."

The property was well known among those working in the area. Currently it comprised an old private house, a coin-operated parking lot, and a shuttered stationery shop next door. The site itself faced a main street and was located in an area undergoing active redevelopment, so the expectation was for development as a high-rise residence. There was no question that all eyes were very much on it, and that if it were to go on the market it would probably fetch no less than 3 billion yen. The owner was a single woman in her sixties who had inherited the property from her parents. Obstinate and misanthropic, she insisted she would not sell the land to anyone and had sent packing every realtor who had come to her door.

"Well that's how it was … ," noted Takeshita.

"And has now anything changed?" asked Gotō.

"Changed? Yes indeed. Big time!" replied Takeshita tri-umphantly. "I shouldn't be gloating over others' misfortune, but the old lady seems to have been smitten with cancer. And here's where she's so true to form: She's refusing every treatment the doctors are recommending. That's just how she is all right."

"So that must mean that she's resigned herself to dealing with her condition all by herself at home," remarked Takumi, glancing at Takeshita.

"You'd think so, but no … She's gone in for what I guess you'd call folk medicine. There's a famous hot spring up north in Tōhoku that's supposed to cure illnesses. It seems that granny has settled in there and is taking hot-stone baths."

"Cancer can be cured with hot-stone baths?" asked Reiko with a straight face.

"That I'd sure as hell like to know myself," replied Takeshita, as he turned to smile at his companions. "The thing to remember is that the house in Nishi-Shinjuku is at the moment empty and that there are very few people other than ourselves who know it."

Given that the owner was single, antisocial, and, to top it off, not even at home, it was unlikely that someone impersonating her would be noticed, and the job would thus be relatively easy. The land itself had everything going for it, and was many times more expensive than the Ebisu property. Takeshita's "A" rating thus appeared to be perfectly reasonable.

Eyes from all sides of the table were now on the man in charge of decision-making, waiting for him to weigh in. Whether or not aware of the attention, Harrison Yamanaka finally glanced up from the various documents, looking thoughtful if a bit distracted, and turned to Takeshita.

"You spoke of the materials you labeled 'C.' Do you happen to have them here?"

"I do," replied Takeshita, with a hint of irritation "but they're all quite iffy, let me tell you."

"I'd be grateful, if you could show them to me."

"Well, as long as you're going to be displeased, it might be faster if you found out for yourself," grumbled Takeshita, clicking his tongue. He roughly grabbed another document from his attaché case and half-tossed it to Harrison Yamanaka.

The sound of pages being resolutely turned over one after another only added to the ponderous mood around the table.

Reiko, who had been sipping Darjeeling tea, put her cup down.

"Why can't you accept Takeshita-san's recommendations?"

The hand turning the page stopped.

Reiko's fingers suddenly flexed slightly, as though they had just received a jolt of electricity.

"Is this not all quite boring?"

As Harrison Yamanaka began to speak, a gleam of delight shone in his eyes, as if he were explaining things to a child.

"As long as you keep fixating on things anyone can do, you'll never face a real challenge. Rather than hills, aim for mountains. Instead of easy tasks, seek out the difficult ones. It's only by conquering seemingly unscalable peaks where everyone else, looking up at the misty heights would despair, that you will find the ultimate thrill, true fulfillment, and satisfaction, beyond any pleasure."

"This is the way you were talking before, but you're still springin' it all new on us." said Gotō doubtfully.

Harrison Yamanaka adopted a studied air of contemplation, laying the documents on the table, leaning on his elbows, and interlacing his fingers, as though praying. His prosthetic finger, clearly visible from Takumi's vantage point, did not move.

"Now we've just heard Takeshita-san's account of the woman in Nishi-Shinjuku. Well, at my age I can't avoid declining physical vitality."

All were listening with rapt attention, as with downcast eyes he continued:

"And as you know, this line of work is terribly demanding. As our bodily strength wanes, so does our willpower. Our instincts grow dull. And when that occurs, one cannot tackle those high mountains. As the challenges grow, so do our adversaries."

The room again fell silent. After a brief period of meditation, Harrison Yamanaka looked up.

"I was once, this is now some years ago, quite caught up in hunting, for which I traveled extensively overseas. It was not for trophies or the like—specimens stuffed and mounted. I was simply drawn to hunting with a gun. Taking a life with my own hands and being grateful for receiving that life. Perhaps I felt that I was experiencing something sacred in that primitive act."

"Nah, what is this, some sort of old tale you're layin' on us?"

As Gotō tried to interrupt him, Yamanaka gently gestured him to silence.

"I also became accustomed to handling rifles during my trips to Africa. Then I went on a week-long trip to Montana. There I was open to any game that could be eaten, and I think it was either moose or elk, coinciding with the hunting season at the time."

Also on the expedition, Yamanaka continued, was a middle-aged Anglo, fat and haughty, along with their young Hispanic guide, fresh out of hunting school. They made their forays from the beautiful lakeside base camp that served as their hub and, mounted on their horses, spent three days in the woods on a quest for prey. When after the second, then the third day, they had had no luck, the Anglo began to complain, whereupon the overanxious guide went off the deep end. What was to be a pleasant hunting trip had turned most unpleasant.

"On the fourth day, it was bitterly cold. We had been out searching for game since morning, alas, again without success. We were eating our lunch in the woods, the Anglo munching on his sandwich even as, red in the face, he berated the downhearted guide in the foulest sort of language, saying, 'I don't wanna have to see you when we're taking a break. So get lost!' The young man then dejectedly moved himself out of sight behind a nearby boulder."

All were all quite attentive.

"We went on eating, listening to the Anglo grumbling, and then there was a scream. At first, I thought the young man might have been stung by a bee, but it was no ordinary cry. We stopped talking and looked toward the boulder. For an instant it looked as though it had bulged up into something bigger, but no … What we saw was an enormous, fully grown grizzly bear.

"It must have weighed nearly seven hundred pounds but it was nonetheless remarkably agile and was dragging the guide, who though fiercely resisting, was utterly powerless. The tethered horses neighed and thrashed about, and the Anglo fled.

"I couldn't have tried to rescue the guide without putting myself in danger. To a ferocious bear, we humans are mere playthings. We had no radios, since they were prohibited there, so calling for help was not an option."

"So did you run?" asked Reiko with the question on everyone's mind.

"No," replied Yamanaka dispassionately, "I watched."

"I looked on from a slight distance as the guide was being mauled, holding my rifle in both hands. Bears, you see, are voracious, not like cats. They eat their prey alive. The guide was screaming as he was being consumed. His eyes were on me, as again and again he pleaded for help. His voice then fell silent, replaced by the sound of the grizzly crushing his skull."

"Yuck!" exclaimed Reiko, as she reached for her cup. Takeshita was, grimly, staring at Yamanaka, who seemed to be suppressing a smile.

"Well now, the grizzly duly finished its meal and appeared satisfied while it picked up from the ground a rag-like chunk of flesh, perhaps a bit of arm or leg. I thought it would then simply lumber off, but no. It suddenly let go of its morsel and turned toward me. In its round eyes I could not read its intent."

Harrison Yamanaka opened his eyes wide. There was something childlike in the way he smiled and bared his teeth.

"Can you imagine, everyone, what I felt at that moment? I had never had such a sensation of being alive, in every fiber of my being. I was in a frenzy as I fired every bullet into the massive body of the beast. After I had brought it down, my mind was strangely calm, even as I was so intensely aroused that I thought my penis was about to burst. Onto the bear's outstretched, flaccid tongue, covered with the guide's blood, I ejaculated."

Yamanaka stopped speaking and stared at a point in the table, as though peering into his own inner thoughts.

"Perhaps I simply cannot put out of my mind the excitement I felt at that moment."

Takeshita, painfully aware of his heart beating, found it difficult to avert his gaze from Yamanaka's ecstatic profile.

Yamanaka once again examined the documents and then turned to face Takeshita.

"What's the situation here?"

Along with Gotō and Reiko, Takeshita peered at the papers on the table.

The property, previously dismissed from consideration by Takeshita, was a large parking lot adjacent to a former rehabilitation facility near Sengakuji Station in Tokyo's Minato Ward. The combined property covered nearly two-thirds of an acre and was a neatly shaped plot of land with no mortgage attached. It faced a three-lane national road running from Nihonbashi in Tokyo to Yokohama. A new station on the Yamanote Line was being planned there, making it a promising area for redevelopment. It was thus an exceptionally rare and potentially high-demand piece of land.

"Oh, but it won't work. The nun who owns it is well known in the area for refusing to sell, and she's still quite in good shape. Besides, this isn't a standalone property. It's under the supervision of an umbrella religious corporation, so we can't touch it. Honestly speaking, I'd say we should stay away from it. It would be just a waste of time."

Takeshita grimaced, looking annoyed at what seemed to be the bother of it all. Harrison Yamanaka was not backing down.

"What's the market value?"

"Well now … around 9 billion, maybe even 10."

"10 billion!" Reiko's eyes widened as she heard the figure.

"Ah, quite impossible then. You'll not be findin' a buyer."

Gōto leaned back on his chair, running his hand through his hair and smiling as if he had lost interest.

Up until then, Takeshita and his colleagues had hatched several schemes worth several billion yen. But they had never gone beyond the drawing board, all fell through before being executed. A deal in the 10-billion-yen range was a mountain they had never even contemplated climbing.

Rain had begun to veil the reflection in the window of the building across the way.

The agitation in the room, far from subsiding, was only growing.

"There might still be some way in. Look into it a bit more," said Harrison Yamanaka pointedly to Takeshita before slowly turning toward Takumi:

"And I should ask for your assistance as well."

■ ■ ■

Descending from the pedestrian bridge, Tatsu joined the human stream that was flowing toward the station.

The cold air of late autumn penetrated the collar of his nylon coat, making him all the more aware of the drowsiness and weariness weighing on his entire body. His black synthetic leather walking shoes might as well have been lined with lead, and each time their rubber soles hit the ground, the hard pavement penetrated to his heels, which had been supporting his weight throughout restless, largely sleepless days and nights.

Just recently he had been called to assist at the local station in a case of embezzlement at a regional bank with a branch in Tokyo. The investigation was seeking to discover how a thirtyish employee had disposed of the money he was suspected of having embezzled from a customer. Tatsu had been helping 24-7 with the backup work when, finally, a break came, allowing him a brief return home.

In times past he had often been obliged to be absent from home for months during investigations. A week or two away did not trouble him, but lately he had been feeling more acutely the physical toll. The insidious decline in his condition was a most unwelcome reminder of the limited time remaining in his career as a police detective.

Twilight, signaling the end of day, was casting a long shadow at his feet and tinting the buses parked at the terminal and the walls of the station building. The crowds were hurrying homeward, swallowed up by the station. Tatsu followed.

To return home to the suburbs he needed first to take a private railway and then change trains along the way. He was contemplating the route as he walked, stop by stop, when a particular location sprang to his mind.

Countless footsteps echoed in the station.

Tatsu leaned against a wall and took out his cellphone from

the inner pocket of his suit. Pausing slightly, he tapped his home number.

There were five rings. Then, just before the sixth, his wife answered. Her voice was hurried, as if she had grabbed for the receiver while still in the kitchen.

"Something came up at work today. I'm sorry, but could you go ahead with dinner without me?"

"Weren't you supposed to finish early today? I'd prepared an oyster hotpot especially for tonight."

Her sigh was mixed with disappointment; she seemed to have been looking forward to eating together, but her tone carried little reproach.

In his twenties, when Tatsu was still a rookie, with three young daughters, the demands of his job, which knew no distinction between day and night, often led to domestic quarrels. He and his wife had even separated once, deeming it impossible to go on. They had somehow weathered the crisis and managed to continue their life together. His wife had long detested his all-consuming detective work, so she had either resigned herself to her plight or simply become accustomed to it, and now demonstrated such understanding as to bring him a change of clothes and vitamin drinks during prolonged investigations.

"I won't be all that late."

Overwhelmed by the sudden intensity of station noise, Tatsu had to raise his voice.

"Ah, when have I heard that before? Is it some urgent case?"

"No, it's not that. There's just something that's been bothering me."

Throughout his career, he had pursued countless cases. Rational judgments and actions did not always lead to resolutions. Sometimes, a mere hunch, seemingly whimsical detours, brought unexpected key information and significant progress.

Ignoring a gut feeling had more than once led to an irredeemable situation, completely cutting off the path to a resolution.

"Your usual baseless hunch, then?" his wife remarked teasingly.

He gazed at the stream of people passing by without replying and smiled wryly.

"Didn't you say that with approaching retirement you'd be taking it easy?"

Tatsu imagined her smiling her own smile.

The post-retirement plan was to enjoy a leisurely cruise. She did not mention it, but he knew she was looking forward to it.

"I suppose that's what the idea was ... "

"Don't overdo it."

"I know," he said to himself by way of acknowledgement as he put the phone back into his pocket.

Tatsu boarded a crowded train and got off one stop before the terminal station that connected to his homeward-bound line. The station where he now found himself was adjacent to a national university. From the exit of the remodeled station building a straight road led to the main gate. He went in as if he belonged there and set across the vast campus grounds.

The sun had already set, and lights were on in the broad expanse of buildings. He occasionally passed groups of students, their cheerful voices ringing out, breaking the silence. Unconsciously he was quickening his pace as he made his way further into the interior. Gone, it seemed, was his fatigue from his office overnight stays.

As he came to the edge of the campus, the sports field came into view. Absent any lighting, it was pitch-black; there was no one to be seen. Stepping onto the running track, Tatsu had a sweeping view of a ten-story, large-scale apartment building on the opposite side. A blend of single rooms for individuals and larger units for families, the complex had balconies visible from his angle. Light emanating from a few of the rooms formed mosaic patterns against the nocturnal darkness.

Tatsu squinted from the shadows as he looked toward the building, counting up from the ground floor as he searched for the room located at the end of the third floor. The occupant or, more exactly, the person who had used the room as an office, was a man in his thirties, one Inoue Hideo, who worked as a real estate consultant.

In July of that year, Inoue had been present as an agent at the site of a fraudulent transaction involving land in Ebisu. The detective in charge had tried to interview him as a key person of interest, but all contact had been lost. Inoue had disappeared, leaving behind an empty one-room apartment with not a single piece of furniture.

It was not only Inoue who was missing. A mediator and the elderly man who had apparently played the role of seller were also nowhere to be found. Because information leading to the arrest of the perpetrators had proven so hard to come by, the case remained unsolved.

Compared to other major scam cases, this one had seemed to inspire relatively little enthusiasm from the higher-ups. A few investigators continued to work it, but perhaps because they were all dealing with other matters as well, no significant progress had been reported.

Amidst the faintly emerging consensus that the Ebisu victims might simply have to accept their losses, Tatsu, while busy with a new case, continued to keep this one in mind. It had involved more than 700 million yen in damages. And its modus operandi had been all too brilliantly clever.

The account into which the embezzled funds had been transferred was in the name of "Shimazaki Ken'ichi," a phony identity, and all the money had already been converted to highly anonymous cryptocurrency, with not a clue as to its ultimate recipient. The forged documents used in the crime had been expertly prepared, and fingerprint searches had yielded no matches in the database. The investigators had scoured surveillance footage around the site of the transaction and interviewed residents near the property itself, but so far no useful information had been obtained.

The evidence was persuasive that professional swindlers were involved. The elderly man posing as the supposed seller was likely to have been a one-time hire, with others devising the strategies and pulling strings behind the scenes. There were not many people capable of carrying out such a scheme. Was this not indeed the nefarious work of Harrison Yamanaka?

No matter how much Tatsu mulled it over, it was all speculation, and he had no choice but methodically to follow the leads at hand. He wanted to track down Inoue, bring the case to a resolution, and, he hoped, find a clue that would lead to Harrison Yamanaka.

Various assumptions drifted through his mind as he soon identified Inoue's room among the rows of apartments. The room was dark, suggesting the occupant was out. It seemed his hunch had proven wrong. The stiffness in his shoulders now easily gave way.

"Just as she said," Tatsu thought with a wry smile and turned to go. He wanted to head home immediately but noted a reluctance in his steps. Before returning to the station, he would, just in case, check out the room. His wife's teasing voice reverberated from somewhere, advising him that the outcome would be the same. But even as he contemplated the seemingly endless futility of it all, he turned his feet toward the building.

He rode an ancient elevator to the third floor and pressed

the doorbell of Inoue's room. As expected, there was no response, and no sound was coming from within. He considered asking the neighbors, but as luck would have it, they too seemed to be out. He could hardly engage in a one-man stakeout, and so he had no alternative but to give up and leave.

He summoned the elevator from the ground floor, stepped into the empty cage, and leaned against the wall, idly watching as the glass-windowed door silently closed, obscuring his line of sight. After a brief pause, the elevator began its descent. Just then, through the window, he spied a figure crossing the corridor, possibly someone who had come up or down the adjacent staircase.

Reaching the ground floor, Tatsu remained in the cage, closed the door, and pressed the button for the third floor. He felt quite exasperated with himself. Standing again in front of Inoue's room, he rang the bell; and again there was no response. He was about to dismiss what seemed to be yet another idle hunch, when he heard footsteps within, growing ever more perceptible. In a few moments, the door opened.

It was a woman who looked to be in her forties. She was dressed in a sweatshirt and gripping the doorknob. Might she be Inoue's woman? The thought occurred to Tatsu, as he observed several moving-company cardboard boxes folded and lined up in the hallway of the room.

"Yes, what is it?" she asked with a wary look.

Tatsu took out his police badge from an inside pocket and briefly explained the reason for his visit. From her reaction it seemed she knew nothing of Inoue.

"Since moving here, have you noticed anything that might be of help?"

The woman put her hand to her chin as though trying to remember.

"There might have been a letter in the mailbox for the previous tenant."

"Where is it now?" Tatsu asked in a sharper tone.

The letter, she explained, had been in a brown envelope, addressed to a different location but then forwarded to what was now her mailbox, located on the first floor. She said that she had, despite pangs of conscience, neglected to inform the building's management company and then thrown it away in the communal garbage.

Hearing that she had discarded the letter that very day, Tatsu hurried to the trash on the first floor, telling himself it might still be there. Digging through the combustible waste, with all the odors of mold and decay, he at last found an envelope smeared with a margarine-like substance. The seal had been broken, perhaps by the woman. To avoid leaving fingerprints, Tatsu carefully picked it up with a handkerchief.

Affixed to the envelope was a forwarding-notice label. Japan Post's forwarding service was valid for a year after an application was submitted and could be renewed annually. It would seem that the would-be recipient had let it all go. The envelope's addressee was "Tsujimoto Takumi," the address in Yokohama. The characters had been penned in proper block-style calligraphy, though the lines slightly wavered, as though the writer were faltering.

On the back, there was the name of the sender, "Tsujimoto Masami," and next to that the address: "Chiba Prison ... "

■　■　■

The withered winter grass glistened in the morning sun. Here and there divots from tee shots by players ahead of him had exposed the soil beneath.

Aoyagi Takashi had taken a firm stance, seeking his center of gravity and relaxing his shoulders, focusing his attention on the ball at his feet. He brought the head of his driver to rest behind it, twisted his hips to raise the driver, and swung vigorously with his right side tightened. The white ball launched with a solid feel through the grip and, cutting through the air, was drawn upward toward wavy clouds floating in the pale blue sky.

The ball, now pea-size in the distance, traced a parabolic arch as it soared past his group of long-time friends, landing almost in the center of the beige fairway, where it bounced twice and rolled.

His playing partners gasped, then cheered.

"It must have gone a good 270," exclaimed one admiringly, having watched through his sun visor as the ball sailed past the flag at the 200-yard mark,

Aoyagi handed the driver to his caddy, put one hand in his trousers pocket, and began walking with the others.

"Do you go to a gym or something?" joked someone else in the group, an accountant, as he regarded Aoyagi, whose toned frame stood head and shoulders above the rest.

"I do have my eyes on a pretty instructor," he replied, looking ahead.

The all but perfectly straight fairway wove through gently undulating terrain. The grass, neatly mowed and trimmed, was surrounded by bare-topped deciduous trees and lush, green-leaved conifers. Aside from a steel tower soaring above the forest, there were no man-made structures of any kind, making it easy to forget, even if only for a short time, that one was still well within the metropolis.

Aoyagi had joined the golf club—located in a hilly Tokyo suburb—the previous year. The membership was worth nearly 2 million yen, enough, when costs like membership transferal fees were added in, to purchase a small car. It was a reward to himself for attaining the position of managing director and general manager of the Development Division of the company where he had worked for so many years. Clearly this had not been a bad move, as he was now able to spend a weekend relaxing with old friends. "It's delightful here. So close to the city center. And here I am playing golf, all thanks to Aoyagi-sama!"

So enthused another old friend, a bureaucrat who drove a hybrid from his government-housing unit in residential Ikejiri-Ōhashi. He was clutching his irons and looking at Aoyagi with his chest thrust out proudly.

"It may well be," joshed another, "that he has proven himself the cleverest of us all by choosing to go into the private sector and joining a major firm."

When enrolling in Chuo University's law department, Aoyagi had had his heart set on a legal career, quite the same as everyone around him. His abundant ambition and lofty aspirations were, however, eventually sidelined as he abandoned his classes and devoted his time to mahjong parlors. He twice was obliged to repeat a year of studies and then managed only by the skin of his teeth to be hired by his current company.

Being in the employ of a large and prestigious enterprise gave a modest boost to his self-esteem, but he himself had utterly no interest in business in and of itself. The dizzying pace of life had him immersed in it nonetheless, to the point that he found it had all seeped into the marrow of his bones. Still, part of him continued to suffer from a sense of inferiority toward those friends who had followed through on their initial aspirations.

"So whenever Aoyagi gets a promotion, let's go for an even more prestigious course!"

"Great idea. So next it'll be 'president and CEO'!"

The men were chattering away as they walked across the grass. A half-step behind them, Aoyagi offered no protest, responding only with a wry smile.

It was the tradition in Aoyagi's company for the position

of president to be held by a member of the Corporate Strategy Department or the Commercial Business Division, both of which generated profits from real estate income from condominiums, office buildings, commercial facilities, and the like. With the unusual selection of the current president, who, like Aoyagi, had come from the Development Division, this tradition was beginning to give way. With the end of his term in office steadily approaching, one could by no means rule out Aoyagi as the lucky man to succeed him. Indeed, while the Commercial Business Division's projections for the fiscal year were not expected to be met by any of its subdivisions, the Development Division seemed to be on track to make its own ends meet. Aoyagi desired very much to rise beyond his current position so as to enjoy a uniquely panoramic view from the pinnacle. Were he to achieve his ambition, he might, he thought, be able to overcome the insecurity he felt toward his friends.

At the beginning of the week, Aoyagi spent the morning in the company's conference room receiving reports from his subordinates. This meeting was important, for it would set the direction of future site development. One by one, the managers in charge of each department explained their progress, projecting visuals on the screen in front of them.

The mood changed dramatically when attention turned to the department in charge of the site for the development of a large-scale commercial facility. A project previously progressing smoothly had stalled in negotiations, and an irreparable rift had developed between the department and the landowner.

"I thought that things appeared to be working out."

Aoyagi, who usually tried not to intervene, could not resist speaking up.

The scale of the project was so large that if there were any delays in carrying out the plan, the result would be worse than a failure to meet the budget: There would also be enormous losses.

Moreover, undeveloped land in central Tokyo was scarce, making it difficult to find an alternative site, particularly for a large-scale project such as the one in question.

As Aoyagi's subordinate explained, it was possible that the delay would lead to the deal's complete termination. Experience said that there would be no easy way out.

A general meeting of all the managers was scheduled for the afternoon, and it would be Aoyagi's task to provide an update on the Development Division; as division head, he would bear a most heavy responsibility for whatever happened. As usual, his subordinate's repeated explanations were all quite beside the point. Gazing sternly at the pale face of the man gave him a sharp pain, as though his stomach were being pierced with a steel needle.

"Sir ... We're getting close to the luncheon meeting."

His secretary approached and whispered in his ear. A single woman in her forties, she had joined the company following her divorce a few years earlier. A platinum necklace peeked out from under the collar of her white cut-and-sew blouse; a scent of the same perfume from the previous evening wafted forth.

"We're not finished yet," he cut her off, without turning to look at her.

As he had anticipated, the afternoon managers' meeting proved to be most contentious, as he found himself hounded for an account of the situation.

"What are we going to do? How are we going to carry out a building project without land?"

The accusations put forth by Sunaga, the head of the Commercial Business Department, were relentless, his voice bordering on anger. Though two years younger than Aoyagi, the two had been classmates. The embodiment of the corporate world's impetuousness, Sunaga had risen to his current position by outpacing a host of senior employees.

He appeared to have the position of president clearly in

his mind. Ever since Aoyagi had become head of the Development Division, Sunaga had crossed swords with him at every opportunity, perhaps seeing him as an obstacle to his own career advancement.

"No matter how you look at it, the responsibility for this all lies on your side. This is bad! Do you get it? Huh?"

Sitting diagonally across from Aoyagi, Sunaga carried on his attack, his eyes glaring. The others at the meeting offered no sympathy, maintaining a cold detachment.

"Yes, I do understand."

"Instead of playing for pity, with that hang-dog tone, how about doing something about it? Now!"

Aoyagi nodded neither yes nor no, without looking directly at Sunaga. The participants having failed to come up with any proposal for an effective solution, the meeting came to its inevitable end, though having run far overtime.

One by one, the attendees left the conference room. The last to remain was Aoyagi, his despondency so heavy as to nearly glue him to his chair. A vague sense of anxiety also weighed him down, with Sunaga's shameless opprobrium still nagging at him.

"Damn!" he muttered under his breath, slamming his fist on the desk, before finally struggling to straighten up and get to his feet.

■ ■ ■

The ceiling lights had been turned off. The small one-room apartment, measuring some seven tatami mats, was enveloped in silence and dark.

"Doesn't constantly watching like that wear you out?"

A voice filled with amazement spoke to Takumi from the vicinity of his feet. Close by, in a sleeping bag, a young member of Takeshita's group had been snoring until just few moments ago and was now sprawled out and playing with his phone. With a shaved head and a boyish face—despite recently turning twenty—he had a strong physique and stood over six-two in height. When changing his clothes earlier he had flashed a tattoo resembling the eight-headed, eight-tailed legendary serpent Yamata no Orochi on his back.

This "Orochi" had been in a reformatory and then, following his release, had hooked up with Takeshita through a slightly older youth from his hometown. Orochi complained that his supposed job was nothing more than that of an errand boy. For this stakeout, too, he had been sent here without being told anything at all about the work.

"I can't afford to be tired," replied Takumi without taking his eye from his night vision monocular. "She might step out while I'm not looking."

The scope, capable of visibility in the dark for well over four hundred yards, was mounted on a tripod poking through a gap in the curtains. From the eighth floor of the apartment, it clearly captured the two-story target, directly a hundred yards away. The monochrome image of the house told him that the front door had remained closed since the entry and exit in the evening. Takumi's hand turned ever so slightly the scope's handle on the tripod, switching the night vision mode to normal.

The entrance opened onto the living room, which faced a courtyard still covered by curtains. The faint light at the edges suggested that the resident had not yet gone into the bedroom.

The target was the residence of Kawai Natsumi, the abbess of Kōan-ji. More precisely, it was her living quarters within the temple's 9,600-square-foot property. Enshrined in the adjacent main hall stood a statue of the Buddha, said to have been built during the Azuchi-Momoyama period and thus over four hundred years old. The concrete exterior of the edifice was grand, almost double the 1,400 square feet of the hall.

Kawai also owned extensive land near Sengakuji Station, a mere stone's throw from the temple. This was the property that had come up for consideration at the recent meeting. Takumi and his team had rented the apartment overlooking the temple in order to carry out overnight surveillance in the hope of learning and taking advantage of her daily routine.

"We're recording all of this, so do you really have to stick around?" asked Orochi, suppressing a yawn.

A cable connected the scope to a laptop; the captured images were then projected onto the screen and recorded for later information sharing and analysis.

"If Kawai went somewhere while we weren't watching, we wouldn't be able to track her."

"But I'm watching the computer too, so, hey, no problem," exclaimed Orochi with a laugh. "The little nun won't be leaving at this hour of the night, absolutely not. We've been watching her for five days, and nothing's changed. Peeking into the life of some spinster auntie is not at all my idea of fun. It would be different if she were a celebrity or maybe someone young and good-looking."

Orochi's tone suggested not only his irritation at being cooped up but also some familiarity and even a neediness. It was less that he had become accustomed to Takumi during their time together than that there was no sense of hierarchy between them, despite Takumi being significantly older, perhaps because their relationship was limited to this one-time assignment.

They had been confined to the small apartment since the beginning of the week. As Orochi grumblingly noted, Kawai's days were utterly monotonous. Even taking into account the abstemiousness her shaven head represented, hers was a life lacking in vibrancy.

She awoke at five in the morning, conducted services in the main hall, and then, depending on the day, spent the afternoon cleaning the temple grounds or tending to the garden. Once she had concluded her evening prayers, all the lights in her room were out by ten. She remained almost all the time at home, and on the rare occasions when she went out, it was usually to take a taxi to a local supermarket.

The temple's main hall, surrounded by dense trees beyond which lay an adjacent park, was usually closed except for rites and ceremonies. There was no stone gate or offering box, nor were there visitors. The abbess had all but no interaction with her neighbors; her solitary life in the large estate resembled that of a mountain hermit engaged in ascetic exercises.

"You're amazing, Takumi-san!" exclaimed Orochi in a tone of admiring wonder.

"How so?"

"I mean, you keep watching, without sleeping. That'd normally be such a pain that one would just go through the motions, since who's gonna notice? Just look at your hair. It's all white!"

"An occupational hazard."

Perhaps due to a lack of sleep, Takumi had lost a surprising amount of weight, despite eating well. He stroked his face and noticed that his cheekbones were protruding.

"Doesn't learnin' a job really just boil down ta how much ya can fuck off?"

Over the last five days, Takumi had repeatedly heard this line from Orochi. He could only imagine how hard he had worked at pulling the wool over the eyes of his reformatory's teaching staff.

"If you keep fucking off, you won't get ahead."

He spoke in a patronizing tone, even as he continued to peer through the scope.

"Do you want to get ahead, Takumi-san?"

"No, not interested in that."

He was not sure what Orochi understood by "getting ahead," but for him it clearly did not mean losing sleep in order to lord it over others or to make a name for himself.

"So it's about the money then?"

Money was important, but it was not the sole motivation. It was not easy to explain to someone who really did not know what was going on. As he was still puzzling over his answer, he heard the door open behind him.

"How're you doing?"

Takeshita greeted them cheerfully as he came in.

"Nothing has changed," Takumi replied. "Nothing so far."

He spoke with his back to the door. Orochi jumped up from his sleeping bag and stood at attention.

"Hey you, don't just stand there. Go over and relieve Takumi-kun."

At the sound of Takeshita's raised voice, Orochi forced Takumi aside and took his place in front of the night vision scope."

"Here's something to eat, if you'd like."

Takeshita positioned himself cross-legged on the wooden floor and took some wrapped octopus cakes and canned beer out of a plastic bag. Takumi sat down in front of him. He looked thinner than before.

"You've lost more weight." Takeshita looked at him with a smile, the corners of his mouth turned up. From his trouser pocket he pulled out an e-cigarette, most likely filled with a solution of methamphetamine.

"If you're feeling bone tired, try this."

"No, thanks. I'm doing all right."

He had no intention of relying on the power of drugs, nor did he need to. Sometimes he felt assailed by drowsiness, but it was not so strong as to overwhelm him.

"Well now, let's have a look at what I've dug up on the little nun."

"What do you have?"

After nearly a week of observing Kawai, Takumi had nothing more on her than the overall pattern of her daily life.

"It seems," replied Takeshita, "that her husband ran out on her."

"Ran out?"

Kawai Natsumi's husband had, according to marriage custom, been adopted into the Kawai family and taken its name. The nun's parents had already died, and as she had no siblings, he was all she had left of her family, apart from a daughter, married and permanently residing in Germany. Husband and wife were clearly not living together.

According to Takeshita, the husband had had no affiliation with Buddhism prior to marriage and had left all temple matters in the hands of his wife, who had also inherited from her predecessor the management of a facility for the support and rehabilitation of parolees. A few years before, the husband had begun an affair with a woman being looked after there and eloped with her.

"Ah, now there's a quaint old story!"

Takumi pulled the tab on his beer and took a little sip.

"And it's always the same old story, men and women, you know …"

Takeshita looked bored and spoke as if he had now come to perceive the reality of the world.

"Is that why the facility was closed?"

The rehabilitation facility had been established to support the reintegration into society of parolees and those who had completed their sentences. It was one of the few women-only facilities in the country. Kawai's husband had been serving as the director. Working in collaboration with the government, it provided housing and meals for a fixed period to those under its care. The entire building was now locked, and it seemed no one went in or out.

"If the man in charge gets involved with a young woman who's just come out of the slammer, well, it's hard to keep the place going. That's the sort of thing the authorities hate the most."

Takeshita speared one of the cold octopus cakes with a toothpick and ate it.

Reportedly, it was just after her husband left her that Kawai had shaved her head and begun to go to great lengths to avoid being seen by others.

"The nun's shock must have been all the greater, as she had apparently been an all-adoring wife."

Takumi nodded in acknowledgment, remembering having several times seen Kawai's downcast expression through his scope.

"What I'm curious about is her financial situation," Takeshita said, as he picked up a stray rubber band and shot it at Orochi's head.

"What do mean by 'financial situation'?"

Kawai was well known in the area as a woman of wealth. In addition to owning the main hall, her living quarters, and the parking lot, all of which Takumi and his cohorts were targeting, along with the former rehabilitation facility, she was the owner of real estate in the neighborhood, both in her own right and through a corporation. She had sold much of the property after inheriting it from her parents, but she had held on to a considerable amount, including some apartment units. Takeshita explained that there were bank mortgages on most of them.

"Why does she need so much money?" Takumi asked.

Kawai's modest lifestyle would surely not require vast expenditures.

"I don't know," Takeshita shrugged as he flicked another

rubber band. It apparently hit Orochi, who was touching the back of his head.

After cursory confirmation of the future course of their surveillance and information-gathering endeavor, Takeshita stood up.

"Have to go. My woman will start nagging again ... "

With a smile, he showed them the e-cigarette he had taken from his pocket.

"Is it all right for you to be using so much?" asked Takumi. Takeshita's health was a matter of concern.

"Yes, Take-san, maybe you should give it up," said Orochi, lifting his face from the scope and looking worried. Takeshita was his boss—he both feared and respected him—but Orochi was also inclined toward frankness.

"Hey," Takeshita snarled, his face contorted, "who d'ya think you're talking to?"

Enraged, he began to kick Orochi in his broad back and utter curses.

"Since when d'ya think *you* have an opinion?"

Though theirs was a corner room, any noise from a ruckus was likely to be heard downstairs and next door. Avoiding unnecessary trouble was of tantamount importance.

"Takeshita-san ... " cautioned Takumi, his eyes then falling upon the laptop screen. It showed the front door, but now the scene was different. Standing there was a man in uniform who was pressing the buzzer. Looking more carefully, Takumi could see that he was a cab driver.

"She's going out!" Takumi shouted and started to run.

This was, since the surveillance began, without precedent. Where was she going? Was she suddenly in need of something or had she fallen ill? There was no answer, but it was vital to find one.

Takumi could hear Takeshita's angry shouts coming from behind and Orochi's hurried footsteps in pursuit. He grabbed his shoes and hurried to their car, parked in the lot downstairs, a brand-new Land Cruiser on loan from Takeshita. Right on his heels was Orochi, who climbed behind the steering wheel, gasping for breath, as Takumi deftly slid into the passenger's seat beside him.

■ ■ ■

The engine started, and the car lurched forward. Kawai's taxi was passing on the street in front of them.

"That's it! That's it!" he shouted, pointing toward the cab and urging Orochi to speed up. From the sidewalk and entering into their path as they were on the verge of leaving the parking lot was a bicyclist.

"Watch out!"

Orochi swerved in panic. The wall on the right came ever closer, and he screamed, as now that dark concrete block took up the entire right rear window; a violent scraping sound reverberated throughout the vehicle. There was no need to see the obvious damage to the body of the car; one's imagination was quite sufficient.

"Oh man, shit!"

As though to taunt the utterly flustered Orochi, the cab approached a curve and promptly disappeared from sight. The Land Cruiser had come to a complete stop.

"What're we gonna do? It's *bad*!"

"Hey, it's OK!" exclaimed Takumi on the edge of genuine anger. "You have to keep after Kawai!"

"Take-san will kill me!"

Orochi, quite beside himself, was gripping the steering wheel with his eyes fixed on the road ahead.

"He won't kill you," replied Takumi. "If things get dicey, I'll join you in groveling. It'll be all right. Trust me."

Orochi stared at him in silence, tearful. He continued to gaze ahead as the car finally began to move.

"I said I didn't want to drive this dumb tank!"

With a dismal roar, the Land Cruiser sped off. They made a sharp turn and were now approaching an intersection and a red light. The cab was already gone. Beyond was the three-lane National Route 15, intersecting the road; a constant stream of cars, their headlights glaring, was passing perpendicular in front of them.

"Which way should I go?"

Orochi turned to Takumi with a desperate look.

If Kawai were going to the supermarket, as was her custom, she would turn right. The supermarket had a fine selection of goods and was open twenty-four hours a day. But she habitually turned off her bedroom light at ten in the evening. Would she be going shopping now after eight? If not, would she go left and head in the direction of Tamachi? What could possibly be there? No matter how much he thought about it, Takumi could not guess what direction the cab had turned. He would have to rely on intuition.

"Left, go left."

The light turned green, and Orochi turned, accelerating past the cars in front of them, one after another, as they looked haphazardly at whatever cabs they spotted. Two intersections further on, there was still no sign.

"There's no one ... " The voice from the driver's seat was tinged with anxiety.

Takumi fretted. Had he guessed wrong?

The car slowed at a red light. In the left lane, the back seat of a cab came into view, and there Takumi saw the profile of a figure he now knew so well.

"There she is! On the left."

Takumi lowered his eyes and stealthily directed his gaze toward her. She was sitting upright, her face, on which sunglasses were perched, turned toward the window.

"She's never been like this!" exclaimed Orochi, twisting himself around to get a glimpse of the cab. "Here it is night, and she's wearing sunglasses!"

It was indeed just as he had said. She was wearing a black jacket; her hat and sunglasses were of the same shade. When performing her duties at the temple she wore a robe or clerical garb, and when she went out in the daytime, such as to the supermarket, she dressed casually in jeans and a cardigan. Although she had sometimes appeared in light-colored glasses, they had never seen her wearing spectacles or hats to hide her eyes.

"Hmm, where's she headed?"

As if in response to the half-spoken question, the cab promptly headed off. The chase went on for a quarter of an hour until they arrived at a hotel in Shiodome. Takumi remembered the place, one of the most luxurious in all of Tokyo, from a visit he had paid to Harrison Yamanaka. The hotel overlooked Hama-Rikyū Palace and Tokyo Bay.

The cab stopped at the porte-cochère, and Kawai got out. From the trunk a porter unloaded a compact suitcase and led her inside.

"I'll be right back," said Takumi, as he saw her go in. He got out of the car and took the express elevator up to the lobby on the twenty-eighth floor. At the open, high-ceilinged reception counter he glimpsed Kawai. Seeing her in modishly coordinated slacks, he could hardly recognize the woman he had observed in her robe or working clothes. Here she displayed a remarkably good and straight-backed posture for a woman of fifty-five. In such a refined ambience, she appeared a most suitable guest.

Takumi looked nonchalant as he passed the counter where

Kawai was standing and from a short distance away pretended to make a phone call as he kept an oblique eye on her.

A few moments later, led by a porter, Kawai began walking toward the elevator hall, headed for the guest rooms. Takumi hurriedly followed, managing to join them in an elevator just as the doors were about to close. The porter pressed 36 and asked Takumi for his floor.

"The same," he promptly replied. The porter gave a deferential reply.

The elevator quietly ascended. Takumi gazed at the panel of buttons, feeling a sudden weighty sensation. Kawai was immediately to his right but only at the edge of his field of vision, her figure unclear and indistinguishable. When following her to various places, including the supermarket, he had been able to spy on her only at some distance, within the confines of the Land Cruiser. Even though he knew she was not mindful of his presence, his body stiffened at the thought that she was now so close he could almost hear her breathing.

The elevator stopped at the thirty-sixth floor, and as the doors opened, Kawai was the first to step out; directed by the porter, Takumi followed.

The corridor of guestrooms formed a T-shape with the elevator hall. Not knowing on which part of the T Kawai's room would be, Takumi stopped, pretending to be on the phone and letting the two move on ahead. Seeing them turn left, he, one step behind, turned right.

Moving as slowly as he could, he heard a door open behind him. Quickly turning, he sprinted down the carpeted hallway and, as that door closed, identified it as belonging to Kawai's room.

He returned to the twenty-eighth floor and with his phone accessed the hotel's website and reserved a bay-view room for that same night.

"I'd like to check in," he asked at the reception desk, giving the male clerk the false name he had just used. With a polite nod, the man went about confirming the reservation on the terminal before him.

"Excuse me," Takumi inquired. "Is Room 3623 available?"

The clerk looked up, puzzled, as though not understanding the need or motive for the specific request.

"I once stayed in that room with my wife," Takumi explained. "I wanted to surprise her."

The clerk flashed a sympathetic smile and began tapping once again on the keyboard.

"Sir, I'm sorry, most dreadfully indeed, but that room is currently occupied."

There was no mystery there: The occupant was, of course, Kawai.

"Those next to it too?" Takumi continued, pretending to be disappointed.

"No, a neighboring room is available."

"Then I'll take it."

Declining the services of a porter, he made his way to the room and went in. He pressed his ear to the wall shared with Kawai's room but could hear neither sound nor voice. Using a glass from the beverage counter, he made the same attempt but again to no avail.

Calling Orochi, he told him to retrieve from Takeshita the concrete microphone in his possession. The voice through the receiver suggested an undertone of reluctance, Orochi being well aware that he had just put dents in Takeshita's car and that the man was now off on a tryst with his lady love. After much coaxing, he grudgingly agreed.

As he awaited Orochi's return, Takumi sat at the entrance

of his room, leaning against the door in order to be able to detect immediately if Kawai stepped out. The oak floorboards were chilly but caused him no immediate discomfort. The carpeted room, with its king-size bed, was dimly illuminated by indirect lighting. Beyond the full-height window lay, in all its glory, though now enveloped in darkness, the broad expanse of Tokyo Bay's surroundings.

Takumi pondered what Kawai was doing in the next room. Why was she staying in this hotel so close to home? She was carrying a suitcase, suggesting she was going off on a trip. The airport was close by, so she could have been preparing for an early-morning flight. Or perhaps it was merely the case that even members of the Buddhist clergy are in need of a change of pace from time to time. A stay in a hotel room costing more than 60,000 yen would certainly allow one momentarily to forget one's daily routine.

He was still lost in thought when Orochi called.

"I'm in the lobby."

He sounded out of sorts, perhaps after being chastised by Takeshita, but at least he had, without incident, succeeded in getting hold of the concrete microphone. As Takumi terminated the call, he heard a door open and close, the sound seeming to come from next door. Had Kawai left her room? He could not be sure. He quietly opened his door and looked out.

Walking toward the elevator hall was a woman, dressed in a tight charcoal two-piece dress that elegantly showed off the contours of her body. Her shapely legs were clad in sheer black stockings, revealing a hint of bare skin. Her steps were light, the crimson soles of her black high-heeled shoes bobbing up and down. Her hair, full and tousled, was pulled back in a short style, shiny dark brown in the downlight.

To judge by the back of her head, the woman seemed to be in her forties or perhaps her late thirties. No, he thought, contrary to his expectations, this was not Kawai.

He put his phone into his trousers pocket, picked up his wallet and key card from the table by the window, and left the room. Before heading for the elevator hall, he put his ear against the door of the adjoining room. There was no sound. Kawai was probably already asleep.

As he was about to move off, he saw that a lamp by the door was lit. Beneath it was a message in small letters: MAKE UP ROOM. At this hour he assumed that the lamp signaled a request for turning down the bedclothes in preparation for the night. Yet this service was normally for when the occupant of a room was stepping out. Why, he thought, suddenly chilled to the bone, would she be asking for it if she were indeed still in her room? So no, she was obviously not there. She had surely gone out.

Takumi rushed down to the lobby, a sickening feeling of sweat running down his back.

When had she left? The door might have softly closed, and he may have been so absorbed in his thoughts that he did not notice it. Sheer carelessness.

Orochi was in the library. Looking quite out of place, his large frame slumped in the sofa, he was fiddling with his phone.

"Did you see her come down?"

"No … ," Orochi replied with a puzzled expression.

Takumi felt suddenly weak and sat down beside him. He had gone to such lengths to keep his eye on the target, but now at this critical moment, he had inadvertently lost her. Perhaps she had gone out to eat. He tried to console himself with that possibility but knew that it was no more than a convenient guess. No working of his imagination would tell him what Kawai was doing or about to do.

"Takumi-san ... "

He turned and glanced at Orochi, whose face now bore a graver expression than he had ever seen.

"Don't turn around suddenly," he said in an emphatic whisper.

"Isn't Kawai right there, behind you?"

Takumi felt his heart skip a beat, then took a deep breath and stood up. Pretending to call someone, he turned around.

A largely empty bar lounge lay before him. A woman in a tight two-piece dress was seated by the window, facing and chatting with a man who looked fiftyish, a cocktail glass in her hand. She was surely the very same woman he had just seen from behind in the hotel corridor. The soft, warm lighting faintly revealed eyes highlighted by dark eye-shadow and mascara and, below, rows of teeth behind red-painted lips. Her features were beautifully sculpted, and she was gazing up with a smiling and youthful expression.

Takumi nearly cried out ... This woman, now so different in appearance and aura as to be mistaken for someone else, was none other than Kawai Natsumi.

. . .

The members of the team continued to follow Kawai's movements and to investigate her background, even as they also sought to identify the man she had been secretly meeting at the hotel in Shiodome.

According to the findings of the task force led by Takeshita, the fifty-seven-year-old man was the leader and director of a well-known theater company in the area. His name was Kuboyama. He regularly put on performances at small theaters, and he had no other source of income. He was separated from his wife and, with no assets to speak of, lived more or less from hand to mouth.

It was not clear how and when Kawai had become acquainted

with Kuboyama. What was known for certain was that, putting on a glamorous disguise, she would dine with him in a high-class restaurant and spend the night with him at a luxury hotel, all behavior hardly in keeping with the ways of a nun. Kawai was not only bearing the costs of these encounters but was also defraying the expenses of the man's theatrical troupe. Her motive for wanting to generate money by liquidating her assets was now clear.

■　■　■

"It's started! Come on, come on!" called out Orochi, gesturing to his companions as he lay on a bed across the room, pressing the concrete microphone against the wall and listening to the sounds emanating from an earphone connected to an amplifier.

In the adjoining room were Kawai and Kuboyama, who, having finished dinner at a fancy restaurant in Moto-Azabu, had then relaxed at a wine bar near Nishi-Azabu Crossing. Tonight's was a different luxury hotel from the one in Shiodome the weekend before. They were in Roppongi. Not more than half an hour had passed since they had returned to their room at eleven.

"Hey, little nun," exclaimed Orochi, "you wine and dine. You eat meat. You gobble up men. My oh my!"

He was flabbergasted, his eyes glazed with sheer excitement, neither indignant nor jealous.

Takumi had been chatting on the sofa but now got onto the bed with Takeshita. He took a pair of earphones from Orochi and put them to his ears.

There was static noise, like the roar of a sandstorm, mingled with the sound of heavy breathing and a steady tap-tap, like the plink of water dripping into a puddle. He thought he caught a faint female voice and then a woman's blubbering, exclamatory entreaties. The sounds of flesh-upon-flesh grew more intense, as though impelled by the screams. The lack of a visual image led him to imagine the scene all the more vividly. Unable to bear it any longer, he removed the earphones.

Takeshita, a sardonic look on his face, tossed his own earphones onto the bed.

"So here we've got us a sugar mama who's even put on a wig. How very touching!"

"I still can't believe it's Kawai," Takumi muttered.

"No matter how old she may get," said Takeshita, grimacing through his ceramic teeth, "a woman's still a woman."

The investigation into Kawai Natsumi now for the time being suspended, the team collected its data and reported the results to Harrison Yamanaka.

"I see," he commented. "A nun and a playwright engaged in an affair. An interesting story."

He had been quietly listening to the conversation, flipping through the documents on the table and nodding, his hand on his goatee.

As though unable to resist the question, Takeshita asked:

"So what are we going to do now?"

Takumi saw Harrison Yamanaka's eyes light up with pleasure as he spun the two rings on his prosthetic pinky.

# 4

Over the phone came the sound of Takeshita's cheerful voice. He was jabbering away as though quite unglued, perhaps again under the influence of drugs.

His listener learned on inquiry that Takeshita's task force had managed to secure a parking space in Takanawa and that the owner of the lot was Kawai Natsumi, the abbess of Kōan-ji. Further, during the negotiating they had apparently obtained some of her personal data.

"Yes, yes, that temple. It's been disaffiliated. There was a public announcement, but I totally missed it."

"What do you mean?"

Takumi was speaking into his phone, his voice markedly reverberating in the hallway of the semi-residential building. Perhaps because it was the weekend in this office district, the area was deserted, enveloped in the stillness of the night.

"It means they've left the sect. Maybe there were some internal wrangles, and especially after that business with her old man, the relationship with the authorities must be bad too."

Takeshita's suppressed laugh could not be muffled:

"Looks like a fine tailwind for us! Is there any good news at your end?"

"No, we're still in the middle of interviews."

After promising to let him know of any progress, Takumi ended the call.

Returning to the dimly lit anteroom, he saw Harrison Yamanaka observing the interview through the one-way mirror. His profile, faintly visible in the peripheral light, was stern as ever.

"How is it going?"

"This one isn't bad," replied Yamanaka quietly, still focused on the mirror.

The two sat in the anteroom, invisible to the interview room, which measured some ten tatami mats and was bathed in bright light. In the center stood a table where, facing each other, sat Reiko and a female candidate.

Reiko had introduced the woman, who worked part-time at a supermarket checkout and also for a call-girl service. She had no criminal record and was fifty-three, making her slightly younger than Kawai. The two were of comparable height, and both had thin lips. She was a bit overweight but all in all still within an acceptable range.

"The vibe is somewhat similar, is it not?" remarked Takumi hopefully. This was the thirteenth candidate since the beginning of interviews for the impersonator role two days before. Some resembled Kawai in appearance but lacked acting ability or quick responsiveness. The team's task was not an easy one: Several candidates had not met any of the criteria. Arrangements for necessary equipment and other materials could not be made without first coming up with the appropriate woman for the job.

"Her manner of speaking also feels right."

Harrison Yamanaka seemed to share Takumi's positive assessment.

Reiko was posing the prepared questions. The voices flowed from the table's microphone to the speaker in the anteroom.

"Well now, there's just one condition …"

Reiko, dressed in a tightknit one-piece dress, crossed her legs again, her camel-color high heels swaying restlessly.

"Would you be willing to cut your hair?"

It was the final question.

"My hair?" came a surprised reply. The woman's black hair was long and straight, reaching down her back, and although it had lost some luster, it appeared to be well maintained.

"Yes," Reiko said, pressing on, "completely shorn. You'd be bald."

"Eh … I … "

The woman's expression grew more perplexed, and no matter how much Reiko attempted to persuade her, she offered no sign of assent.

The anteroom door opened, and Reiko, having escorted the woman as far as the elevator, walked in.

"I thought she was fine, but … "

Reiko leaned back in the opposite chair. Her gesture of brushing her long hair back attested to her fatigue at having carried out interviews since noontime.

"Still, going along with being bald is a tough condition," said Takumi in a consoling tone.

"What if we try a bald wig? Like the ones they often use in the movies, where actresses have them put on with special makeup."

Reiko made the suggestion half-seriously.

"But unless we apply Hollywood-class makeup, we're likely to be exposed," replied Yamanaka, who had been listening to the two.

"The next one's the last one, right?"

"Yes, she hasn't called to say she's been delayed, so she should be arriving soon," said Reiko, glancing at her phone.

If they were unable to fill the job, they would be obliged

to come up with a new batch of candidates. Another search for women of the same age as Kawai, especially those willing to cooperate in a high-risk endeavor, would mean going beyond the immediate area to other regions. Spending unnecessary time would not only increase expenses but also alter the situation. The whole underpinning of the plan designed by Yamanaka might collapse, further diminishing the prospects for the success of an already challenging project.

A little earlier than scheduled, a candidate by the name of Taniguchi appeared. Takumi remained in the anteroom with Harrison Yamanaka to observe the interview.

Sitting across from Reiko, Taniguchi had an overall slender form and appeared to be taller than Kawai. With her large eyes, despite her jowls, she resembled Kawai more than any of the other women before her. She exuded intelligence, and her attire appeared to be more refined.

"You might have heard this already," said Reiko, her voice carrying over to the anteroom, "but what we want from you, Taniguchi-san, is to impersonate someone, attend a business meeting, and act. That's all. The fee is 3 million, with thirty thousand in advance, the rest to be paid on successful completion of the job. Is that acceptable?"

"Yes, that's fine," Taniguchi replied clearly, though to Takumi she seemed more tense than confident.

"What, if I may ask, Taniguchi-san, is your normal occupation?" inquired Reiko, as she continued with her questions. There was almost no prior information about the woman. Reiko only knew that Taniguchi had heard of the job from a friend who in turn had an acquaintance whose illicit lover had acted as the indirect go-between.

"Um ... I'm a full-time housewife."

"So may I assume that you don't do any part-time work?"

Taniguchi nodded.

Reiko was surprised, as was Takumi.

Among the candidates they had interviewed had been several housewives, all of whom were forced to do some sort of part-time work, either in the demi-monde or as cleaning ladies in commercial facilities. Their appearances all faintly bore the shadows of life's hardships. In Taniguchi there was no sign of anything like that.

"We hear you've had financial troubles," Reiko said bluntly.

Taniguchi averted her eyes and faltered.

"There's no need to talk about it if it's difficult for you, but perhaps we can help."

There was silence, the heavy atmosphere seeping through the mirror into the anteroom. After a few moments, Taniguchi looked up and spoke.

"I ... incurred a loss in forex trading."

"How much of a loss?"

"About ... 14 million yen."

She had gotten into foreign exchange trading at the suggestion of a friend and, seeing the surprisingly large unrealized profits, had been quickly hooked. She had cashed in insurance policies and time deposits and emptied a savings account in order to invest it all. One morning her currency holdings crashed, leaving her with a huge unrealized loss. All of her assets had melted away, and the forex firm was demanding an additional collateral to the tune of several million yen.

"I couldn't tell my husband."

"Indeed," Harrison Yamanaka murmured, as Takumi, sitting next to him, nodded. Most interviewees had some number of skeletons in their closet. When strangers not legally bound to each other in any way were working together, such injuries and defects could actually form a basis for trust. Because when push came to shove, one could simply poke away at those skeletons. It was this that made Taniguchi, who had a respectable family and seemed to have led an upright life, trustworthy for the job.

The interviews continued. Taniguchi read aloud a set of questions and answers that could be used to identify Kawai. There was also a simple memorization test. The candidate's appearance was close to Kawai's, and her ability to memorize personal data, her acting skills to convince the other party that she really was Kawai, and her quick-wittedness in responding to unexpected situations were all judged to be fully in order.

"There is just one last condition."

Reiko broached the subject with a bit of a flourish.

Takumi watched the exchange across the way, spontaneously leaning forward, his breath now shallow. Harrison Yamanaka also seemed to be slightly on edge.

"Are you willing to have your hair cut short? We'll cover the expense."

"Yes, I'd be willing," Taniguchi replied unhesitatingly. Her hair was a shoulder-length bob, entirely in a subdued color, indicating that she made frequent trips to a hair salon.

"When I say 'short,' I mean having it all taken off with clippers. You'll be bald. Are you sure you'll be all right with that?" Reiko asked, a note of doubt in her voice.

At a loss for words, Taniguchi looked down at her hands; she had, it seemed, not expected anything so drastic. Reiko was clutching her elbows, anxiously awaiting a response. The anteroom was likewise quiet.

Taniguchi nodded her head: "Yes, I can do it … Please, allow me."

The woman's decisiveness was palpable. Her cheeks relaxed and she broke into a smile. Takumi remained silent as he looked at Harrison Yamanaka.

■ ■ ■

A ray of light was falling onto the small stage, no more than twenty tatami mats in size. In the spotlight, the lead actress stood barefoot. The program informed theatergoers that she was playing the role of a women's liberation activist, following her instincts and leading an unrestrained life. Her white thighs peeked out from a disheveled splash-pattern kimono, and her hair was loose, as though she had just indulged in a sexual encounter.

"Please, please, let us die together! Leaping from this place, we shall abandon our carnal selves and thereby surely be done with it all!"

Her tense monologue reverberated through the rapt silence. The theater was nearly full, with over two hundred and fifty attendees facing the two sides of the stage. Takumi was in the last row, steadily staring forward. The peculiar scent of the hair dye he had used before his arrival could be intermittently detected in the air. Next to him sat Harrison Yamanaka, who, with his legs crossed, was observing the actress with a cool indifference.

Kawai Natsumi, seated on the opposite side, was blocked from view by the shadows of other audience members and the wall. When Takumi had glimpsed her in the lobby before the performance began, she was wearing a wig and a long, beautifully contoured skirt, and her high-heeled shoes clicked as she walked.

"No one in this world told me in what form happiness would appear. But it has set me free."

The actress knelt down on the stage as if drained of all her strength and stared into the distant void. Her mouth hung slightly open, a rich smile upon her face and her hands outstretched, as though caressing the air.

Harrison Yamanaka smiled wryly.

"Oh God, you are surely there! My wish, my wish is ... just to love this mad freedom, with all its pain. That is all!"

One by one she bent her fingers to form fists with both hands. Her kimono slipped from her shoulders, revealing her right breast.

In Takumi's mind's eye, the figure of Kawai, perpetual strumpet, was superimposed on the fictional activist and the playwright who had created her.

The spotlight faded, followed by thunderous applause. And now the entire theater was illuminated. Following the lead actress and seven other performers, Kuboyama, Kawai's lover, appeared in the stage wing, looking quite satisfied with the event. Repeatedly they all politely bowed in response to the audience's acclaim.

In the crowded lobby the performers greeted the members of the audience and took photographs with those they knew. Kuboyama, too, was chatting merrily with some of the people involved, and, off in a corner, Kawai was likewise present.

After a short time, Kuboyama was alone. Kawai came up to him, and the two began to exchange friendly words, quite oblivious of their surroundings. Perhaps they were confirming their plans for the rest of the evening. Takumi had already learned that they were to meet at a hotel or restaurant the next evening, when there was no performance.

Takumi put on his plain-glass spectacles and went over to engage them in conversation while they were still together.

"Just wonderful!" he exclaimed. "It really struck a chord with me. It's a classic theme, but I think it's a novel interpretation of something that has never been done before."

Up close, Kuboyama's simple face suggested the guileless nature of a man who had devoted himself to a single pursuit. Takumi felt at least a glimmering of why Kawai was attracted to this playwright.

Kuboyama bowed awkwardly, unable to hide his bewilderment at these compliments from the stranger in a suit.

"Forgive me. I should have introduced myself before. I am a consultant for this foundation …"

He handed Kuboyama one of the dummy business cards he had prepared. In addition to contact information, it gave the URL of a fictitious foundation. Accessing the site would bring up a stylish website where one could browse through its various activities.

Perhaps out of prudence or deference, Kawai was about to walk away. Takumi immediately handed her his business card as well: It was essential to keep her there.

"The foundation has decided to focus more on supporting education, and we should very much like to pass on superior skills and knowledge to the next generation. For that endeavor, Kuboyama-sama, your cooperation would be deeply appreciated."

Takumi began cautiously. If Kuboyama rebuffed him, the team would have to rethink its plan.

"How precisely?"

The tension in Kuboyama's face was fading. Standing next to him and listening, Kawai appeared to be pleased as well.

"We are thinking primarily of educational institutions, such as local elementary and middle schools. We would like you to convey to the pupils there the appeal, the charm, of the theater. The format would be up to you: lectures, workshops, as you wish …"

"I see. Theater is indeed ideal for cultivating artistic sentiment."

"As for the location, one possibility that we are considering is Okinawa. Would that be possible for you?"

The minimum requirement here was a place that would be inconvenient for any return to Tokyo, where the team's project was to be carried to completion.

"Okinawa would be fine."

When still at the beginning of his career, Kuboyama had for three years been active in the capital city of Naha, as could be seen on his website. In a magazine interview some years before, he had spoken of his love for Okinawa.

"In addition to the honorarium, we shall compensate you for your airfare and accommodation—for two."

"For two?"

"Since you're making such a journey. The view of the sea from the hotel is spectacular, and it's better to have someone to dine with. It could be your manager or a family member. In any case, do bring someone along. Anyone will be fine."

Speaking loudly enough for Kawai to hear, Takumi gave her a subtle nod. She was turned toward Kuboyama with a most loving look.

■ ■ ■

A few days after his conversation with Kuboyama and Kawai, Takumi traveled to Okinawa with Harrison Yamanaka. There they met by previous arrangement with the prefectural board of education, offering free support for a liberal-arts-related lecture. The proposal was accepted without reservation, Kuboyama's achievements as a playwright being perhaps less consequential in that regard than Harrison Yamanaka's advance scheming with a politician from the area, a former baseball player with whom he sometimes enjoyed occasional drinks in Ginza. Yamanaka had succeeded, without arousing suspicion, in aligning the lecture schedule with that of the project.

"Lucky for us that things seem to be going quite smoothly," said Takumi, as he reached for a thin slice of flounder. It was kelp-cured fish from Nagasaki. The firm flesh, dipped in salt from Yonaguni-jima, burst with flavor in his mouth.

Harrison Yamanaka put his beer glass back on the fancy Japanese-paper coaster.

"They have no reason to refuse. The ministry bureaucrats are also pushing theater education."

Takumi and Harrison Yamanaka had been working separately but were meeting that evening at a sushi restaurant on the outskirts of Naha. Inside the establishment, with its L-shaped counter, groups of customers were enjoying their food and drink.

"With Tokyo-style sushi like this, I'd be happy to take on more work here."

A husky and annoyingly loud voice came from a man sitting diagonally across the way. Takumi and Yamanaka, engrossed in discussing their plans for when they were back in Tokyo, found their conversation thus not infrequently interrupted. Glancing over, they saw a casually dressed man in his sixties drinking sake and recognized him as a well-known TV personality. He had finished his sushi and was chatting with a businessman, most likely a local patron.

"Oh no! I forgot about *him!*" the celebrity exclaimed and called to the proprietor behind the counter.

"There's someone I want to get food for. Can ya scramble up some sort o' bowl dish? Leftovers would be fine. Even just a bit o' vinegar rice topped with pickled ginger will do."

The chef, who normally did not serve such dishes, hesitated but then put some vinegar rice into a small round dish and generously sprinkled it with sushi toppings before placing it on the counter.

"Ah, a great feast has arrived! Much too good for the likes of 'im." The man chuckled as he made a phone call.

"Hey, your eats are here. So make it snappy."

Soon the door opened, and a young man with a buzz cut, dressed in a jersey, sat down next to the older man. Chopsticks now in hand, he was no doubt his lackey. Politely expressing his thanks for the food, he dove into the dish, only to be slapped on the back of the head.

"Hey there idiot! This isn't some sort o' beef-bowl joint, ya know!"

The restaurant suddenly fell quiet. The young man, still with his mouth full, bowed his head, as the older man resumed his boisterous chatter with the customer. The mood was constrained, and the conversation between Takumi and Yamanaka talk became disjointed.

"Hurry up an' finish it!"

The man swatted the youth's head with even more force than before. The earnest-looking proprietor intervened, only to be met by scornful laughter.

"No, chef. I have to do this, really goin' after 'im. Ya know yerself what rigors ya had to go through. The boy has handed over his life to me. He knows what's comin' to 'im."

Seated at the far end of the counter was an early middle-aged couple, tourists, it would seem. Not until this moment did they exchange expressions, apparently more surprised at the man's harshness and his blatantly outmoded master-servant mentality than at their happenstance glimpse of a celebrity.

"It's like his face was almost buried in that bowl!"

Their mirth proved contagious, and the two men now smiled as well.

Harrison Yamanaka kept his amused expression and set down his chopsticks.

"Such is show business … In my younger days, having left the syndicate, I was at loose ends and so found myself going with what was then a trend: I set up a talent agency, gathering young girls languishing in Ginza and Roppongi clubs. Of course, we were quite lacking in know-how, so things didn't go terribly well. The reality was that it wound up being a kind of place to buy drugs. I developed my own supply chain, and, while pretending to do business with the girls, sold the stuff left and right. With all the pent-up demand in the entertainment industry, I was flying high. The clients were mainly show-biz-related, but an older guy from my days with the syndicate, somebody who'd once screwed me over, heard about it and wanted some for himself. I obliged, of course, giving him the family discount. He got addicted and met a messy end. Karma, you know."

He stared at his prosthetic right pinky, holding it with his other hand as though to adjust it.

"I'm not talking about those two guys over there, but if asked, would you be willing to devote your life to someone else?"

"By 'devote' do you mean to be like a servant?"

Takumi was sipping top-grade sake from a brewery in Kyoto. The bracing aroma filled his nostrils, and the subtle, fruity sweetness melted on his tongue. A cozy atmosphere had returned to the restaurant.

"Just between you and me … Takeshita-san is about to double-cross us."

"Takeshita-san?" Takumi asked, quite taken by surprise.

"If he does, will you back me?"

Caught off guard, Takumi turned directly toward Yamanaka, only to see his familiar face, ready to enjoy a nice chat.

"Well what exactly is he up to?" he asked carefully.

"It seems he's going to try to keep our upcoming profits all for himself."

The money from the fraud they were attempting was expected to be on the order of 10 billion yen. The amount to be allocated to Takeshita was incomparably larger than from any previous projects. Takumi could not understand why Takeshita would have the audacity to make off with it all. Was that really his intent? He could make no sense of what he had just been told.

"Takumi-san, will you side with Takeshita-san or with me?"

The question seemed to have been posed in earnest.

It was after meeting Harrison Yamanaka that Takumi had entered the world of land swindling. Once a scheme had been launched, he followed the instructions given to him. He had come to a measure of trust in Yamanaka, as he had with Takeshita, Gotō, and Reiko, with whom he had had a shorter relationship. This was possible only as long as they shared a clear and common objective. Without their work together, they would be mere strangers. He had no intention of taking sides, nor did he intend to act according to the logic of friend or foe.

At a loss for an answer, Takumi saw Yamanaka's face break into a happy smile.

"I'm just joking. Takeshita-san would never betray us."

Takumi gave a vague nod and downed the rest of his sake. The taste and aroma had disappeared; it was more akin to bitter, off-flavored water.

■ ■ ■

The next morning in the hotel lounge, filled with fresh natural light, he had breakfast and then checked out. Harrison Yamanaka, who had been staying in a room on an upper floor, had already left; there was a message saying he had suddenly changed his itinerary and decided to go on a short trip to a resort hotel in the north with a hostess he had met at a club the night before.

As he stepped outside, Takumi felt the warm winter air on his skin. He informed the doorman of his destination and was soon climbing into a cab.

"Here on business?"

The driver, a seemingly good-natured man of some years, spoke with a hint of an accent as he turned the wheel. Takumi wondered what sort of business he might be imagining. Business? Yes, he supposed what he was doing was indeed business.

"This your first trip to Okinawa?"

"My second. The first time was quite a while ago. I'm surprised at how much the city has changed."

"Oh, and has it! When you look back at the old days, it's different all right. Nowadays there are these big cruise ships, and Chinese tourists are coming here in droves. They grab all the cabs, so we're chewed out by the regulars when we're all taken."

Perhaps because it was outside of commuting hours, the roads that had been jammed the night before were now surprisingly empty. The cityscape outside the window quickly faded into the background.

Takumi looked at his watch. His Haneda-bound Tokyo flight was scheduled for a little after noon. If he continued straight on, he would arrive at the airport with too much time to kill before boarding.

"Excuse me. Does this road go in the direction of Senagajima?"

The driver was looking back in the rearview mirror as Takumi caught his eye.

"No. This new road takes you straight to the airport."

"Sorry, but can you take me to Senagajima after all?"

"Of course. Let's do that then."

With a loud click of his turn signal, the driver turned left at the intersection. Takumi plopped back in his seat and gazed out the window. Raindrop-stained concrete buildings, the monorail gliding overhead, a large Malayan banyan tree spreading its branches and leaves by the side of the road, a lion-dog statue glaring at him from a red-tiled roof, blue sky peeking through a mass of clouds ... These ever-changing snippets of scenery overlapped with deep-seated memories ...

"Hmm, not so bad today ... "

The driver was muttering to himself as he turned the wheel.

The way to Senagajima took them along a palm-shrub-lined marine road. They passed the occasional car in the opposite lane.

On holidays, this road was packed with tourists, and the volume of traffic increased dramatically.

"Look. There's a new hotel, built just a while ago. There're a lot of stores all around. That's changed everything."

"So it seems …"

It was before the company went bankrupt. Takumi was with his wife and son, enjoying event-filled but tranquil days on the island. Their three-day, two-night trip included a friend's wedding. It was not yet spring, and, like today, it was cloudy, but the city was awash in warm air and sunlight.

On the last day of their trip, as they were driving to the airport in a rental car, his wife told him of a place along the way that she wanted to visit. While in high school, she had lived in Naha for a time with her parents, there on business, and it was now Senagajima that she wanted to see. It was at the time still a quiet place, with only a rectangular baseball field, a batting center, and a modest video arcade.

They had parked their car in a lot next to the road and sat on the seawall with their son on their knees. The shallow water extended out into the distance, and the ocean surface was glistening with gold in the dazzling evening light. The sound of the waves was constantly lapping at his ears, and at regular intervals huge airplanes were roaring overhead.

Since their arrival, his wife had kept up a stream of chatter, but now for the first time she was quiet. She had told him that when she was a teenager, she had, in the aftermath of various happenings, come here to stand in the twilight. Her features had stood out clearly as she silently gazed at the sun while it set over the Kerama Islands.

"The beautiful sea …," his wife had murmured, her profile gilded in the sunset. "Will we ever see it again?"

She had placed her head gently on his shoulder. He was sure

there had been no deeper meaning in her words. He had in turn silently leaned against her thin shoulder. He had felt the warmth of his son's sleeping breath, as the boy lay on his chest, and the scent of his wife's hair. He had had no doubt that his ordinary, peaceful life would go on forever.

"Are you getting out here? If you want to take a look around the shops, I'll wait for you."

The driver's voice drew him back. The man was looking at him through the rearview mirror as the car slowed down.

Tourist groups were milling about, taking photos against the background of the shallow waters or of the airport across the way and licking soft ice cream. He caught the sound of their fragmented chatter and the innocent laughter of the young people, all students it seemed.

"No, please take me to the airport. I have work waiting for me."

Takumi closed his eyes. His cheeks were twitching. The bustling noise outside the car faded away, replaced by the roar of a jet plane passing directly overhead.

∎ ∎ ∎

After registering at the entrance, he sat down on a bench in the waiting room.

In parallel rows sat other visitors, waiting for their numbers to be called. Next to him, a man with a pin in his lapel that identified him as an attorney was craning his neck, a weary expression on his face. A blonde woman in front of him was nervously picking and tearing at the ends of her dry, wavy hair with her abnormally long-nailed fingers.

Tatsu gazed idly at the back of her hair, completely black at the roots, and thought about the man he was about to meet.

According to the past investigative and trial data he had read beforehand, as well as various news reports, Tsujimoto Masami, aged sixty-eight, had been sentenced to twenty-three years in prison for murder and residential arson. He had now been incarcerated in Chiba Prison for four years.

A failed business venture had left Tsujimoto in debt, and in a murder-suicide attempt he had started a fire in his home that took the lives of three people: his wife, who was living with him, and his son's wife and son, who happened to be staying at the house at the time. The number of victims alone was a measure of his crime's gravity. Judicial precedent called for the maximum sentence. There had, however, been extenuating circumstances: The defendant had fully confessed his guilt from the outset, had been suffering from depression and insomnia, had no previous criminal record, had not planned his crime, and had immediately attempted to extinguish the fire. He had thus been spared the life sentence demanded by the prosecution.

Tatsu was focused on the attitude of Tsujimoto Takumi, who was both Masami's son as well as a bereaved survivor, related to both the victim and the perpetrator. Taking the stand in that capacity, Takumi did not speak of any desire for severe punishment, saying only that he could not forgive the defendant. He had nonetheless continued over the years to have his mail forwarded, as Tatsu had deduced from having recently found a letter from the father in the trash. Takumi had little need of mail from his old address, and if he had wished to receive messages sent from the prison, he could simply have provided his new address.

Tatsu sat up when the official in charge called him in.

In the visiting room, through an acrylic panel, he sat facing Tsujimoto, who, dressed in work clothes, looked healthier than he had imagined. Perhaps he had adapted well to prison life. His hairline had receded, but he was not excessively thin; his complexion, though wrinkled by age, was by no means sallow. There did not appear to be anything the least disreputable about him, the light in his eyes suggesting a frame of mind hovering ambiguously between enlightenment and resignation.

"What brings you here today?" he asked, apparently having been informed of the detective's visit.

"I should like to inquire a bit about the incident ... "

Tatsu had been prepared to be rebuffed, but Tsujimoto replied that he was open to any questions. His apparent disinterest and detachment—he had not even asked what the purpose of the interview might be—made Tatsu less relieved than perplexed.

Tsujimoto's memory was sharp and clear; his replies to Tatsu's questions were precise and detailed. Resting his hands on his knees, he reached back into the past, groping for words, a downcast look on his face. His appearance, together with the strange tone of his voice, conveyed the depth of his remorse.

"You have said that you were motivated not only by the debt into which your company had fallen but also by your strong sense of responsibility for the bankruptcy. It appears that it came about as the result of your own transactions. What exactly were they?"

"We were to purchase medical equipment from a major manufacturer, with the intention of distributing it to a leasing company. But the entire deal turned out to be a sham."

Tatsu looked up from the documents he had been perusing.

"So you found yourselves left with defective products?"

"No. I thought that the person with whom I was dealing was a physician working for one of our clients. In fact, he was a broker posing as a doctor."

Seeing Tatsu's puzzled look, Tsujimoto explained in an almost stoically detached tone how it had all happened. Tatsu stopped moving his pen, acutely aware of something incongruous here, though what that was he did not know.

"Did any of your family involved in your company's

management contact you after the incident, either through visits or with letters?"

Tatsu had learned in delving into the case that Tsujimoto's next-of-kin, including his brother, the representative of the company, had disappeared.

"No," came the answer with a shake of the head.

"So you don't know where they are or what they are doing?

"I'm ashamed to say that I know nothing. There is a family grave in Yokohama, but I don't even know what became of my wife's remains."

It was natural to assume that Takumi, who was closest to the victims, had taken care of arrangements in the aftermath, including the funerals and various administrative matters. Yet from Tsujimoto came not so much as the mention of Takumi's name. This was a glimpse into the delicate feelings of the father toward his son, the grieving survivor.

Tatsu asked for and received the relevant temple's address and wrote it down in his notebook.

The attending prison guard, feigning sleep while sitting behind Tsujimoto, leaned back in his chair and glanced at his watch. Even though the visit involved an investigation, Tatsu could not keep Tsujimoto there indefinitely.

Tatsu reached into his inside pocket, took out a margarine-stained envelope, and held it close to the acrylic panel for Tsujimoto to see. His face, until now expressionless, showed agitation.

"This is your handwriting, is it not?"

"Why ..." Tsujimoto was staring at the envelope, his mouth slightly agape.

"Unfortunately, it seems that this letter did not reach your son."

Tsujimoto put his hands, which had been on his knees, on

the table. The little to middle fingers of his left hand were fused together and bent crooked. In some places his right hand had lost its pigmentation, with a fresh scar from a skin graft. Tatsu subtly returned his gaze to the other man's face.

"I'm looking for your son, Takumi-san. Do you have any idea as to his whereabouts?"

There was no clear evidence that Inoue Hideo, suspected of managing the transactions in the Ebisu case, and Tsujimoto Takumi were the same person. All that was certain was that Inoue had used an apartment at the address in question as his office and that Takumi had had his mail forwarded there.

Shortly before his visit to the prison, Tatsu had learned that the old man who had impersonated the seller in the Ebisu case had been hiding out in Nagasaki. And he was told that this same man had, with no final note, committed suicide, hanging himself from a doorknob in his apartment. With each passing day, more and more clues were slipping through the investigators' fingers. This was no time to be excessively concerned about the accuracy or relative importance of information.

"Why, officer, why are you looking for Takumi?"

"Hmmm, I can't … "

"What … what has he done?"

Seeing that the detective was not responding, Tsujimoto looked down at his hands in some kind of realization. He said nothing more, refusing to answer any further questions.

▪ ▪ ▪

"JR? Japan Railways? Nah, I don't think that's going to work," Takeshita said as soon as he had taken his seat.

With that, the already lagging conversation gave way to silence. The dishes there in their private room were almost completely untouched, with only occasional sips taken from the beer and Shaoxing wine in each of their glasses. Off and on, Takumi could hear the sounds of customers downstairs.

Takumi glanced at Takeshita, diagonally across from him, and immediately noticed that he was much more hollow-cheeked than before; his pupils were strangely bulging, and the whiteness of his ceramic teeth, visible through his open lips, only accentuated the unhealthy pallor of his skin, which had apparently long gone unexposed to the machine in the tanning solon.

As if attempting to dispel the glumness, Takumi ventured:

"But isn't it true that JR has gone in big for, whatever, the redevelopment of the pedestrian plaza?"

"No, it seems they've backed off. No one knows why, but it may be that they looked into the general neighborhood or even Kawai herself. Besides, they don't need any land for the redevelopment of the station and, from the outset, may not've even been interested in the project."

"JR isn't one to be taken in by such a foolish-soundin' name as 'Takanawa Gateway,'" remarked Gotō, sitting next to them. "And even leavin' that aside, it's JR that's holdin' the cards here. It won't be easy for us."

Gotō dipped his pork entrails into a spicy miso paste. There was again a lull in the conversation.

With snow flurries in the central Tokyo sky, Takumi and his cohorts were meeting for the first time in several months. At the end of the year they had been preparing for the supposed sale of Kawai's property by spreading the story that it was being offered for the price of 10 billion yen. There had, however, been few bites, and no company or broker had come to the negotiating table.

"What about TATA Hotel?" asked Reiko, nervously fiddling with the curly hair hanging down onto her chest. "And what about the hotels in Hong Kong or Singapore? You said they were interested."

Apparently Taniguchi, hired as the impersonator, was constantly pestering Reiko about when the work would begin. Further postponement, it was clear, might lead her to back out, and there was always the possibility she might run to the police.

Takeshita turned to Reiko and shook his head.

"Nah, it's a dead end for the lot of 'em."

"TATA. It's just got taken fer a billon's worth o' land in Roppongi, so it's surely bein' ever so cautious. 'Tisn't a good time."

Gotō was munching on dumplings and sipping Shaoxing.

"What then are we going to do?" continued Reiko whiningly, still staring at her hair.

"I have an inquiry from a broker," replied Takumi, licking the lip of his glass, well aware of the anxiety in the air, "but from there it's not going to be easy."

The number of companies able to purchase land valued at 10 billion yen was limited, and apart from enterprises such as TATA Hotel that actively own and develop real estate properties, the only contenders were large corporations like general trading companies, major general contractors, leading developers, and railway-related real estate companies, along with real estate fund investors.

"It may be that we've got ourselves a hook that's too big to bite."

Gotō, a wry smile creasing the corners of his eyes, unfolded a warm hand towel and wiped the grease from his balding forehead.

"So what are you going to do?"

Takeshita's gaze fell on Harrison Yamanaka, who had remained silent for some time. Takumi and the others likewise turned their eyes to the project's mastermind.

"Let's wait and see," he said in a calm and even tone. "The land is not at all bad."

"But how long are we supposed to wait?" asked Takeshita with persistence.

The cost of the project to date had been substantial. Although Yamanaka was responsible for most of the expenses, Takeshita had been obliged to pay for a portion of the stakeout and for his separate team's explorations. Although he would be reimbursed in the event of success, with failure there would be no guarantees. Such was no doubt not the only reason for Takeshita's impatience. His religious corporation had recently been charged with tax evasion and incurred a hefty fine, causing its revenue base to collapse. It was now facing cash-flow issues.

Harrison Yamanaka was as nonchalant as ever: "Until a buyer comes along."

Takumi watched the exchange between the two men with bated breath, constantly thinking back to the suspicions Yamanaka had confided in him at the sushi restaurant in Okinawa.

"What if one doesn't show up?" came the retort.

Yamanaka beamed with pleasure: "I'll wait until one does."

Takeshita's face was flushed with rage as he clutched his glass before letting it fall to the bare concrete floor, where it shattered most spectacularly.

"Don't go messin' with me!" he shouted, standing up and growling. "It's been a month, a month! If there's no action in another month, I'll pull out. Listen! If that happens, you're gonna pay me all the expenses and ten percent of whatever you make on the deal. And if you don't come through on that, I'll see to it that you're finished in this business."

Takeshita left the room just as a middle-aged woman, apparently the establishment's owner, came in.

"What the matter? Not to be making trouble in my place!"

With her strong Chinese accent she sounded ever so slightly gentle, as if scolding a child.

"Sorry. We've broken a glass." Yamanaka said with a deliberately amiable smile.

"I don't like it when the police come, you know. Oh, and then this … A customer just came in, with something to give you."

From her apron pocket she took out a phone in an organizer case, a throwaway phone it seemed. It was a bit larger than the one Yamanaka usually used. The leather case was dyed orange, and there was a dial padlock on the cover, preventing unauthorized use.

"Just this time," she said. "This is no baggage service here."

Thanking her, Yamanaka tucked the case into his inside pocket.

"I've never seen 'im like that before," remarked Gotō once she was gone.

Reiko was frowning and looking at her feet, where glass fragments were strewn.

"I really don't care for the rough stuff. If you're going to get into a fight, leave me out of it."

"So the plan remains unchanged?" asked Takumi.

"Of course, unchanged …," came Yamanaka's serene reply.

∎ ∎ ∎

"What's the matter with you?" Aoyagi shouted in anger.

It was past noon, and the mood on the development headquarters' floor was tense. The staff members all looked exhausted as they went about their work.

An unexpected setback in a major project was forcing Aoyagi's company to seek most urgently an alternative development site. It was from the outset an impossible task. If there was still any land remaining in the metropolitan area suitable for their purposes and meeting their 7-billion-yen budget, it would have long since come up for discussion. Aoyagi knew perfectly well just how difficult the situation was but could not resist venting his rage and frustration.

He crossed the floor and headed for Development Department #4 in a corner by the window.

While other departments were bidding on land through trust banks as intermediaries or making purchases from major brokerage firms, this one alone was dealing with small real estate firms, so-called "land sharks," which for the most part specialized in rights adjustments. Aoyagi had once been a member of Development Department #4, and his success there in completing redevelopment projects by teaming up with these skilled land-grabbers is what had won for him the position he now held. If there was one place that could pull off the impossible, this was it.

"What's up?"

Most of the workers had left. The few remaining paused in their tasks and looked up at Aoyagi, vacant looks on their faces.

"How much longer are you all going to sit there like bumps on a log?"

In a fit of anger, he slammed his fist against the steel cabinet next to him. A muffled thud broke the stillness and echoed throughout the tier. Nearby a young member of the department shrugged and went on staring at the computer on his desk.

After speaking briefly with a familiar face, Aoyagi left the company and headed for an old building near Higashi-Nihonbashi Station, where in a small office on the third floor he found a handful of employees huddled together at work.

At a desk in the back sat Hayashi, wearing suspenders. As ever, for what he lacked in stature he made up in girth, the flab around his abdomen suggesting that under his shirt was a flotation ring.

Reclining his round body against a high-back chair, Hayashi was staring at the ceiling and talking loudly on the phone. On his forehead were beads of sweat, and his breathing was labored, likely due to pressure on his airway. Seeing Aoyagi at the entrance, he briefly raised his hand in acknowledgment.

Hayashi had worked for a railway-affiliated real estate company before setting up his own business as a land shark and in that capacity was widely known in the world of property developers. He was at the very least among the top five land sharks in Tokyo. Intelligent, bold, and skilled in negotiation, he was knowledgeable in the relevant laws and, working the tax system, was able to pull together difficult projects that would drive other contractors to despair.

Land development, inextricably linked to urban redevelopment, often attracted criminal and other malignant forces greedy for huge profits. Hayashi was undaunted in his efforts to cross swords with such groups, using laws and regulations as his shield to ultimately turn them into compliant commodities. Even the likes of a major corporation man such as Aoyagi could confidently do business with him.

He had been waiting on the sofa at the side of the room when, on the completion of his call, Hayashi sat down across from him; when his phone immediately rang again, he put off the caller.

"You look as busy as ever."

"I'd be dead if I weren't," Hayashi, who had just turned seventy, replied with a smile, his eyes burrowed deep in the flesh of his face.

Urban land development necessitated negotiating with many landowners and tenants and thus required huge sums of money, even if only just to pay for the land itself. With large-scale projects such as those in which Hayashi was involved, the developer was obliged from the outset to secure the cooperation of investors with ample funds. If he did not receive a favorable response from the risk-averse, Hayashi would aggressively pursue the project nonetheless, even when it meant raising funds through illegal loan sharks or sponsors. As substantial as the annual sales volume was, the money outflow was no less absurdly stupendous.

"I'd like to know whether there is any way we can work out something soon. We are willing to make as many concessions as possible."

Sensing Aoyagi's uncharacteristic state of mind, Hayashi smiled knowingly, but did not inquire as to the reason for his impatience. Aoyagi pressed him to describe various ongoing projects. None of them, it was clear, would meet Aoyagi's budget, or, even if they did, would not meet the current fiscal budget deadline.

"What's going on with the deal in Shibuya?"

"Shibuya, that cursed place?" came Hayashi's reply.

"Yes," Aoyagi nodded.

The property he was referring to was well known in the industry. If the deal were finalized it would create a group of lots covering some 2.5 acres in a prime location in the heart of the city, facing a major thoroughfare. The development budget would easily exceed 100 billion yen.

"I haven't given up on that one yet, but it has a long history, doesn't it?"

It was during the bubble economy that talk of redeveloping the area had begun. Various schemers, including major corporations, foreign funds, brokers, Diet members, and criminal elements had been involved. At one time, there were reports of threats from gangsters, and bullets had flown in broad daylight. The death toll, including unreported victims, had been high.

"I'd like to go, if I could, just to check out the situation from time to time," said the veteran land shark, without mincing his words, "but that would be, well, difficult."

Aoyagi had seen Hayashi as the most promising way out of

his dilemma, but now that path too was gone. He expressed his thanks and got up from his chair.

He now paid visits to other influential land sharks but found none of them holding out hope. As he emerged from the subway at Roppongi Station, he gazed at the city in the evening darkness, bathed as it was in glittering electric light. There were endless throngs of people in the all-enveloping cold winter air. He fastened the front buttons of his long coat and weaved his way through the crowds on his way toward Nishi-Azabu.

He looked left and right as he walked. The city was undergoing a constant process of renewal, aptly reflecting the state of current society and the spirit of the times. There remained nonetheless dilapidated buildings and small edifices. The inefficiency in land use was obvious, restricted as it was by various laws and regulations that set an upper limit on the size of buildings to be constructed. But while a single lot could accommodate a building of no more than three stories, a combination of several lots would allow for a skyscraper. The ratio of common space could then be reduced, with dramatically increased rents and a boost to the economy of the surrounding area.

Although the situation had somewhat improved in recent years, tenants-rights policies were still strongly in place throughout the country. Sometimes 100 to 200 million yen in compensation had to be paid just to evict a small stand-up soba noodle shop or a cafe in front of a railway station. Unscrupulous dealers would attempt to boost the eviction fee by buying up the business rights of such owners. If major firms like Aoyagi's had to negotiate solely on the up-and-up, there would never be enough time or money for it.

To Aoyagi's left, a cylindrical high-rise came into view, blue illumination flickering up and down its exterior.

Without the aid of land sharks, it had taken the Mori

Building Company nearly twenty years to redevelop the area that had come to be known as the Roppongi Hills. The more time it took, the more money it cost. Hayashi was not shy about claiming that if he had been involved, the project would have been completed in half the time. He was probably right. Land sharks had always been necessary, and now, at least for Aoyagi, they were almost the only ones to whom he could turn.

He walked down the hill and opened the door of a members-only lounge near the Nishi-Azabu intersection. He was then shown to a sofa where a stern-looking Matsudaira was sipping a drink. On his face was a curiously coarse smile. With his arm around a bar girl next to him, he seemed to be in fine spirits, his right hand kneading her breast, his left hand ceaselessly running up and down a thigh peeking out from her short skirt.

"Sorry. I didn't mean to barge in on you," said Aoyagi, as he sat down on the sofa, his cautious apology intended to gauge the other's reaction.

"Well, well, Aoyagi-san, let's have a drink. It's been a while."

With a hint of condescension, Matsudaira handed him a glass of champagne. Although not as large a player as Hayashi, he had clearly had his own extensive career as a land shark.

After a perfunctory toast, Aoyagi began:

"Well, to be quite frank ... "

"Ah, what is it now?"

Aoyagi noticed a sharp glint in Matsudaira's eyes. The woman, still next to him, was smiling, the corners of her mouth turned up, her own eyes glazed over.

The real estate company for which he had worked was well known for its "Osaka ardor," as a wry expression went. Aoyagi had dealt with Matsudaira on numerous occasions, as he was able quickly to rejigger complicated land rights situations, provided he was properly paid. As time went by, with greater emphasis given to compliance with laws and regulations, Aoyagi's relationship with Matsudaira had been curtailed, as his aggressive methods and ties to unsavory forces had come to be seen as problematic. His company had eventually gone bankrupt, leaving him to reestablish himself as an independent shark.

Matsudaira listened quietly as Aoyagi opened up to him about his urgent need for a large plot of land and then spoke, mumbling to himself, as he stared at the glass in his hand.

"They shove off all their dirty work on others, who then do it, but with only them coming away with happy faces. And when things get dicey, they chop off the lizard's tail. And now when they get themselves in trouble, they come running to us again ..."

He turned his eyes to Aoyagi, who with a stiff face bowed low.

"There are some very nasty folk out there who have it in for us, so watch your back, Aoyagi-san."

Matsudaira's now suddenly jovial tone was all the more alarming.

"I understand," he continued, a deliberate chill in his voice, "what the job entails. If there is any movement at the site, I'll be right in touch."

Aoyagi took his leave and returned to his office. There were still many there, doing overtime. He checked the newly arrived emails and reviewed all the properties he had previously dismissed. The situation was such that he was obliged to accept some risk. He called the in-house representatives of those properties that caught his attention to inquire about their current status. Their replies were uniformly grim.

Checking his personal phone, he saw several exceedingly long text messages, all from his wife. He paused and read through them; they concerned his junior-high daughter's future. His wife, he was now hearing for the first time, wanted to send her to Keio

University's affiliated high school in New York. As he read on, noting that the annual expenses, including dormitory fees, would come to some 6 million yen, he felt, with wrenching annoyance, that he was caught up in a story about someone quite other than himself.

Concerning his children's education, he had never argued with his wife, who was older than he was and lacked a university degree. She seemed to believe that boosting the children's academic accomplishments would somehow put a feather in her own cap, the benefit being primarily to herself, not them.

As if to nip in the bud any objections, she had laid out some of what she had heard concerning the advantages of overseas education, noting, "Besides, you've been happy to tell me that your salary will go up if you become president. And you're on the verge of that, right? It's all been decided. No?"

He could feel the tone of resentment oozing out of the phone he was clutching. He returned his gaze to the monitor on his desk, so distracted that he could no longer concentrate on his work. It was not just fatigue and lack of sleep. He left his seat and headed for the break room downstairs

He stood by the window, sipping canned coffee, the buildings beyond made visible in every corner of the room by the vast amount of electric light emitted. Somewhere in this sprawling city, there had to be a piece of land he had yet to see.

Behind him he heard a door open.

"Well, what's become of you?"

The voice was tinged with the hint of a sneer. He turned around and saw Sunaga for the first time since he had been denounced at the recent management meeting. Sunaga sidled up next to him, unrestrainedly gaping at his exhausted face.

"Come on. Give it up. There's no use in biting and kicking. It's over."

Aoyagi fixed his gaze on the window and was silent.

"You can say goodbye to any chance of the presidency," said Sunaga, lowering his voice, as though conscious of his surroundings. "If you play ball on that, I'll let you stay on as director."

A directorship was an attractive position; only a handful of those among Aoyagi's many contemporaries could aspire to it. His salary would be much higher than those below him, and the retirement age extended by five years. Post-retirement benefits were also generous, and there was no shortage of possible jobs into which he might parachute from on high. Yet the messages from his wife and an image of his daughter's face now flashed across his mind, even as the cheers and praise of his friends seemed to echo in his ears. No, he would not be satisfied with the status quo.

"Forget it," he replied tersely.

"Do whatever you like; be a fool. But I'm going to level with you: There's no way you can get away with your lies. Your clinging to your petty pride is so grotesque that I actually feel sorry for you."

Aoyagi heard the sound of Sunaga's shoes edging away behind him.

He had put his empty can in the trash and returned to his seat when a call came in on his cellphone. It was a golfing friend from the other day, telling him he was having a drink in his favorite bar nearby.

"If you're there in the office and have a moment, come on over."

Along with the cheerful voice on the other end, he heard someone singing out of tune.

He was surprised to find it was already ten-thirty in the evening.

"How are you going to get any work done if you're as gloomy as you sound?" asked his friend.

"I'll be there in thirty minutes."

The cozy bar with one booth and a counter was bustling with tipsy customers who had come off work. Aoyagi sat down at the counter next to his friend. From the young kimono-clad woman, the proprietress, he ordered a strong whiskey-and-water as she handed him a hot hand towel.

"I guess this is what people look like when their dissatisfaction reaches maximum compression. Is something wrong?" asked the man, giving him a teasing look. The customer in the singing box had just finished his number, and applause filled the bar.

"No, it's nothing serious."

A barmaid new on the job handed him his drink, which he downed in a single gulp.

"Well now, how do you do?"

The man sitting next to the friend was around forty and was craning his neck to look at Aoyagi. He had a trendy haircut, with both sides cut short; his skin was dark and oily. Though of diminutive stature, he had a muscular build that was apparent even through his pinstriped suit. There was an intimidating air about him.

"Pleased to meet you," he said with a fawning smile. "I've heard so much about you, Aoyagi-san."

"I told Sonezaki-san here that I had a friend who's an executive at Sekiyō," interrupted the other to explain. "He has wanted so much to make your acquaintance." Both were regular customers and chatted here whenever they met.

"As it happens, it looks like a plot of land in Sengakuji is coming up for grabs," remarked Sonezaki, leaning in to bring his face closer.

A bit startled, Aoyagi listened as he was told that the owner wanted to sell a large plot near a new station on the Yamanote Line. It appeared to be in good shape and would easily come within the company's budget. This was the first time he'd heard of it.

"I think that I could be your point man, so if you're interested, let me provide you with all the details."

The man got up from his seat and with a practiced hand drew out a business card from his inside pocket. Leaning forward in acknowledgment, Aoyagi accepted the card in exchange for his own.

"Well," said the friend, as he watched Sonezaki walk out of the bar, "that worked out well, now didn't it?" He seemed to regard the encounter as his own accomplishment.

"He's here quite a lot, isn't he now?" he noted, turning to the mama-san. "You know he doesn't come off as mean or snide, so he's popular with the girls. And he's got quite a voice and sings well."

"He's a customer from way back. Even though he's young, he already runs several companies. He handles his drink extremely well and is quite the charmer." This the proprietress said with an air of pride as she handed him a whiskey-and-water.

Aoyagi looked down at Sonezaki's card. The name of the company was not familiar to him. The back showed a real estate business among several others. He wondered whether his own company in the past had had any dealings with Sonezaki.

Someone was singing a Shōwa-era pop song; the bar staff members were clapping along. Aoyagi stared silently at the company name: AKUNI Holdings.

# 5 ▬▬▬▬▬▬▬▬▬▬▬

As soon as he came in, he saw that the place was much cleaner. The piles of empty bento boxes and plastic bottles were nowhere to be seen. The cracked concrete of the earthen floor extending to the entrance was exposed, illuminated in the soft glow of a light bulb.

"What's going on here?" exclaimed Takumi. "It's so neat and tidy!" Nagai, who was just on his way to the back room, stopped. In his arms was his black cat, its eyes shining like marbles.

"We're about to enter a new season," he remarked, a friendly smile on his keloid-scarred face. His long hair was still pulled back in a bun, and on his head like a hairband was the pair of black sunglasses he had used to conceal his lightless left eye. In front of Takumi, he had for some time stopped wearing a mask.

"You didn't have to go the trouble on my account."

"It's got nothing to do with you, Takumi-kun."

He sounded ever more cheerful.

It had been here that Takumi had first come to ask Nagai to do some work, and since then they had become friends. Whether or not there was any business to attend to, Takumi would drop by on occasion, using a box lunch he purchased along the way as an excuse. Recently, however, the timing had not been right, and his visits had become less frequent.

"What is it you've brought for me today?"

Nagai was sitting cross-legged on the floor, his right eye on the plastic bag in Takumi's hand. A black cat jumped out of Nagai's arms, wagged its tail, and made off toward the front door.

"Dumplings. The world's best."

"Where are they from?"

"When it comes to dumplings, they have to be from Ohsho."

"Yes, for sure," replied Nagai in joshing tone, a twinkle in his right eye, "though I've never tried them myself."

Over the cold dumplings they bantered about day-to-day matters and then, when nearly done with their meal, turned to matters of work.

The current project's target was a plot of land near a new station on the Yamanote Line. Nagai's task was to distribute the money that the scheme would bring in. If all went well, the amount would be far greater than ever before. Harrison Yamanaka wanted the participants' predetermined portions to be deposited to their accounts so as to be untraceable.

It had been decided to use the same fictitious account as before, again following Nagai's idea, and to convert the money into safely anonymous virtual currency and then launder it all through an exchange on the dark web.

"How much is it going to be this time?"

"They're aiming at 10 billion."

"10 billion?" exclaimed Nagai, his right eye widening.

"So your share will have at least an extra zero attached to it."

"Well then for you it's going to be quite fantastic, isn't it?"

Without so much as a nod, Takumi silently sipped from his plastic tea bottle. Harrison Yamanaka had promised him several billions of yen.

"What're you going to do with that kind of loot?" asked Nagai with evident interest.

"Nothing. Things won't change."

"You don't sound terribly happy about it."

"Oh, I'm happy."

Out of the corner of his eye Takumi could see Nagai staring quizzically at him, though he posed no further questions.

The phone rang. Nagai grabbed his phone and stood up, hesitating for a moment before answering.

Takumi capped his plastic bottle and relaxed, his hands behind his back. His eyes were drawn to the mounted aquarium tank before him. There had been a dramatic change in its layout since his last visit. The tropical fish had increased in both number and variety, many of spectacular color. He was struck by their sheer vibrancy.

As he continued to gaze at the tank, he became aware of Nagai's voice at the other end of the room.

"I've just had dumplings … Yes, from the guy I told you about. He brought them specially for me. The best dumplings in the world."

The conversation did not seem work-related, and his tone was cordial. Takumi wondered who it might be. He had never heard of anyone else with whom Nagai was in contact, including, of course, anyone in his family.

"We're still talking, so I'll call you later," said Nagai, concluding the conversation and returning to Takumi.

"Who was that?"

Nagai seemed hesitant to respond.

"It doesn't matter."

Nagai remained diffident, his gaze wandering restlessly. Then, as though to accede to Takumi's curiosity, he went to his desk and computer display and with a well-practiced hand tapped the keyboard.

"We met here."

Looking over Nagai's shoulder, Takumi could see a virtual-reality three-dimensional scene. Responding to Nagai's typing, a wizard knight, his face obscured by a hood, was running about a mountain field. There, holding a long sword and an axe, stood an avatar, likely controlled by another player.

"You say you met someone there … Is that who you were talking to?"

"Yes," replied Nagai.

She was, he explained, a woman close to his own age. They had met some six months ago in this online game and then teamed up, thereby becoming friendly to the point of exchanging telephone calls. Surprisingly, she was aware of his current situation, that he had been severely burned and lost sight in one eye.

"It seems that such things happen … " Takumi glanced at Nagai's profile and let out a sigh of relief. He had apparently been assuming that Nagai would go on alone for the rest of his life.

Nagai shyly explained that the two were calling almost every day just to talk of nothing consequential. She was, he said, a graphic designer working in Tokyo, and though that meant that they could easily meet in person, for now they only knew each other through their voices.

"So you don't actually get together?"

Nagai was staring at the display, absentmindedly typing away. A clacking sound rang in the room over the hum generated by the tank.

"We get together here."

"I'll bet she wants to meet you," Takumi said, forcing a lighthearted tone.

"I say it's better not to put reality on display."

Nagai's stony reply suggested he had from the outset ruled out the possibility.

Perhaps he was still haunted by the break-up with his former fiancée.

"Go on. Meet her. You both need to show some guts."

"It's none of your business. Leave me alone!"

Nagai's voice was tinged with irritation. He went on pounding the keyboard, the sound growing louder.

"You want to see her, don't you?"

"You just won't let go of it, will you?"

The tapping on the keyboard stopped, and they both fell silent, the low hum of the aquarium motor hanging in the air. The cat must have jumped, as there was the sound of something falling to the earthen floor.

"Please take care of the crypto-currency matter."

Putting the dumpling container into his shopping bag, Takumi headed for the entrance. The cat leisurely moved passed him across the floor and made its way to Nagai, still standing behind him.

■ ■ ■

"Shall we take a cab?" asked a subordinate following close behind, a concerned look on his face.

Above them was the concourse plaza in front of the station. Taxis were waiting for customers at the terminal nearby.

"No, we'll go on foot," Aoyagi replied without turning around.

The route was the same, but walking instead of using a car allowed for a significantly greater amount of information to be gathered. The city was rapidly changing. Aoyagi had passed through here many times by car and had a fair sense of the area, but assumptions were hazardous. The dubiously reasoned conviction that one knew it all rendered even visible things invisible.

With his four subordinates in tow, Aoyagi made his way along the three-lane thoroughfare. Cars were ceaselessly coming and going in the heavy traffic, and with every breath he caught the whiff of exhaust gas.

On both sides of the road stood tall buildings, as if viewed from the bottom of a ravine. There was scarcely any trace of the town that had once prospered here along the old Tokaido Road. Still, if one looked carefully, one could see the earthen walls of old temples and samurai estates scattered along the alleys, remnants of a bygone era.

"It's straight ahead, sir."

One of his men walking beside him looked down at the map on his tablet and informed him that the site they were about to inspect would be facing them just down the street. The property, visible from the sidewalk, now consisted of a parking lot and what remained of a closed facility.

Aoyagi had already had two business meetings with Sonezaki, who had told him about this property there in the bar. At first, he had been wary of the man's strikingly intimidating appearance, but from their conversations he found him to be quite the sort of low-profile businessman one might encounter anywhere. Although there had been no previous transactions between Aoyagi's company and the real estate division of AKUNI Holdings run by Sonezaki, his firm had developed a wide range of event and restaurant businesses; although unlisted, its total annual sales for the previous fiscal year had amounted to 3 billion yen. A credit check revealed no issues that would hinder the transaction.

They had passed the entrance of the Toei Subway Line's Sengakuji Station when a tiger-striped construction-site fence came into view. An announcement placard explained that JR East, the railway company, was undertaking the project of constructing a pedestrian walkway linking a new Yamanote Line station and Sengakuji Station.

On the other side of the fence, across the alley, a tall, paneled fence covered an area of nearly three-quarters of an acre. Looking through the gaps one could see an expanse of asphalt that appeared to have been used as a parking lot. Apparently the Tokyo Metropolitan Bureau was planning to renovate Sengakuji Station.

The redevelopment of the area in preparation for the opening of the new station was steadily progressing. By the time construction was completed, the station's appearance and ambience would be dramatically altered.

Aoyagi stood between the two construction sites with his back to the national highway. A dark, culvert-like alleyway, so narrow as to allow only a single line of cars to pass, lay beneath an overpass surrounded by several railway tracks and a rail yard. It continued on for nearly three hundred yards, its ceiling so low that a man as tall as Aoyagi could well hit his head on it. Cabs overestimating their clearance often wound up with smashed dome lights. Drivers passing through the vicinity were familiar with the road, as was every real estate agent seeking to do business in the area.

"When are they gonna get rid of this hazard?"

"Um, well ... "

The blood drained from the face of the man standing beside Aoyagi, as he began to shuffle through the documents in his bag.

"Didn't you study up on this?" Aoyagi muttered.

Seeing his irritation, the other men likewise fretted.

"I'm sorry, sir," came a response. "Uh, yes, that seems to be the plan. It'll be gone."

"Do you think you can get your act together? I'd hate to see you go crying to the Employment Service Center."

Aoyagi shrugged and moved on, heading down the street once more.

They were probably on their way home from school. A group of high-school girls in matching uniforms was heading toward them. The girls passed the silent Aoyagi and his team, the sound of their light laughter trailing after them. The wall of buildings blocking the left side of the street now gave way, and there was a clear view.

"It's over there, sir," said the map holder, pointing the way.

A coin-operated parking lot separated by a U-shaped fence lay before them. On an adjacent lot stood sedately the three-story building that had once been a rehabilitation facility; in the front yard Yoshino cherry trees were broadly extending their branches. The huge property was there, just as was indicated on the land-register map and the guide map.

"So there actually was such a place … ," muttered Aoyagi to himself as he stepped into the sprawling parking lot.

One could see at a glance that it could accommodate some seventy cars, but though it was the middle of a workday, only about ten spaces were now occupied. Such was a most uneconomical use of the land. Next to the lot, trains were ceaselessly click-clacking to and fro over the rail joints.

The land was located in a commercial district and had a floor ratio of 600%; when the site of the former facility was included, the total area came to nearly two-thirds of an acre. It was exceedingly rare for such a large piece of land inside the circle of the Yamanote Line to come up for sale, where developers were in never-ending competition. The property was close not only to the subway's Sengakuji Station but also to the new station that was to open in only a few years, thereby creating demand for both condominiums, hotels, and other accommodations.

To judge from current market conditions, the price per tsubo would be approximately 12 million yen. Were condominiums to be built, and estimating a high profit margin, the sale could be expected to bring in nearly 25 billion yen, with a gross profit of several billion. The Development Division's budget would, of course, then be met.

"Can we really afford to … ?" Aoyagi murmured to himself half in disbelief.

Aoyagi and his team conducted their on-site inspection of the land and found there would be no major problems regarding the construction of condominiums and the like. The boundary with the neighboring land was fixed, and there were no obstructions or power lines in the way. The rehabilitation facility was closed, so there were no evictions or related concerns. The coin-operated parking lot only needed to be contracted out.

Was it now just a matter of the seller?

According to the registration, the seller, the owner, was not a corporation but rather a local resident operating a nearby temple. The rights were simple, and nothing questionable had turned up. A business meeting with Sonezaki was scheduled for the following week, but poor health was preventing the seller from attendance. Detailed conditions were yet to be drawn up. In real estate transactions, victory went to the swift, and it was not uncommon for sorrowful would-be buyers to lose by a hair. Aoyagi was determined to get this property as soon as possible, even if that meant compromising on some terms and conditions.

"The thing under construction over there looks like Takanawa Gateway," remarked one of his men, consulting the map in his hand.

Over a passing train and at some distance, a spanking new up-to-date structure could be seen. Its immense exterior shone white in the sunlight.

The redevelopment of the former rail yard, including the new station, was proceeding at a remarkable pace. It was on a much larger scale than Aoyagi had imagined. He walked up to the fence and looked in at the station-to-be. Next to it rose a tall crane, with the skyscrapers of Shinagawa in the background.

Some two or three hundred years before, in the Edo period, this entire area beyond the tracks had been under water. The land was later reclaimed, and the scent and sound of sea and shore had ceased. Today, there were no waves to be seen, only artificial landscapes completely obstructing the view. Aoyagi was made keenly aware of the limitless potential of the city, as it continued to develop.

"Why didn't you tell me about this place?"

He turned and looked sharply at the man in charge of the area. It was inexcusable that this possibility had not even come up for discussion.

"No, it was just that ... we didn't think it would ever come up for sale ... "

At Development Division headquarters, each area was assigned one by one to staff members, who then were constantly endeavoring to deepen their ties to the local community and to gather information. If a property had potential, it was the responsibility of the person in charge immediately to report it.

"Well now ... " the clearly flustered and confused assignee began.

"What is it?"

"It's, it's strange, but I haven't heard from anyone that the owner of the property was intending to sell it. I'm also a member of the neighborhood association, so I'm sure that any such rumor would have gone around."

Aoyagi checked his impulse to give an angry retort, as his underling did not appear to be making excuses for himself. The man continued in a weak voice.

"The property owner seems to be a bit of a recluse and has always stayed away from the neighborhood association."

The roar of the trains grew ever louder, as a cold gust of wind blew through the parking lot. The tops of now budding Yoshino cherry trees were silently swaying.

"Get it, even if you have your doubts," said Aoyagi, as though trying to reassure himself.

■ ■ ■

As Takumi finished speaking, Gotō, who had been sipping Harper's on the rocks, set down his glass on the table beside him.

"We've hauled in quite a big one, we have. Now it's gettin' interesting, wouldn't ya say?"

A smile appeared on his face, obscured though it was in the semi-darkness of the room. The walls in front and in back of him were lined with books, their spines faintly illuminated in the dim light. The private room, closed off behind a hidden door, had only a sofa set and a table. In the background, jazz piano music was softly playing.

"I think I've seen advertisements on TV. But is it really all that good?"

Sitting with her legs crossed on the sofa across from him, Reiko took her lips away from her champagne glass as she spoke.

"Sekiyō House is in all Japan one of the most outstanding developers. As a partner, it's right up there with this thirty-year-old Talikser."

Harrison Yamanaka, who was seated next to Reiko, his nose hovering over the tasting glass, had intervened to reply. His brown suit, custom made by a Neapolitan tailor, had chalk stripes in a similar hue. Elegantly cinched at his neck was a bright persimmon-colored silk tie.

Holding up a glass of Tanqueray gin and tonic with a squeeze of lime, Takumi added:

"And the interested party is the head of the board of directors and is taking the initiative on this. That ought to smooth the way forward."

"Great! Seems we're gettin' down to business all right … " exclaimed Gotō as he cracked open some pistachios.

"I do think that we stand a good chance," said Takumi.

Sonezaki of AKUNI Holdings, a collaborator on the project and an acquaintance of Harrison Yamanaka, had informed them that Sekiyō House had expressed considerable interest in the land by the new Yamanote Line station and wanted to begin discussing conditions as soon as possible.

"So when will the initial negotiations begin?"

"Next Thursday. At 2 p.m.," Yamanaka replied.

Talks were to be held in the conference room at the company, with Takumi and Gotō in attendance.

"Weren't ya asked to bring the seller?" Gotō asked in a skeptical tone.

Sekiyō House had, through Sonezaki, requested that Kawai, the owner of the land, be invited to the negotiations. Again citing her poor health as an excuse, Sonezaki had begged off.

"In any case, this one's quite a special deal. There's no reason not to go all out on this. So let's get moving and wrap it all up."

Yamanaka tipped back his tasting glass and turned his gaze to Reiko.

"Any problem on your end?"

Reiko took a bite out of a strawberry, dipped it into her champagne, and shook her head with an unconcerned expression.

"No, no problem at all."

She had apparently been meeting regularly with Taniguchi, the impersonator-to-be, and making progress in preparing her, particularly in regard to the memorization of personal data and her acting performance. She had had her head shaved bald and a passport photo taken. They had also had the good fortune of learning that Kawai's passport had expired and had thus clan-destinely gone about having her legal domicile and residence certificate changed in order to apply for and obtain a new one. Such had not only the advantage of being a first-rate form of identification; it was also difficult to trace since, unlike a driver's license, the number of the document changed each time that it was renewed.

"Takumi-chan, we need to ask Taniguchi-san to clear her schedule, so let me know as soon as you decide on a date."

Taniguchi had reportedly stopped complaining to Reiko now that she had been told that her "stage appearance" was in the offing.

More drinks were ordered as the discussion continued con-cerning subsequent strategy, arrangements, and the best negotiat-ing path. In the center of it all was Harrison Yamanaka.

Gotō, beginning to feel the euphoric effects of the alcohol, laughed, the half-melted ball ice in his wavering glass making a crisp clinking sound.

"Well now, this time, it could be ... Ya never know ... "

"Now don't be suggesting that things are bound to go wrong ... After all we've done, this is not going to fail."

Reiko's voice, too, exuded confidence, reflecting her aware-ness of how suddenly the outlook for the endeavor had changed.

"On the other hand," said Yamanaka, by way of caution, "without Sekiyō, we'll be in a bit of a bind, as companies able to consider such a huge undertaking are few and far between. Taku-mi-san's team has got to do some heavy lifting for us."

He said this as he put a dry martini to his lips. Though he had just consumed another strong drink, he seemed not the least intoxicated.

They had been listening to Gotō going on and on about Sekiyō when through the door came a steady thud-thud, the intensity of the sound suggesting persistent kicking. From beyond came voices angrily exchanging words as the thick panel slid open, and then—seemingly defying the protests of the restaurant's dismayed staff—in came Takeshita. Those seated in the room fell silent.

From the speakers on a shelf came the sound of a familiar jazz standard, a plaintive tune played on piano and bass, and this only added to the oppressive atmosphere. Takeshita stood silently at the other end of the room, his face obscure in the dim light. He too, it seemed, had been one of those set to attend the meeting, only to be told at the last minute that something urgent had come up and that it had been canceled. Seeing Harrison Yamanaka, he sat down next to Reiko, pushing her legs away.

"Now ya must've heard, Takeshita-san," said Gotō his voice restrained, "the one-and-only Sekiyō appears to be hooked."

Takeshita was staring at Harrison Yamanaka, his lips slightly parted, as though deaf to all sound around him. His profile, faintly seen in the orange light, was gaunt and bloodless, his eyes unfocused.

Takeshita was mumbling something.

"Money … Gimme money!"

"If we succeed in the project, money will come in," replied Yamanaka, apparently unperturbed.

"I need it now … Cash!"

With a snarl, Takeshita grabbed at Harrison Yamanaka, twisting his tie and soaking his brown suit with drink, but the latter merely smiled, as though signaling to the others not to intervene and not to worry.

"Hand it over!" Takeshita shouted, his hand tightly gripping the other's tie. "All of it! I'll trash this place!"

Reiko wrinkled her brow and moved away from Takeshita. Gotō sat frozen, still holding his whiskey glass. Takumi, too, was unable to move from his slumped position. The low, plaintive sound of the bass guitar still reverberated.

"I understand," said Yamanaka. "I'll give you what I have on hand and transfer the rest later. How about that?"

He pulled a wad of ten-thousand-yen notes from his wallet. Takeshita silently shoved them into his pocket and staggered out, an ear on his cellphone.

"We'll need to have him meek and mild until this is all over," said Yamanaka, his mouth so dry that his tongue was stuck to the roof of his mouth. He laughed as he murmured to himself and adjusted his tie. The jazz tune ended, the static from the record sounding like wood sputtering in a bonfire.

■ ■ ■

As he made his way into the tatami room at the back of the restaurant, he was greeted with cheers and applause by his eagerly awaiting hosts.

"Congratulations, Tatsu-san!"

His colleagues, both contemporaries and junior officers, had taken time from their hectic schedules to honor the retiring detective with this evening's reception.

Tatsu shyly acknowledged their good wishes with a smile and took his place at the head of the table. Once the waiter, to all appearances a student, poured drinks, the organizer of the event delivered a pompous speech before proposing a toast.

"Sorry. Excuse me please!"

The restaurant's close-cropped owner emerged from the kitchen, holding an enormous boat-shaped dish of sashimi.

"Detective Tatsu, we are so grateful for all your tireless endeavors. Please enjoy this small token of our appreciation with all those here assembled."

This most thoughtful gesture was met with wild cheers from

the entire room. Tatsu expressed his thanks to the owner, whose eyes were red with tears. Years before, Tatsu had received word that a man he was investigating was a regular patron here. He had taken the owner into his confidence and then frequented the restaurant day after day, secretly gathering information. Since then, the two had cemented their ties, both publicly and privately. When the owner's second son expressed his desire to become a police officer, Tatsu had acted, in his official capacity, as a go-between. It was through the support of people like this owner that he had been able to carry out his work.

"Tatsu-san, we have a small gift for you."

A younger colleague handed him a commemorative plaque with a snapshot of himself, no doubt taken some years before. It showed him scribbling something in his notebook during an investigative meeting. Embossed at the top was a police badge. For over forty years he had seen such insignia every day, but the sight of one now on the plaque was deeply moving.

"Now we feel," continued the young man, "that as you have caused your beloved wife all sorts of annoyance and loneliness, we hope that henceforth you two can spend some quality private time together in this matching lingerie."

And then he held up for all to see a pair of racily contoured lace underwear. Hoots came from all around.

"Hey, knucklehead," Tatsu exclaimed in mock protest, as he accepted the gift, "I'm always wearing something a hell of lot flashier than this!" There was more hysterical laughter.

Then came more drinks, with loud shouts of gaiety flying back and forth.

"Are you going to take on a new job somewhere?"

A junior colleague next to him was filling Tatsu's empty shōchū glass.

"No," came the reply, "not at the moment."

That month he and his wife were planning to take an all-around-Japan cruise. He wanted to make up for the heartache caused by the many nights he had been away from home. What would he do after that? An acquaintance had asked him to join his company as a trouble-shooter. He had not yet responded.

"You should take it easy," the young man advised him. "A relapse could bring the curtain down with a bang."

"I'm not yet so decrepit that anyone needs to worry."

Tatsu was managing his high blood pressure with medication, but his liver and kidney function numbers were as bad as ever. His physician had given him strict orders to avoid to the extent possible anything stress-inducing.

"I shall strive to carry out my life as a cop without any regrets, just like you, Tatsu-san."

Though it was a simple, casual remark, it stayed with him, drifting through his mind. As a detective, Tatsu had been involved in countless cases and had managed to solve most of them. Some culprits, however, had eluded him, and there were cold cases, with Harrison Yamanaka, the land swindler, in particular still appearing in his dreams. He had not while still on the job been able to arrest him a second time or get to the bottom of the Ebisu case. He had done everything he could with the limited time he was given and the poor hand he had been dealt but had nonetheless been unable to break through.

As he tipped his glass and took another sip of shōchū, his eyes fell on a poster on the sand-textured wall announcing the opening date of an antique market. It was on that day, seven years before, that Tsujimoto Masami had committed the crime that had cost Takumi his family.

After meeting Tsujimoto in Chiba Prison, Tatsu had grown curious about the circumstances surrounding the bankruptcy of his company and had dug into the matter on his own. Tsujimoto had told him he had been tricked by a broker posing as a doctor into purchasing medical equipment. From the huge loss incurred, the company had gone into a tailspin and collapsed. The broker had taken great pains to gain the trust of the company as a whole and of Tsujimoto in particular by carrying out several small but genuine transactions.

The company had gone to the police once the fraud was revealed, and a few months after the bankruptcy the broker was taken into custody, only to be released after the charges were dropped. He had left the country sometime thereafter, and his whereabouts were now unknown.

There were still several people involved that he had not been able to interrogate, and there remained a mountain of information that he had been unable to confirm. He had handed over all his investigation's data and documents to his colleagues, but given their already heavy workload he had no idea to what extent the case would be pursued. With the passage of time, priorities steadily shift downward. Tatsu sensed that this case, too, was fading into the background.

If it were allowed, he would happily carry on with it, but that, he supposed, would be willful and selfish on his part. A retiring police officer becoming obsessed with a particular case or a particular criminal was no different from bringing one's personal feelings to the fore at a crime scene. Those nurtured in the bosom of an organization were bound by its rules and were obliged gracefully to accede to junior colleagues coming up in the ranks and to trust them to bring about justice.

He took a swig from his glass to wash away the regret that day by day had been growing since his retirement. A longtime colleague leaned in drunkenly to him.

"Tassan, I'm going to miss you!"

"Rubbish! I'll still be pestering you for help!"

As they were laughing and pouring each other drinks, the phone in Tatsu's trousers pocket rang. The call was from an old acquaintance, a journalist who had been in the Philippines for some time. He had originally been working for a newspaper but had become so persistent about following a serial killer case that his employer had lost patience with him. He was now freelance, covering a wide range of stories, mainly in Southeast Asia, and was publishing reportage in several media outlets.

"Tatsu-san, have you got a minute."

"Hold on a moment."

Tatsu excused himself and moved toward the relatively quiet entrance.

"So? How did it go?"

His voice spontaneously grew louder. It was not just the congratulatory speeches from his friends that now intensified his mood.

"I've found him. The broker. He's told me everything."

■ ■ ■

Final confirmation having been made, he headed off in the early afternoon to Sekiyō, together with Gotō. They had just turned down a narrow alleyway behind an area of office buildings when a Western-style building reminiscent of a time now past came into view. An old signboard at the entrance read: "Established in 1926." He had been to this coffee house before.

Ignoring Gotō's objections, he went in. Before him lay a vaulted expanse. The interior was reminiscent of a church, and even at this time of day the light was dim. One could detect the faint smell of decaying wood. Speakers as tall as a man stood against the back wall, and the air was filled with the solemn sound of a pipe organ, as though rising from the depths of the earth.

"What the hell is this place?"

Gotō was standing motionless beside him, dumbfounded.

The seats were arranged as if in a theater, all facing the speakers, and a few lone patrons were listening to the music. He went upstairs, where the seats were tiered, and sat down in the first row where he could hear the best audio quality.

"Nah we're not to be out for drinkin' tea!" exclaimed Gotō reproachfully. "Are ya goin' or not?"

The appointed time for the meeting with Sonezaki and the others was fast approaching.

"No loud voices are allowed here … Let them wait. We have the initiative. Keeping them in suspense is just what we need to do."

"Well now, Takumi-kun," said Gotō with a wry smile as he lit a cigarette, "you're becomin' more an' more like Harrison."

Picking up a pen, Takumi promptly wrote down his request on a scrap of paper and handed it to the young waitress who had come to take their order.

"Just between you and me," Gotō began, looking at the aged speakers and speaking earnestly, "I'm thinkin' o' making this my last. I don't need any more money. I've made quite enough, I have. And I'm old. As long as I can live quietly with my family, that's all I'll be wantin'."

This was the first Takumi had heard of this. There had been not a hint of it before.

"That Harrison is bad news. He's insane. The other day when he got into a row with Takeshita-san … He was smilin' through it all … And I dunno how old Sasaki met his end in Nagasaki—or, honestly now, what's gonna happen next … "

"You're not getting cold feet, are you? There's no way I'll let you get away with backing out now!"

Perhaps taken in by the cafe's eerie ambience, Takumi spoke

grimly. Even as he tried to stifle rising anger at feeling left in the lurch, his words burst forth, as though an inner dam had broken.

"Yeah, yeah, I know. Don't give me that look!"

Gotō averted his eyes and reached for his glass of water.

As Takumi sipped the coffee that had been brought, the organ music came to an end.

"The music you have requested will be played next." The waitress from downstairs was holding a microphone. She was all business, well aware that here it was music that was the main event.

"Hey, just like a show pub, it is!"

The waitress put a finger to her lips to signal silence as Gotō gleefully teased his neighbor.

"Bach, Orchestral Suite No. 3 in D major, BWV 1068, 2nd movement. Conductor Ozawa Seiji. Performed by the Saito Kinen Orchestra."

The waitress put down her microphone, and soon the air was pulsating with the sound from the speakers. Takumi sank deep into his chair and surrendered all thought to the multilayered musical waves emanating from the string instruments.

The morning tomorrow would mark the day when his mother, wife, and son had been reduced to ashes. Every year, as the anniversary of their deaths approached, he found himself irresistibly drawn to this music. One year he would listen to it on earphones on his way to the cemetery; another year he would have it played here.

"Nice piece!" said Gotō, apparently listening as well.

The performance came to an end, as the lingering notes of the strings faded away. In the silence that followed, the men stood up.

They arrived at Sekiyō House, which stood facing a main

thoroughfare. Sonezaki of AKUNI Holdings was waiting for them in the reception lobby.

"Let's go!" he exclaimed, his face clearly showing his enthusiasm. Acting as the go-between, he had been promised ten percent of the take in the event of success. He appeared to be a most effective negotiator.

As they entered the room, all of those representing Sekiyō House rose from their seats.

"Please accept our apologies for keeping you waiting. We are very sorry our arrival was delayed," said Takumi by way of a perfunctory greeting before reaching into his Dulles bag for his business-card case. Gotō was likewise prepared, and so the process of exchange began.

"Thank you," said Gotō standing on the other side of the table with a charming smile as he handed a card to each of the junior staffers, playing his prearranged role.

From the five Sekiyō representatives, a remarkably large number for the occasion, came not a hint of annoyance at the delay, and the general ambience, far from being chilly, was one of sincerity and courtesy. Just as Sonezaki had predicted, the seriousness with which Sekiyō was approaching the project was palpable.

Takumi had greeted the division chief when his eye caught that of the last man to present his business card. He appeared to be the oldest in the room. Although not as tall as Orochi, with whom Takumi had carried out the stakeout of Kawai's residence, he stood a head above the others and displayed a muscular physique. Takumi could sense that the entire Sekiyō staff, including the division chief, were most mindful of him.

"My name is Aoyagi. I am in charge of the Development Division. I very much look forward to working with you."

Aoyagi bowed and presented his business card. This was the

man who above all would have to be persuaded. Determined to remain calm and not to yield to the pressures of the moment, Takumi responded with a low bow.

"I was there the other day and was once again impressed with what a splendid site it is."

The division chief standing opposite Aoyagi had now taken the floor, a bland expression on his face, clearly aware though he was of Aoyagi's quiet but stern and steady gaze.

"Our company is most interested in acquiring the property. We should like, however, to hear, if we may, how Kawai-sama came to her decision to sell."

The implied meaning of his words was clear: "How is it that you people, coming out of nowhere, were able to persuade an obstinate and antisocial landowner to let go of her property?"

"Well no, it's not such a hefty issue at all."

Gotō was standing next to Takumi as he spoke.

"Now while I don't wish to be delvin' into private matters, Kawai-san has recently become ever so enthusiastic about cultural activities, the theater in particular, and she thought she'd like to lend her support to such endeavors, even if that means givin' up some of her own wealth. And that is why she came to me for advice."

Gotō's eloquence was so convincing as to belie the weakness he had just displayed in the coffee shop. As though to suggest that she was regularly consulting with him, he displayed several pamphlets of performances organized by Kuboyama that Kawai had actually invested in.

"Both the parking lot and the facility next to it were originally intended by those from whom she inherited the property to be used for the good of the greater community. But then came various problems with the facility, and Kawai-san herself lost some of her vim 'n' vigor."

To Gotō's suddenly murky explanation, the staff members of Sekiyō House were nodding their heads in understanding. They were perhaps aware that Kawai's husband had run off with a resident of the facility.

"The theater immediately came into the picture. You may be unaware, but theater costs a bundle of money once you get into it. The budget just for invitin' famous actors goes sky-high. Still, that's a pittance when compared to Kawai-san's resources. She thought that instead of just givin' money to her favorite theater company, she would contribute in a way that was, um, broader and more sustainable."

"Ah … " exclaimed the division chief, appearing to show interest. He listened to Gotō's argument, which had been prepped by Harrison Yamanaka.

"I'd like you to keep this confidential. But, if truth be told, they're plannin' to build a theater."

Gotō took a tablet device from his bag, switched it on, and placed it in the middle of the table. The division chief and his colleagues leaned forward and peered at the screen, where they saw an image of a rough sketch taken with a camera. It was a watercolor, depicting a theater of innovative design, with forceful depictions of the exterior, floor plan, and cross section.

For a suitable fee, the team had commissioned a sketch from an architect, a young man accused of plagiarism and currently in hiding. There were four stipulations: (1) the seating capacity was to be about one thousand; (2) the budget was to be unlimited; (3) the acoustic design was not to be taken into account; (4) the designer was to demonstrate his talents to their fullest and to work as if such a theater could actually exist. He had gone all out on the endeavor and met the deadline, the result exceeding expectations.

"The building has six floors above ground and two below, with seating for a thousand when the balcony and wheelchair space is considered. There'll also be a restaurant and a lounge. It is Kawai-san's wish to have countless numbers of people enjoy this dedicated theater hall for countless years to come."

Gotō spoke with great fervor as he pointed to the sketch.

"Where will this theater be built?" came a question from the section chief, sitting next to the division head.

"Nothing firm's been decided, but Kawai-san said that Shimokitazawa would be an ideal location. There's a lot of redevelopment goin' there, and, above all, it's a theater district."

"Well, yes, Shimokitazawa ... "

The manner in which the section chief was nodding his head suggested skepticism. Why, he seemed to be asking, would it not be built on the land she already owned? After all, if Kawai used her land, there in front of the new Yamanote Line, as collateral, she would be able to borrow sufficient funds from financial institutions. Moreover, the convenient location in the heart of the city would be quite advantageous for the operation of a theater.

As though intuiting the doubts on the part of the Sekiyō staff, Gotō went on to explain:

"Kawai-san did want to spare herself all the trouble and to build on the present site, which is all very convenient, bein' right in front of that new Takanawa-what's-it-called station. But, you know, there was an awful lot that happened with the site, which is to say, the facility. I trust you'll understand. She wants to let go ... It's a matter of her feelings ... "

There was a fervor and poignancy in Gotō's tone; he was clearly assuming that Sekiyō knew all about what had gone on at the facility.

"Now, now, I must apologize for sounding doubtful. We can

indeed understand the situation. What you say about the theater is quite inspiring, and we should like very much to aid in that cause."

"Well, it's not my story to tell, but if you're still concerned about the matter, you might look into it yourselves and consider why the facility wound up closin' its doors."

Gotō's disgruntled expression prompted a flurry of dismay among the Sekiyō staffers. The section chief was now attempting to assuage him.

"And so it was, when Kawai-san consulted me about her wish to sell, that I went to our financial advisor, someone she's also known a long time."

Gotō now introduced Takumi, to whom attention now turned. He bowed and took from his Dulles bag a set of documents.

"As you may have already heard from Sonezaki, AKUNI Holdings has already completed a sales contract with Kawai-san, with a deposit of 30 million yen."

He handed the contract, stamped with a forged seal, to the general manager.

"Here are Kawai-san's ID, her seal registration certificate, property disclosure statement of important matters, and a letter of attorney."

The ID included a photo copied from a passport showing a tonsured Taniguchi, the impersonator, the resolution of the face reduced so as to make it blurry when copied. In the margin of the document was written: "As a judicial scrivener I hereby certify the seller's identity as evidenced by said seller's passport." Along the seal, Gotō had signed his name, using his pseudonym.

The director entrusted the submitted documents to two young subordinates at the end of the row, who then set about verifying them.

Takumi could sense his breathing become shallow and his heart rate rising. He knew he should not give undue attention to what was now occurring, but he was nonetheless anxious. Gotō too was looking on nervously.

There would probably be no doubts about the forged contract, a private document, to say nothing of the legal seal registration certificate. If a question were raised, it would concern the passport photo.

A different photo of Taniguchi had been posted on a fake website that had been covertly produced in order to introduce the temple's head priestess, and although its existence had been communicated to Sekiyō House, if anyone there should happen to know the face of the real Kawai and to raise the issue, the entire venture would go crashing into the rocks.

A copy of the passport was passed to the first person in charge, then to the second, another junior staffer, who stared at the photo page for what seemed much too long. At last, the manager discreetly cut him off and looked toward Takumi:

"So in regard to the figure you have in mind ... "

The young man who had had his eyes on the passport now reached for the seal certificate, as though to indicate he had no further issue. Having now passed a major hurdle, Takumi felt his shoulders relax and could now speak without hesitation.

"First of all, by way of background, the property is situated within a group of lots, a circumstance that is quite rare along the Yamanote Line, and is in very close proximity to Sengakuji Station. As you know, a new Yamanote station is scheduled to open in the next few years, at which time the surrounding area is expected to change and develop dramatically."

There was a hint of pomposity in his words, to the mild but clear irritation of his listeners.

"Under normal circumstances, the expected value would be

reflected in the price being proposed, however, in this case the seller, for reasons already given, has left it to us to consider a reasonable range."

"Specifically … ?" the director asked, unable to hold back.

"The prevailing price of land in the area has currently risen to about 12 million yen per tsubo, and in some cases it has gone even higher. If we assume that amount, the total value of the land, covering altogether 810 tsubo, would be approximately 9.7 billion yen … So the final amount would be 14 billion."

The face of the division chief clouded over as he heard the figure, which far exceeded the upper limit of expectations. His colleagues too, no doubt anticipating rough sailing in the negotiations ahead, looked no less glum.

Seeing that the director was about to speak, Takumi jumped in:

"The land is what it is, and there may well be others willing to buy it at that price, but as we are blessed with Kawai-san's benevolence, I would propose 11 billion."

He could feel the tension in the room ease with this proposal.

With Harrison Yamanaka it had been agreed in advance that negotiations would center on the 10-billion figure. The decision was based on the knowledge that Sekiyō House was, for whatever reason, urgently in need of a large amount of land. There was no need to offer a bargain price.

The section chief quickly tapped his calculator and showed the figures displayed on the liquid-crystal display to the division chief and to Aoyagi. With a ballpoint pen the section chief pointed to a document he had brought and silently gestured Aoyagi for his approval before turning to look back.

"I wonder whether we might agree on 9.8 billion," suggested the division chief, his polite words carrying a resonance no doubt cultivated over the course of many negotiations.

In offering a concrete figure, the company was suddenly revealing all the more clearly the reality of its position. It was now willing to pay the staggering sum of 9.8 billion yen. Takumi's heart was racing. The difference of a few million yen was of no concern; with a little more of the bargaining game, the deal would be done.

"Kawai-san has done as much as she can for us, so now we shouldn't go 'n' be greedy, what with Mitsui and Nomura about to come forward."

Gōto, who had sat watching, his arms crossed, was now engaged in bluffing.

Mention of the would-be competitors was cause for renewed agitation, and again there was silent discussion on the Sekiyō side. In a dour tone, the division chief then said:

"What would you say to 10.2 billion?"

This was 400 million more than the amount offered just a moment before. All the trouble that previous projects had caused the team seemed by comparison now to be utterly absurd. They were undoubtedly close to the point of Sekiyō's true upper limit.

"10.8 billion!" said Takumi with as much force as he could muster, feeling his temperature rising, surprised at his own burst of excitement.

"10.8 billion … " The division chief was frowning, though whether he was in earnest or putting on an act was impossible to discern. Takumi sensed that any further bartering would not end well.

"Well now, I understand … I would propose that we share the pain and split the difference. That is, how about 10.3 billion?"

He then asked for feedback from his own negotiating partners, who offered no objection.

The parties now collectively agreed to a purchase agreement between Kawai, the seller, and AKUNI Holdings, the

188 | KO SHINJO

intermediary, and, at the same time, between AKUNI Holdings and Sekiyō House, the buyer.

"There is, however, one condition. Kawai-san is, for various reasons, feeling pressed to sell the property. We should like to have the contract signed by the end of next week and the settlement made by the end of the week thereafter. Would that be possible?"

Such would, under normal circumstances, be unthinkable. But the team was nonetheless compelled to hurry the process along. The more time it took, the greater the likelihood of most unwelcome information coming in from outside the company, and that could well result in rocking what was supposed to be a steady ship.

The division chief looked perplexed.

"We understand your concern," said Gotō to put him at ease, "but the fact is that if a decision is not made quickly, others'll be movin' in. Kawai-san is in need of the funds now."

The clearly flustered section head was whispering something in the ear of the wavering division chief. From across the table Takumi looked on.

"I understand."

The voice was Aoyagi's. With his gaze fixed on Takumi, he continued:

"While the settlement might need more time, we shall make every effort to accommodate your wishes."

Never in all the business negotiations Takumi had been involved in had he ever seen in a gaze such a cold, animalistic look. His heart was pounding and now he felt his limbs grow tense, as he found himself unable to look away from the eyes of the man before him.

"Nevertheless, we too have conditions. As the head of the

Development Division, I cannot give the green light to the contract in this setting alone."

He paused before saying in a more challenging tone:

"Please allow us to meet with Kawai-sama."

■ ■ ■

Seated to his left, Gotō had opened his mouth wide to nibble on the lobster in his fingers.

"Now I'm gonna order some meat. I dunno when Reiko-chan'll show up."

His voice was filled with irritation. She seemed to be behaving the same as ever, but then perhaps she was getting butterflies in her stomach. The second meeting with Sekiyō House was to be held in two days, and Reiko was to bring Taniguchi, the impersonator. Were they successful in their deception, they would be garnering 10.3 billion yen in one fell swoop. It was a critical moment.

Sitting to the right was Harrison Yamanaka, who had rolled back his sleeve and was looking at his watch.

"Yes, let's do that. If possible, I'd like mine fresh off the grill."

A pure white tablecloth adorned the round table, the downlights producing a bright halo upon it. The vibrant red of the lobster, arranged on large plates, caught the eye, and champagne filled each glass, creating a luxurious atmosphere. With no message and the appointed time having passed, Reiko's seat alone remained with the napkin neatly folded on the plate.

Takumi wiped his mouth with the napkin on his knee and looked up. The interior of the spacious, softly lit restaurant was filled with customers at every table as far as the eye could see. The lively conversations of people enjoying dinner rebounded from the Art Deco–style ceiling as a pleasant murmur.

He called over a passing waitress and ordered sautéed spinach as a side and the signature T-bone steak.

"They've got nothin' but good-lookin' women here. If Reiko-chan sees 'em, she's bound to be jealous. Maybe that's why she's late."

Gotō tilted his glass back, as with a persistent eye he watched the back of the waitress.

"I wonder whether something's happened."

Normally, such things wouldn't matter, but tonight was different. Reiko was the one in charge of looking after Taniguchi.

"It's the usual, isn't it? She'll be arrivin' with excuses like her shoppin' took longer or she's had a fight with a guy, somethin' like that."

Gotō grabbed the neck of the champagne bottle and carelessly tossed the liquid into his glass. He returned the bottle to the ice bucket and turned toward Harrison Yamanaka with a probing gaze.

"More importantly, how's Takeshita-san doing?"

Takumi had not seen Takeshita since the last meeting, and this evening he was again absent. Flashing through his mind was the image of the man's face as he grabbed Yamanaka by the collar and demanded money. Perhaps it was the drugs, but his eyes had been unfocused and erratic. It was impossible now to see him as anything but disturbed. He was madness personified.

"It would seem that his health is not quite in order. There is, however, no problem with his subordinates, as Takumi-san has been managing them from the beginning."

Harrison Yamanaka was moving his knife as he calmly gave his response.

Before coming to the restaurant, Takumi had had a meeting with Orochi, who said he had not recently seen his boss Takeshita.

Asked where he might be, Orochi had replied with a shrug that as usual he was probably out chasing some woman.

"Takumi-san, what about the key?"

"I've made arrangements for tomorrow night, as during the day there are the eyes of the neighbors to consider. I've also received a call from our people in Okinawa, who report that Kawai and Kuboyama have checked into their hotel."

Yamanaka nodded with an expression of relief and reached for his glass.

As they discussed the status of their progress, the last of the champagne was poured, with a bottle of Opus One then being uncorked just as the steaks arrived.

"The meat here's fantastic. Got a real meaty taste!"

Gotō was chewing away, ceaselessly busying his knife. Harrison Yamanaka heard the remark and nodded with satisfaction as he savored his medium-rare steak, its flavor blending with the wine he was sipping.

"It's just this sort o' grub that I cannot do without. Come on, Takumi-kun, get yourself some more!"

With his knife still directed at his plate, Gotō became aware of a presence behind him. Turning about, he saw a woman making her way from the entrance. Accompanied by a member of the restaurant staff, she was wearing a tight, knee-length dress of navy-blue lace. Her breasts, disproportionately large for her slender figure, made her all the more striking. It was Reiko.

She sat down directly across from Takumi, making no move to unfold her napkin.

" … Just won't listen. Just won't listen … Not a word … "

Reiko was staring at the large plate of lobster and using both hands to hold on to her bangs. Her long, translucent, ice-gray nails dazzlingly reflected the downlight's glow.

"Reiko-chan, it's another guy, is it not? Men, you know, you've gotta think of them all as children. It's all right. You'll be makin' up soon ... So let's toast now."

Gotō poured some wine into her glass.

"I went all out to persuade her, but it's all quite impossible."

She was muttering without making eye contact with anyone. They had never seen her before with such a desperate expression.

"Has something happened?"

Reiko looked up from the table as Takumi spoke.

"It's impossible. She says she can't do it."

"Says she can't do it? What the hell's that?" exclaimed Gotō, his relaxed expression vanishing.

"Taniguchi says she can't go along with us."

The table fell into heavy silence.

"Can't go along? But she's already been paid the advance, and she was fully committed. Why all of sudden?"

Before realizing it, Takumi was now impulsively grilling her. It was all quite unexpected. Taniguchi had recently been said to be highly motivated, diligently memorizing Kawai's personal information.

"She talked about her debts, right? Well, it seems they all came to light."

Reiko, with furrowed brow, was incessantly running her fingers through her hair.

When asked why, Taniguchi said that her family had discovered a collection notice sent to her from a creditor. And when they asked her about it, she confessed to having run up debts. On hearing of her situation, her parents had, it seemed, decided to assume the burden. Thus, Taniguchi's motivation for cooperating with the project was now gone.

"Sorry, Takumi-chan, but can't we postpone this for a bit and reschedule?"

"And look for someone else? Now?"

He thought of how difficult their search had been before finding Taniguchi. Even if they quickly found a suitable substitute, they would be starting from scratch with all the preparation, from acting practice to fabricating materials. Furthermore, as Kawai and Kuboyama had already arrived in Okinawa, they would have to reconceptualize the entire plan.

"Now that may be quite a tall order. The other party's in a hurry, and we can't wait forever. If we go to hemmin' and hawin', the whole endeavor could be crumblin' at our feet."

Gotō's observation was accompanied by a bitter expression, as he smothered his meat with creamed spinach.

"There is the distinct possibility that the police may get involved with Taniguchi, and that further tells us we haven't the luxury of time."

Harrison Yamanaka said this with a contemplative look, as he drank his wine.

"I suppose asking the woman who at the interview refused to have her head shaved would also go nowhere ... "

There was no response to the murmurs from Reiko, who appeared to be taking much of the responsibility upon herself. No one was speaking. Grasping the stem of her glass, Reiko took a sip.

The mood became one of profound emptiness and futility. It was clear that something painstakingly built over a long time had been shattered and scattered before their eyes.

Cheers erupted nearby. A waiter was presenting a cake adorned with sparklers and candles to a nearby party. Basking in the light was a smiling couple, as staff members sang "Happy Birthday," with guests at the surrounding tables joining in. Takumi and his companions appeared to be left out, abandoned in a conversation-less space.

With eyes blurred, Takumi was staring at his glass as the

clapping stopped. His eyes then met those of Reiko there on the other side of the table. Faint afterimages passed through his mind, as though superimposed on his retinas.

"Wait a moment ..." he murmured, still staring at Reiko.

"Somehow ... Don't they look similar?"

"What do you mean?" Led by the direction of Takumi's gaze, Gotō turned his head sideways.

"Hmm, I think so too," said Harrison Yamanaka, now chiming in, as he looked at Reiko. Gotō seemed to have caught on as well.

"Now that you say so, it wouldn't be impossible. Just fiddle with the makeup, the hair, the boobs ... They're about the same age too."

"What are you talking about?" asked Reiko coldly.

"If you were to do it, Reiko-san ... You would already know the situation. You were doing all the memorization work with Taniguchi-san. It wouldn't be such a challenge, and we could go on as planned."

A copy of the passport submitted to Sekiyō House had had the resolution of the photo area reduced. By digitally manipulating photos of Kawai, Taniguchi, and Reiko, it might be possible to come up with something they could use. Even if it was now too late to get a passport, they might still have enough time to forge a driver's license.

Harrison Yamanaka was looking at Reiko's head. Her hair, exposed to the light, was brown and hung in loose, wavy curls down to her breasts.

"No way! I absolutely won't do it!"

"If I could, I'd take your place. But it's really necessary, it is."

Gotō was dotingly stroking his own sparse hair, as he spoke. He turned to her, overwhelmed as she was. There was no remaining option.

"Reiko-san, can you somehow see your way to do this? It'll

be fine. Hair grows back, you know, and that's better than nothin', is it not?"

"What're you saying, you with hair like slats in a bamboo blind. It's impossible. If I went along with this, I'd sure to be caught first thing!"

Reiko might well have understood, better than anyone, the risks that impersonation entailed.

"If you take the job and all goes well, I'll throw in 100 million as a bonus."

Harrison Yamanaka said this is in a measured and soothing voice. Of the expected 10.3 billion yen, roughly 3.3 billion was to go to Yamanaka, three billion to Takeshita, 1.2 billion each to Takumi and Gotō, 1 billion to Sonezaki, and 600 million to Reiko. Yamanaka appeared willing to pay 100 million out of his share. This was vastly more than the 3 million that had been promised to Taniguchi.

"No way!" said Reiko again flatly. "I won't do it unless its 100 million upfront and 500 million if we pull it off. The original 600 million is separate."

She muttered the numbers without making eye contact. It was obviously an unreasonable demand. It was still unclear whether they could even secure the down payment, let alone the entire 10.3 billion. An awkward silence prevailed.

Leaning back in his chair, Gotō scratched the back of his head, a wry smile on his face. Harrison Yamanaka seemed to have been caught off guard and was sipping his wine quietly.

"All right. I'll guarantee the upfront payment and the success bonus."

It was Takumi who spoke. Gotō and Yamanaka turned in his direction.

"Takumi-kun, d'ya really mean it?" asked Gotō, as he sat up straight.

Without replying, Takumi turned to Reiko:

"If I pay, you'll definitely do it, am I right?"

There was no response. Reiko sat with her arms crossed, her gaze turned away in a stern expression. In her eyes was a flicker of indecision, suggesting neither joy nor apprehension.

.  .  .

It was a steep road. Exiting the station, he immediately saw before him a densely packed residential area, houses in the distance rising up as a sheer wall. Here and there, fresh greenery was sprouting between the houses and on the cliff-top, lending to the scene a lingering hint of the wild.

Holding the map he had printed out, Tatsu set out to climb the hill. The road, just wide enough for a single car, wove through the gaps between the houses. In a small park surrounded by family residences stood an old cherry tree, now in leaf, basking in the dazzling sunlight. Beneath it sat young mothers with children, chatting with one another as they lunched.

In the inner pocket of his worn jacket his cellphone vibrated. His wife was calling.

"I'm done at the home and am on my way now. But there seems to be a train delay, so perhaps I'll find a coffee shop and wait."

Her breathless voice came through amidst the background noise of what sounded like a train station. They had planned to shop for clothes at a Tokyo department store. Attendance at a dinner party on their upcoming cruise required proper attire, and what they had was unsuitable. Tatsu's wife had since that morning been visiting her mother at a nursing home in the suburbs; he was to meet her later at the entrance to the store.

"Uh, about that," he said, looking up at the cherry tree, "I'm sorry, but I can't make it. Just pick out something appropriate." Fluttering in the breeze, white blossoms, not yet fallen, were peeking through the green. From nearby came the sound of a child crying.

"What do you mean? What are you up to?"

"Well, uh ... "

He looked down at his feet. His shoes, poking out from beneath his slacks, were lost in the shadows on the dry asphalt.

"Is this your usual baseless hunch?"

Her voice was demanding, almost laughing in disbelief.

"I do hope that I'm wrong."

"How long are you going to go on playing detective?"

She sounded exasperated. He could imagine her rolling her eyes on the other end of the phone.

"I'll be fine for tonight."

Their three daughters were organizing a retirement celebration.

As long as they could remember, he had been consumed by investigations, even on holidays, and had never been one to play a fatherly role. He had known next to nothing of how they spent their days or of their youthful struggles: such he had left to his wife. Now all three were employed and living their own lives. There had even recently been the happy news from his second daughter, married to a coworker, that she was pregnant.

"Don't be late. The girls are looking forward to it."

She seemed to be the one most eagerly anticipating the event.

Tatsu returned his phone to his pocket and again looked down at the map.

He continued to follow the gentle slope and, after losing his way several times, eventually saw on his right a densely wooded cliff. A steep stone staircase, cutting through a tunnel of trees, led to a tiled gate, small and antiquated, through which, having breathlessly climbed the stairs, Tatsu now passed.

Various plants were being cultivated within the snug temple grounds. A stone path led directly to the main hall. Tatsu made his way across the flagstones and rang the bell at the side of the temple's living quarters. A few moments passed before a man of his own age, presumably the head priest, appeared at the door.

"I've not been here before. I would like to visit a grave."

As Tatsu spoke, he realized he had come empty-handed. Though he had abruptly changed his plans and come on the spur of the moment, it occurred to him that he might at least have stopped to purchase some flowers.

"Yes, of course. Please come in," replied the priest calmly. "Do you know where it is?"

"No. It's the Tsujimoto family grave."

"Ah, the Tsujimotos ... "

The priest's face seemed to cloud over ever so slightly.

Tatsu purchased incense and was then guided to the back of the living quarters. The cemetery stretched out over a small hill, with the graves arranged in steps along the slope. The paths were well maintained. There were no other people, and though all was still, there was no sense of gloom, perhaps because of the bright · sun.

The Tsujimoto family grave was in the highest section. Standing in front of the gravestone, Tatsu could see the basin-shaped town below and even make out the bay, surrounded by an industrial complex.

"Who visits the grave?" he asked the priest in a casual tone.

"Once a year ... A relative comes. Around this time ... Always leaves everything quite clean. We have a good rapport."

Alone now, Tatsu sat in front of the grave and lit the incense. The vase on the gravestone was empty. To judge from the ashes in the incense holder, it would seem that no one had been here recently.

Looking downward, he saw a parking lot for visitors and a bench set up in one corner. From here, one could easily see people coming and going.

Leaving the grave, he sat down on the bench and drank a can of cold vending-machine coffee as he extended his gaze beyond the fence.

Smoke was rising from the factory area; the surface of the bay was shimmering in the sunlight. The faintly tinted sky towered above him as a dry, gentle breeze playfully swayed the large camphor trees on the temple grounds and the shrill call of a bush warbler periodically echoed through the valley.

Tatsu put his hand into his jacket and pulled out an envelope slightly stained with margarine, the one he had taken on his own initiative just before he was about to retire.

"Will he come?" he murmured to himself, his eye on the path to the right. "Probably. No, certainly."

An hour passed. Then two. There had been no visitors. A woman who appeared to be the priest's wife had gone out shopping and then returned ... Perhaps he would not be coming today. Until Tatsu sat down on the bench, he had hoped that indeed he would not come. Yet now he noticed in himself a vague sense of disappointment. His contradictory feelings were irritating.

"Excuse me ... "

Turning around, he saw the priest looking at him.

"Have you finished visiting the grave?"

There was a tone of suspicion in the question. Tatsu's police badge might have dispelled his doubts, but he had surrendered it on his retirement.

"Well no, this is such a pleasant place ... I was thinking how fine it would be if my wife and I could find our final resting place here. I'm not here to cause trouble. Let me assure you."

The priest, seemingly still unconvinced, walked away. Tatsu

wondered whether he might be reported and yet was not inclined to leave, deciding to deal with whatever came.

The shadows at his feet gradually lengthened as the light in the sky began to fade. The temperature dropped, and the chill of the bench seeped through his slacks. His muscles were stiff; his buttocks ached. He looked at his watch and realized he had been sitting there for nearly four hours. His dinner appointment with his daughters came to mind: If he left now, he might make it just in time.

The bay turned crimson and was then blotted out in the dusk. He watched the lights flickering in the houses below and felt gripped by the frustration of time passing all in vain.

"Perhaps he won't come."

He chided himself for carrying on with baseless, self-centered delusions. What was he so obsessed about? It was time to go.

He was about to stand up when, still holding his empty can, he heard a faint sound. It was neither the distant rumble of a car nor, from the camphor tree on the cliff, the rustling of leaves. He turned his head to the right and saw someone moving toward the cemetery. He followed the figure with his eyes and then, having momentarily waited, slowly and calmly arose.

He returned to the cemetery and saw a man in front of the Tsujimoto grave. His white hair was set off by the dark hue of his suit. His eyes were closed, his hands clasped in prayer. He opened his eyes again as he noted the sound of footsteps.

Whatever that white hair might lead one to think, it was a man in his mid-thirties who was looking back at him. As Tatsu observed more carefully, he could see a resemblance in the eyes and nose to Tsujimoto Masami, whom he had met at the time of his prison visit. The man was also similar in appearance to Inoue Hideo, captured in several security camera photos, though their angle was bad and the image fuzzy.

"You are Tsujimoto Takumi-san, are you not?" inquired Tatsu in low voice.

"And who might you be?"

"A policeman."

Takumi managed to suppress the pangs of conscience surging in his throat.

"What is your business with me?"

He appeared to be so composed as to be utterly unconcerned. Maybe there was no connection to the case.

"Last year there was a criminal hoax involving land in Ebisu. A company was defrauded out of 700 million. Do you know anything about it?"

Takumi averted his gaze, pondered for a moment, and then replied:

"No, nothing."

Tatsu silently stared into Takumi's eyes, their crystalline lenses cold and emotionless. As he gazed, he felt he was being dragged into a deep darkness. The cast of those eyes reminded him of Harrison Yamanaka, who had maintained both his silence and an eerie smile as in the dead of night he was being grilled there in the interrogation room.

"You're lying," Tatsu muttered, still glaring at the other. "You know … about the case, about Harrison Yamanaka. You know about it all. That day, you pretended to be a nonexistent consultant named Inoue Hideo and used a man posing as the landowner to steal from a real estate company."

"I don't understand … On the basis of what evidence are you making these accusations?" Takumi's face was without expression, revealing no sign of agitation.

"I don't need any. I simply know. You can bet on it. And that face of yours is lying."

Tatsu's shoulders were slumping, as though the strength were being drained from them, belying his strong words.

"You're a land swindler," Tatsu whispered, as if to make it clear to himself.

The sound of a train passing below the hill echoed through the valley then faded away, and momentarily the silence returned.

"This is all voluntary, am I right? So are we done now?"

Takumi reached for the bucket and dipper that lay at his feet.

"About the medical equipment company that your family used to run ... I've looked into why it went bankrupt."

Takumi, still gripping the bucket, froze.

"There was a broker pretending to be a doctor, whom you introduced to your father, the company manager. He tricked your father into a massive loss with a phony deal."

Takumi remained silent, his gaze fixed on a corner of the city spread out below the graveyard.

"That man was an old-time henchman of Harrison Yamanaka, dealing drugs and engaged in fraud. Did you know that?"

For a moment, a change seemed to creep over Takumi's face, illuminated by the white light of a lamp.

"He approached you from the start, am I right? At the bar in the Hotel New Grand in Yokohama. He'd had his eye on you all along."

The journalist who had cooperated in the investigation had reported that the broker was now in the Philippines, engaged as some sort of pimp with Japanese males as his targets. When contacted by the journalist, he had admitted to ensnaring Takumi's family company, all with the help of Harrison Yamanaka. Apparently a dispute over dividing the spoils had led to his holding a grudge against Yamanaka.

Takumi remained silent as before, keeping up his air of indifference.

"I don't know what your intention is in associating with the likes of people like Harrison Yamanaka. Just remember: He's the one who brought your family to ruin."

Takumi's hitherto spiritless eyes suddenly widened with emotion. A wild and confused light flickered for a moment before disappearing. He did not reply, but his cheeks were now twitching, as if suddenly infested with a swarm of insects.

"I have visited your father. You could at least respond to one of his letters."

The envelope he now took from his pocket bore the name, in meticulous script, of Masami's son.

"My contact information is in there too. If you are inclined to talk, please get in touch ... "

To the white-haired man, whose twitching face was still staring wordlessly into the darkness, he handed the envelope before walking away, his back stiff with nervous tension. He could scarcely breathe, overwhelmed by an indescribable sense of futility. Picking up the empty can he had left on the bench, he descended the hill.

■ ■ ■

To Tsujimoto Takumi-sama:

The Stewartia trees visible from the exercise yard within the facility have turned a brilliant vermilion, fully ushering in the autumn season. These days I keenly feel the swift passage of time. How have you been?

It is difficult for me to believe that more than six years have passed since the incident in which I committed my irreversible transgression. No matter how many days and months go by, the fact that out of sheer selfishness I took the lives of our family, which above all I should have cherished, and moreover destroyed your life, even after you had devoted all your strength for us all, will never fade away. It should never have happened.

Reflecting on the depth of my folly, I am ashamed to be alive. Perhaps I should atone for my sins with my own death, but even that might well be a selfish and cowardly act. No matter how much I pile up words to express my sorrow and thoughts of remorse, such is now meaning-less—no more than empty noise within these walls. Now, all that is left for me is to live in disgrace, doing nothing more day by day than expressing my unpardonable shame, as I should.

My only concern is about you. How have you been since what happened? I have no right to ask anything of you, but if you could find it in your heart, a single word … No, words are unnecessary. Even a blank piece of paper would be profoundly appreciated if you could send a single message.

I am truly sorry for repeatedly sending you letters. As the cold season approaches, please take great care of your health.

Sincerely,
Tsujimoto Masami

■ ■ ■

"Hey, it hurts. I think it's too tight." Reiko's impatient voice rang out in the car.

"Say what ya want, but all you've got is some cotton cloth wrapped round ya. If it's not tight, there's no point to it," replied Gotō, disparagement in his voice.

The taxi was heading south on National Route 15.

The soft afternoon sunlight streamed into the passenger seat.

Narrowing his eyes, Takumi gazed through the windshield at the scenery. It had been at the end of the previous year that he had gone down this road with Orochi at the wheel, tailing a taxi taking Kawai to her hotel. It felt like long ago.

"Are you all right? We'll be there soon."

Turning to the back, he could see how Reiko was conspicuously concerned about her chest area. For a moment, seeing her transformation afresh, he had no idea who she was.

Her long hair had been mercilessly shorn, revealing the neat contours of her scalp. Her usually thick makeup was applied sparingly, with no eyeliner, eye shadow, or even lipstick. Her eyebrows were lightly drawn, and gone were the Cartier earrings that hung like a string of diamonds, her colored contacts that enlarged her irises, and her false eyelashes. Her hastily assembled clothing, based on Kawai's usual attire, was loose, making it hard to discern the contours of her body. The cotton band wrapped around her chest, half-concealed by a scarf around her neck, made her bust less conspicuous.

"This is ridiculous. I'll end up laughin' during the negotiations. You look too much like a nun," exclaimed Gotō, glancing at her while biting his lip.

"If you do, I'll kill you," replied Reiko, as with a painful expression she adjusted the band.

"Reiko-san, I've informed the other party that you're not feelin' yer best," he said reassuringly, "so don't be afraid to speak up if you start to feel uncomfortable. We'll take care o' things."

The meeting with Sekiyō House was to take place in a hotel lounge. If they could convincingly present Reiko as Kawai and obtain confirmation of her identity, any minor issues that came up could be resolved.

A call to Takumi came from the separate team in Okinawa. The speaker was in an utter panic.

"Bad news! The woman is flying back by herself today."

"Today?"

Kawai and Kuboyama were not supposed to return from Okinawa to Tokyo until two days later.

"What's happened?"

"Don't know exactly, but she's already at the airport."

Kawai had apparently already passed through the security check at Naha Airport and entered the restricted waiting area. She was likely returning to Tokyo on the same airline, the ANA flight departing at 2:25 p.m.

"So, what is her expected arrival time?"

"If everything is on schedule, she'll be coming into Haneda at 4:55."

Considering the thirty-minute drive from Haneda Airport to Sengakuji Station, she would be back home by around 5:30 at the earliest.

Takumi hung up and glanced at his Garmin watch. The LCD displayed the current time, 2:06, along with a heart rate of ninety-five.

"What's going on?"

Reiko's anxious voice came from the back seat.

"Kawai has changed her plans and is returning today alone," he explained.

"That's bad. What are we going to do?"

Gotō could not hide his surprise at the sudden change of events.

"The meeting with Sekiyō House starts at 2:30, and even if it goes long, there shouldn't be a problem. We'll go on as planned. But let's leave the matter of the temple's main hall out of the discussion."

Just to be on the safe side, Takumi decided to arrange for

someone to go to Haneda and call him when Kawai arrived. The mood in the car was now somber.

"There it is!" Gotō said, leaning forward and pointing ahead. The calm he had displayed only moments ago was gone.

The row of buildings on the left had given way to a large parking lot, and now an old three-story building came into view. This was the property owned by Kawai and much sought after by Sekiyō House. A train was passing on the other side of the parking lot. Ahead of the train, the station-to-be, Takanawa Gateway, was under construction.

What sort of fantastical tower was Sekiyō House designing for the site, Takumi wondered. Before he could look more closely, the scene was all swept out of his field of vision.

"By the way, Takumi-chan, were you all right yesterday? Did something happen?"

It was Reiko's voice.

"We met up yesterday so I could check my clothes, and it went on for a while. You seemed to be in a hurry to leave."

He was reminded of his visit to the grave the night before, the old detective's words intermittently replaying in his mind.

"No, no, nothing at all," he replied, his eyes fixed on the road ahead and his mouth shut. He needed to concentrate on the task at hand.

The cab turned right at the intersection, sped up the gently winding slope, eventually coming to stop at the hotel porte-cochère.

**2:22 p.m.**

It was still a little early. Sekiyō House staff had not yet arrived at the lounge.

They were led to a sofa at the back, where the three sat down side by side.

The spacious lounge was filled with spring sunlight, the glass walls reaching to the ceiling of the atrium. Looking to the side they could see the expansive lawn and garden.

"Shall we first order some drinks?"

As he spoke, Takumi glanced at Reiko, seated next to Gotō. He blanched.

"Reiko-san …" His eyes were locked on her fingertips.

"What?" she queried, distracted by the seasonal desserts, whose featured item was strawberries. She did not look up from the menu.

"Ah, nah, I don't believe it!"

Gotō, too, was looking at Reiko's hands. All of her nails protruded well beyond her fingertips and were still coated with ice-gray nail polish. Preparations had been so hasty, with all eyes trained on Reiko's hair and face, that no one had noticed the obvious incongruity.

"Oh no! What are we going to do?"

Reiko, the fingers of her hands spread apart, was staring at the two men, then at her watch.

**2:25 p.m.**

There was no time. Should they push for delaying the start of the meeting?

"For now we can at least do some trimming. We can ask for a nail clipper at the front desk," said Takumi with a reassuring nudge.

"Hold on! Hold on!" exclaimed Gotō, almost bellowing, as he grabbed Reiko's arm to pull her back onto the sofa.

"Oh no! They're here!"

At the lounge's reception desk stood a crowd of men in black suits. Aoyagi was surely the tallest man in the room.

"Just don't let them see your fingertips!"

So saying, with bated breath, they waited for the party to approach them.

**2:27 p.m.**

Recognizing those awaiting him, Aoyagi quickly led his group their way

"Our apologies for keeping you waiting," he said most cordially, followed by his deferential subordinates.

Sekiyō House was represented by, leaving aside the judicial scrivener (apparently a close associate), the section chief, the general manager, and Aoyagi, the latter having full authority over the transaction. The expression on his face remained mild, even as his restless eyes were fixed on Reiko.

Without anyone taking their seats, they reached into their bags with well-practiced ease for their business-card holders. It was imperative to keep Reiko from having to go through this ritual.

"Under the circumstances, with this number of people, might we dispense with the exchange of cards? If such are, after all, necessary, I can later pass them on myself to Kawai-san."

The Sekiyō House staff, caught quite off guard by this diversion, stood motionless.

"You see, Kawai-san's health is not the best," Gotō added by way of explanation, looking at Reiko sitting next to him with an expression of concern. Appearing ill at ease, the Sekiyō men sat down at the opposite side of the table.

Having left the section chief to order drinks, Aoyagi began speaking.

"Thank you very much for taking the time to meet with us."

The polite bows of the entire staff almost seemed to be directed at Reiko alone. Her shaved head had apparently had its effect; there was no sign of suspicion.

"Well now, to get down to business, given our limited time, we should like to take the few and simple steps to confirm the identity of the relevant person." Aoyagi smilingly made his proposal, as he spontaneously shifted his gaze from Gotō to "the relevant person."

Reiko nodded timidly, a nervous glint in her eye, as seemingly trying to bury her nails she plunged her fingers into her handbag in search of her forged driver's license. Around the table conversation had ceased, with all eyes now focused on Reiko's hands.

Takumi felt a most unwelcome outbreak of perspiration. Gotō too had lost his composure and was staring at the handbag under the table.

"I wonder," remarked Takumi suddenly, as he looked toward the window, "whether you gentlemen are aware that this hotel holds a cherry blossom festival every year?"

On the lawn of the garden stood a lone cherry tree. Beneath its broad branches, three middle-aged women were taking photos.

"When every year the blossoms of the tree you see there emerge, for the hotel it marks the beginning of the season, though now the tree is fully in leaf."

He had learned all of this during a preliminary visit to the lounge and was now grateful to the female staff for, though unbidden, informing him.

With everyone's attention diverted to the garden, Reiko dropped her license from her handbag onto the floor. Gotō picked it up and nonchalantly handed it to the judicial scrivener, who discreetly set about checking the watermark. Though the license had been hastily prepared, initial scrutiny was unlikely to expose it as a forgery. The man then turned to comparing the photo with the face of the person before him. As though eager to join in the inquisition, Aoyagi kept his unreserved gaze on Reiko.

Takumi was acutely aware of the tension in his body. If the fakery came to light, all would be over. No matter how many images had been manipulated to make Reiko resemble Kawai, they were far from reality. The only convincing sign was a shaved head.

Clutching the strap of her handbag, Reiko was looking glumly out at the garden.

"You are then Kawai Natsumi-san. There is, may I assume, no mistake about that?" The question was posed in a businesslike tone, with no hint of suspicion.

"Yes," Reiko replied, her voice faltering slightly. For someone usually so spirited, she now sounded surprisingly delicate.

"Your date of birth then, if you please," the scrivener continued, glancing down at the license and documents.

In the 38th year of the Shōwa era, July … "

She coughed and bent forward, the last memorized detail having momentarily escaped her. Gotō quickly held up three fingers on his lap, unseen by the others.

"I'm sorry … July 3rd."

That was her only stumble, and she now proceeded to breeze through the questions about her zodiac sign and current address. As the questioning appeared to continue, Gotō intervened.

"Sir, as I've said before, Kawai-san is ailin'. Can we then keep this brief?"

At a loss for words, the scrivener silently grimaced, then wordlessly looked to the Sekiyō staff for approval. He had now at last concluded his questioning.

It seemed that lingering doubts had been put to rest. Although the staff had appeared eager to avoid the slightest offense to "Kawai," their true intentions had remained from the outset quite inscrutable. That feeling only intensified as Aoyagi intermittently cast sharp glances at Reiko, much to her discomfort.

"Well now, Kawai-san ... May I speak then o' the matter we've discussed ... ?"

With Reiko's consent, Gotō placed several documents on the table, all advertisements for suburban condominiums developed by Sekiyō House. Despite the company's efforts, sales had been sluggish, with many completed units still on the market.

At this time, in exchange for your company's speedin' the contract and for the various favors we're askin', Kawai-san is to consider purchasing several of these ... "

"Oh? How many are we talking about?" asked Aoyagi, much surprised.

"As long as the amount is under 1 billion, as many as ya want. We need to keep some funds for the theater hall."

Gotō's reply caused quite a stir among those members of the staff who until that moment had kept their thoughts and feelings to themselves.

Harrison Yamanaka had correctly intuited that Aoyagi and the rest of the Development Division might very well be indebted to the sales department for huge sums and would thus be most eager to conclude a contract as soon as possible. The tension that had been building around the table abruptly began to dissipate.

"I saw your sketch of the theater hall. It's splendid."

It was Aoyagi who made the comment. As the stern look in his eyes receded, they could see his eyebrows furrowing.

"Who was the architect who drew it?"

"It's by ... "

Reiko, at a loss for words, stared down at her hand, unable to answer the question, ignorant as she was of architecture in general, to say nothing of sketches. Here was another ill-favored turn of events.

"Kawai-san?" came a sudden voice.

The table was quiet, as all eyes turned toward the speaker.

Two men had paused as they passed, both shorn of hair and clad in black monk's robes: a detachment set up in advance by Takumi and his team.

"Gathered for a tea ceremony or the like?"

One of the disguised, a man in his sixties, as though an old acquaintance, was giving Reiko a friendly smile.

"Well, as it happens … " Reiko replied, bowing her head in greeting.

"We're on our way to partake of eel at Nodaiwa with Yamanaka-san and company. You should join us sometime. I shall let you know how we fared."

So saying, he took his leave, together with his companion.

The Sekiyō House staff appeared to have observed the exchange without suspicion and brought the questioning of Reiko to an end. It seemed that the team had successfully dispelled lingering doubts. But it should not have taken so much time.

"Well then," he said cheerfully, as though attempting to bring the meeting to a close, but then immediately heard another voice:

"Excuse me … "

It was Aoyagi. Hesitant at first, he directed an ever so forceful gaze at Reiko.

"The fact is that documents such as these have been regularly arriving at our end."

From his page he took several A4-sized pages and placed them on the table. They appeared to be notices posted as certified mail, the sender being a landowner: Kawai Natsumi.

"The assertion is the same in all of them, essentially that this transaction is completely baseless and counterfeit, that we are being deceived."

It was out of the blue.

"Ah, that's nothin' but some mischief maker, sendin' anonymous letters. You shouldn't pay it any heed!"

Gotō struggled to refute the charge. But apparently Kawai had somehow had wind of the project.

"Interference of this sort isn't the least unusual. Everyone's greedy for the spoils and will do anything to get 'em. Kawai-san, you didn't produce any of this, did you?"

Looking at the notices to which Gotō was pointing, Reiko shook her head.

"No, you see, the person herself is sayin' it's fake. This is insulting, it is."

"Yes," replied Aoyagi, "but I must honestly say that given that such materials have emerged, we cannot help but proceed with caution."

As Gotō had become more assertive, Aoyagi's own pugnacious fervor seemed to cool.

Unable to restrain himself, Takumi now chimed in.

"I've heard that the temple's main hall houses a most magnificent principal image, from the Azuchi-Muromachi period, is it not?" he asked, before turning to Reiko: "I know that it's rather forward, for which I must apologize, but is it possible for us to visit the temple?"

"Do you mean now?" asked Reiko, taken aback, as she turned to Takumi. Gotō too appeared surprised. Now that Kawai was due back in Tokyo earlier than expected, this was a move they would otherwise have wished to avoid.

"Just for a short while," Gotō said, nodding to Reiko by way of encouragement.

"Thank you. And if it's all right, perhaps we can all go together. After all, it wouldn't do to have complete strangers showing you about inside the main hall."

Aoyagi happily agreed to the suggestion and now put the materials back in his bag.

**3:12 p.m.**

In separate taxis, the two groups were heading for the

main hall that stood next to Kawai's residence. Takumi's phone rang. The call was from the team in Okinawa. The voice coming through the receiver sounded even more agitated than before, reporting that the 2:25 ANA flight Kawai was supposed to be on had been canceled due to equipment problems.

"What's with Kawai then?" asked Takumi, losing his composure, as Gotō and Reiko, who had been talking in the back seat, fell silent.

The caller replied that she had not shown up. Passengers on the canceled flight had emerged from the restricted area at Naha Airport, but with no sign of her.

"What does that mean?"

In a disheartened voice, the caller suggested she might have already departed on the 1:15 JAL flight. If that were the case, her expected arrival time in Haneda would be 3:40.

Takumi glanced at his watch.

**3:26 p.m.**

It was too late to go back now.

"What's going on?" asked Gotō, unable to hold back, as the other hung up.

"It's unconfirmed, but it seems that Kawai might arrive home earlier than we thought."

"How much earlier?" asked Reiko anxiously. Takumi glanced at her, astonished to see that she was now wearing white gloves borrowed from the driver.

"The earliest she can get there is around 4:00 … in thirty or even twenty minutes. Well no, it will be later since she'll have to pick up her luggage."

The mood in the car was tense, with no further words exchanged.

**3:32 p.m.**

Having arrived at the temple, the passengers in the two cabs left them idling at the front as Reiko with a stiff face led the group through the gate and into the less-than-spacious temple grounds, her long sleeves suggesting that her white gloves too were plausible as a protection from the sun.

"Good afternoon."

A large, close-cropped man in the working clothes of a priest paused in his task of watering the trees and plants to greet the visitors. This was Orochi, posing as a member of the temple staff. Aoyagi and his team reflexively returned the salutation.

**3:36 p.m.**

The main hall had not so much as an offertory box and seemed more like a treasure repository. Reiko stood before the normally closed front door and opened the padlock with the duplicate key that had been prepared in advance. Removing her shoes, she followed Aoyagi and the others into the tatami-matted interior. The blended scents of rush grass and incense wafted through the air. The dimly lit hall was of simple construction, the floor covered by some fifty mats. This was the first time for Takumi and his team to enter the edifice.

A statue some three feet tall was standing on an altar at the back. Natural light was streaming in from the entrance, softly illuminating the Buddha's serene expression. Everyone stood silently gazing at the statue, and a sense of tranquility pervaded the room as the viewers seemed momentarily to put aside their business.

**3:45 p.m.**

Standing in the rear, Takumi still had his eyes on the Buddha, when Gotō, who had stepped out, tapped him on the shoulder.

"Got a call from Haneda," he said with concern. "It's dire. The nun's just taken a cab and is on 'er way here."

"What? How can that be?!"

"The plane arrived early. Anyway, we have to get out of here right away."

**3:48 p.m.**

Takumi approached Reiko, who was repositioning some articles next to the altar, and offhandedly informed her.

"Kawai's on her way here. Please wrap things up."

"Now?"

Reiko turned around and looked at the men in suits, their gaze on the statue. Aoyagi now was the first to speak:

"I am quite moved. I don't know how to put it, but just looking at the Lord Buddha puts my heart at rest."

In his eyes appeared a glimmer of sincerity.

"The other day I happened to go to the library, where I learned from materials there that this statue was once stolen, back at the end of the Edo period."

This was the first any of them had heard of this, including Reiko, the would-be nun. Unable for the moment to bring the gathering to an end, she felt her face tighten up.

"A foreigner was much taken by the statue and sought to abscond with it as he prepared to leave Japan and return to his native land. Tricking a young courtesan with whom he was entangled, he persuaded her to aid him. Now the woman was secretly in love with the foreigner, so though at first hesitant to comply, she eventually ventured out on a night of the new moon and carried out the plan. Later, the statue was returned to the temple here, and though the woman was suspected of the crime, the kindness of a priest rescued her from blame."

Aoyagi paused, enjoying the recounting, before continuing on:

"Such an example of doing good for the sake of the world has been handed down ever since, has it not?"

"Indeed … "

Reiko was momentarily overcome by the grand storyteller, who was clearly pleased with himself. Takumi glanced at his watch.

**3:54 p.m.**

They had not a moment to spare. He was about to request on Reiko's behalf that they leave when Aoyagi spoke up once again.

"Unfortunately it seems that the courtesan, her love being unrequited, was so stricken with grief that she wound up taking her own life. I read that there is a stone monument on which her name appears. It is not O-taki but rather O- ... "

He looked at Reiko calmly, as though to elicit an answer. The hall fell silent, as none of those assembled could identify a person whose very existence had been unknown to them.

They had run out of stratagems and were too distracted by the pressure of the moment to think of more.

"Yet it couldn't be helped."

The words came blurting out. Reiko was staring at her feet, as though lost in thought. What was it that could not be helped? All seemed perplexed.

"The girl had fallen in love," Reiko said with a faint glint in her eye. "And no one can lie to one's own heart. If you fall in love, it doesn't matter whether the beloved is a foreigner, if he has a family, or if that love is doomed."

The words sounded just as though they were coming from Kawai, whose husband had run out on her and who had been carrying on an affair with a playwright. Such were also the feelings of Reiko herself, who had remained single all her life.

"Shall we go now?"

As Reiko headed for the exit, the others silently followed.

**4:02 p.m.**

"Thank you all very much for meeting with us today."

Looking satisfied, Aoyagi got into the awaiting cab along with his subordinates.

"Oh, oh, I almost forgot!"

The section chief, having first closed his door, now rushed

from his passenger's seat to present as a gift to Reiko a paper bag containing sweets from Toraya. He bowed most courteously. Reiko, beside herself with vexation, clenched her teeth as she struggled not to allow her face to show how inwardly she was seething. Yet now at last the cab was set to depart.

After watching the car disappear from view, Takumi rushed back to the gate to lock it.

**4:06 p.m.**

The key did not turn easily and was perhaps misaligned. In his agitation, he felt his fingers rebelling against him, as though they were those of another. Hastily trying to reinsert the key, he dropped it.

"What are you doin', man?"

Gotō's angry shout made things all the worse. Takumi's hands were shaking; he tried again and this time succeeded, before quickly getting into the remaining cab.

**4:09 p.m.**

Sweat was forming on his forehead, and his mouth was dry, as though coated with sand.

The middle-aged driver unhurriedly asked for the destination. "Just go!" he barked in reply.

A taxi approached from the opposite direction, slowing as it passed. The passenger, a woman wearing a familiar hat, was removing her sunglasses and, phone in hand, openly weeping. For what reason? Perhaps it had to do with her lover, Kuboyama, still there in Okinawa. As Takumi looked back, he saw the vehicle come to a stop in front of the Kawai residence.

He checked his watch.

**4:10 p.m.**

The breath he had been holding was now escaping through his nose. His heart rate had jumped beyond 140.

"It's all so stupid … " Sitting in the backseat, Reiko sighed listlessly.

With no particular destination, the taxi merged onto the national highway. Takumi was leaning back into his seat, his sweat-soaked shirt clinging to his body. He stared at the brake lights of a compact station wagon running just ahead, feeling dazed.

"Oh, I forgot to tell you."

It was Gotō's voice, sounding exhausted.

"It seems Takeshita-san is dead."

# 6 —————

The long *kotatsu* table with its sunken leg warmer was set with cooking pots over burners; in the air was the light fragrance of kelp broth. Through the window came the scattered glow of nighttime Ginza's countless neon lights.

"Ultimately, it all comes down to whether, to the very end, you can truly believe in yourself," declared Aoyagi, gazing contentedly into the portable burner's blue flame. "Data, market conditions, what so-and-so said, common sense ... Honestly, none of that matters to me. Those who are swayed by such considerations are just dumb shits."

His subordinates, who, half in their cups, had been merrily caught up in the festivities, stopped to listen to his words, their faces filled with gravity and awe. The feeling that he had brought them completely under his spell filled him with immeasurable satisfaction.

"No matter how desperate the situation, no matter how much others look down on you, no matter how disgusted you are with yourself, as long as you can go on, deep down, believing in yourself, everything will work out. Such people are strong. They can survive anything."

Aoyagi, more talkative than usual, spoke to each of his men in turn.

"Even this time around, everyone said it was impossible. It's always like that. 'It's impossible to find such a piece of land; it's effort wasted.' Maybe some of you here had already given up. But I always believed it was possible. I was certain. I never doubted myself, not even once. I never abandoned myself, even at my lowest point."

The acquisition of the land in front of the new Yamanote Line station had been concluded a few days earlier. Despite some initial misleading advisories, a meeting at a hotel with the landowner Kawai Natsumi, verification of her identity, and a visit to the temple where Kawai served as priestess all convinced them of her authenticity. The transaction, including the sale and transfer of ownership, had proceeded with unusual speed, despite some cautious voices within the company. Ultimately, Aoyagi, with the help of the head of the legal department, forcefully pushed through the decision.

The door opened, and thinly sliced Tajima beef was brought in on a large plate. The younger employees set about cooking it at the table.

"What is to be done with the land?" asked a younger colleague next to him, glass in hand, who worked in the management section. He was among those who had contributed to the negotiations. In his earnest expression was something ever so slightly different from respect for a superior who had overcome great obstacles: He seemed to be fawning.

"Nothing's definitive, but it looks like a hotel may be built."

Upon acquiring the land, the company had immediately created a cross-departmental special team. The project would likely proceed with this team at its core.

"Would you care for a drink, sir?"

From across the table, Aoyagi's secretary, her eye shadow

rendering her gaze more alluring, was concerned about his nearly empty glass.

"Oolong tea please," he replied curtly, quickly averting his gaze. He felt a stirring in his lower abdomen, aware of the Viagra stashed in his pocket.

The celebration had reached its peak and now wound down as the participants took their leave.

"Here, consider this as a little extra," said Aoyagi, handing a few 10,000-yen notes to one of his subordinates as they all variously headed off for a second round of partying. He then boarded a taxi alone. His destination was the high-rise hotel he had recently been frequenting.

Upon arrival, he went straight to a room upstairs and rang the bell. After a moment, the door opened, and the secretary who until a short while ago had been huddled around a hotpot with the rest of team now peeked out.

"Well now, a reward for all of your hard work ... "

Without so much as a deferential nod, she gave him her usual vivacious look, as though testing him. She released the doorknob and disappeared into the back of the room. Aoyagi stepped inside and followed her. The soft feel of the carpet under his feet gave him a visceral sense of his accumulated fatigue.

She was standing by the window, her back to him. He quietly drew near and wrapped his arms around her from behind.

"With this, you'll be made president, won't you?"

"Probably ... "

He buried his face in the nape of her neck. The mingled scents of her hair, makeup, clothes, and skin, all conveying a certain sweetness, tickled his nostrils. It had been a long time. Though familiar, they irresistibly stirred his desire.

"So then you'll find a job for me?"

She gripped Aoyagi's thick arms with both hands. Her face, illuminated by the pale light of the floor lamp, was reflected in the window. She looked intensely anxious.

Aoyagi silently nodded as he squeezed her slender body, feeling the elasticity of her buttocks through the thin fabric of her tight skirt. Thanks to the drug he had taken, his penis was throbbing, becoming painfully stiff, as he relentlessly pressed it against her behind.

"That means that I won't be just an errand girl and that I'll be transferred to the next project, right?" She sounded needy.

He withdrew her arms and through her white blouse squeezed her breasts, rubbing his thumbs over their promontories. Her slender jaw rose, and she emitted a longing sigh. Restraining her as she wriggled, he put his other hand under her skirt and roughly rubbed her inner thighs. As he drew back to stroke her deeper from below, she leaned against him, the sound of her exhaled breath turning to a squeal.

"Tell me you'll make me a member of your team. If you don't, I won't see you again." Her brow knotted as she made her plea.

"I will."

He placed her hands up against the window as he ran his own hands up her satin skirt, relishing the smooth feel of it, then yanked it up, the voluptuous contours of her black underwear defining her shapeliness.

"Are you full ready to do it, you little slut?"

Aoyagi was breathing unevenly as he got down on both knees on the floor and plunged his face into her backside. Her cries of pleasure increased as he opened her sweat-damp legs and, through a gap in her underwear, thrust his tongue into her moistness. Her moaning grew all the louder as she gave in to ecstasy.

■ ■ ■

A waitress, dressed in an old-fashioned uniform, placed an antique cup and saucer on the scratched table and walked away.

Takumi sipped his second serving of coffee and looked out the window.

Perhaps because he was several stops away from the terminal station and its huge downtown surroundings, there were, even now at dusk, few people walking about. A sparse number, workers finished for the day, were being drawn into the subway entrance. Their shadows, stretching across the surface of the asphalt and fading moment by moment to the color of twilight, formed a one-of-a-kind, mottled pattern. As he gazed at the street scene in the afterglow, he was endlessly reminded of the recent months.

The massive scam targeting the land in front of the new Yamanote Line station had often been faced with crises that could have brought disaster to the project, but they had, by the skin of their teeth, succeeded in ensnaring Sekiyō House and swindling the company of almost all of the money they had initially hoped to take. Amounting to 10.3 billion yen, the funds had been immediately converted to virtual currency, laundered, and distributed to each team member's clandestine account. As of yesterday, Takumi had received his share.

The endeavor had not only been the largest in scale since his first days as a land swindler; it was also the toughest in terms of its degree of difficulty. Now that he had overcome the severe challenges and obtained more money than he could spend in a lifetime, he felt in a certain sense fulfilled. Even so, he felt weighed down, sluggish, perhaps, he thought, because of Takeshita's death.

According to one report they got, Takeshita had been found dead in a love hotel, the victim, it appeared, of a drug overdose. Though he had brought it on himself, his sudden demise no doubt bore down heavily on all those with whom he had had a deep connection.

Perhaps this is why the usual banquet to celebrate the successful completion of a project had not been held. Takumi had not seen Reiko since the day they had escorted Sekiyō House into the temple; he had not seen Gotō since the day of the settlement. And when he tried to call them, there was no answer.

Harrison Yamanaka had contacted him several times after the settlement, asking that Takeshita's share instead be transferred to his account for safekeeping. Takumi had replied that he would make the arrangements as instructed and concluded their conversation by proposing that they have dinner together sometime soon.

On the phone, Yamanaka had treated the news of Takeshita's death with a perfunctory expression of regret. Given Yamanaka's past actions and temperament, Takumi was inclined to think there was nothing strange about his apparent detachment. On the other hand, when he recalled Yamanaka's frequent clashes with Takeshita, he was dogged by the suspicion that the man knew something about how he had died.

He remembered the old detective's words: "He's the one who brought your family to ruin."

That day, he had been quite taken by surprise on meeting the cop there at the Yokohama cemetery, to which without fail he made annual visits. The man had probably ascertained the anniversary, anticipated his appearance, and then waited for him. About his personal matters, including the family company's bankruptcy, he had seemed very well informed. Still, without proof or evidence of swindling, he had not taken him into custody, and this suggested that he was as yet unable to finger him as being involved with Yamanaka and his fellow fraudsters. Could it be he was merely attempting to trap him into a confession?

If, however, the old detective's words were true, he had been doubly deceived by Harrison Yamanaka. He had hoped that by living as a swindler in the present he had been freed from the past, and yet, could it be, that ultimately he had remained for all that time thoroughly bound up in it? No, that could not be!

No matter what society might think of him, he would, for his own sake, go on doing what he was doing. There was no other option. But even as he mumbled all this to himself, he could not suppress the suspicions that flashed across his mind.

At the store entrance he heard a clerk's voice loudly greeting the arrival of a customer. A large man in a trendy jersey was standing there. It was Orochi. As Takumi raised his hand in greeting, Orochi saw him and immediately strode over.

The young man sat down across the table from Takumi, a pouch under his arm. This was the first time the two had met since Orochi had posed as a member of the temple staff in the presence of the Sekiyō visitors. Takumi had heard that he had been sent to help with pre- and post-funeral arrangements for Takeshita. The rites had been held before family members only. Wary of the authorities, Takumi and the other members of the team had kept their distance.

"It must have been a tough time."

"It couldn't be helped. All junkies meet a bad end."

He spoke as though referring to the death of a total stranger. Takeshita's relatives, it seemed, had been quarreling over the inheritance and their other rights and interests, while scornfully ignoring the lowly Orochi.

"What are you going to do now?"

Now that Takeshita was gone, Orochi appeared to have been left to decide on his own what to do. He said he had no intention of involving himself in any of the groups that Takeshita had led.

"I have no plans," he said. "What should I do? I might become a sushi chef. You can use your skills anywhere in the world, like in Ginza restaurants. And I hear you can make a bundle at it."

Takumi frankly told him that learning a craft requires steady and persistent effort and that he did not think the other had the temperament for such.

"Your thinking is out of date," came the reply. "You don't have to go through all of that nowadays. You just watch a video or attend some sort of school. Easy as pie."

Orochi burst out with a lighthearted and cheerful laugh.

"What about you, Takumi-san?"

Just a few days before, he had booked a flight to Taiwan. The stupendous sum defrauded from Sekiyō House meant that the police investigation could be expected to be more intense than usual. Just to be on the safe side, Takumi had decided to leave Japan. He would climb the peaks, towering more than ten thousand feet, and then take a Southeast Asian tour.

"Oh, before I forget …" Orochi extracted a bundle of photos from his pouch.

When Takumi became aware that Orochi was helping to sort through Takeshita's belongings, he had asked him to save anything that might reveal something about Takeshita's past, rather than throwing it all away. He had no high expectations. In the end, Orochi had not been allowed to touch any of the computers or phones that might contain various data, as the higher-ups in Takeshita's circle had had access before anyone else. Even though Orochi had come away with only photos, such was still better than nothing.

Takumi thanked Orochi, saying he would like to buy the photos rather than pay him for his time and effort.

"No need for that. They were all to be thrown out anyway."

"No, I can't just let it go. Please take this."

Somewhat forcefully, he thrust a department store bag into Orochi's hand.

"Takumi-san … is this for real?" Orochi exclaimed as he

peeked inside, then rolled his eyes. The bag contained 3 million yen, cashed in an underground bank from overseas. Takumi was determined to give the money to the man who had, without compensation, done so much for him.

"Yes, for real," was his reply, in imitation of Orochi's tone. He now began looking one at a time at the more than two hundred photographs.

The prints, from various times, were chronologically a disorderly mix of years past; some were faded, as though developed from film, while others were relatively new, produced from digital images. The images were all quite ordinary, most from golf competitions or resorts at home and abroad, with a tanned Takeshita smiling into the lens with a woman or his friends.

Takumi sped up his search. With only a few photos remaining, his hand stopped at one. There was a date in the lower right corner. It was not recent. It was probably taken at the front entrance of a venerable restaurant in Yokohama's Chinatown. Against the backdrop, with imposing bamboo planted on both sides, stood three men, as seen in a long shot. The one smiling on the left was Takeshita, the photo taken before he acquired his ceramic teeth (most of his natural front teeth were missing, most likely due to tooth decay or too much paint thinner). In the middle stood Harrison Yamanaka, wearing a well-tailored suit, clasping his hands behind his back, and displaying a serene expression. Takumi had had no idea that the two men had been associated with each other for so long.

He then looked at the small man on the right. Straining his eyes, he almost let out an involuntary scream. Here somehow was the face of a man he had never forgotten, the face of a man who had once often shown him kindness and given him words of encouragement.

"Did you find anything of interest?"

Orochi, who had been contentedly playing with his phone, looked up.

"No," Takumi calmly replied and returned his gaze to the photo.

■ ■ ■

The following week, he set out early in the morning for the suburbs.

"It's all right to take everything?"

A junk removal man, wearing a shocking-pink polo shirt and gloves was peering at the storage unit, as though estimating the value of the contents.

"Yes, please go ahead."

On hearing the reply, the man began moving with practiced skill the "unneeded items" out to the light truck parked outside.

Takumi also stepped into the small storage room, measuring less than four tatami mats.

He had rented the space some time ago as a makeshift storage facility. Inside he had set up shelves of various sizes, now crammed with mountaineering gear: boots, clothing, rainwear, backpacks of various sizes, tarps, and ropes bundled according to length and thickness. He had grown quite attached to it and taken it on many expeditions, and always treated it with care.

Tidying up his personal belongings had continued over the past few days and was now at last coming to an end. The day before, he had moved out of the one-room apartment he had been using as a nest and disposed of the Suzuki Jimny he had driven into the ground. He had also had his ticket for Taiwan refunded. This had been his last task.

As he glanced at a shelf cluttered with sleeping bags and titanium mugs, a folding knife caught his eye. It was one he had constantly used ever since his first camping excursions. It weighed heavily in his hand as he gripped its severely worn brass and cherry-wood handle. From the meticulously sharpened 3.5-inch blade he unfolded came a dull glow. He closed it, then tucked the knife into his back pocket.

After watching the truck drive off, he took a train to Yokohama. Arriving at the station, he leisurely strolled the afternoon streets until he reached a familiar park. It had been years since his last visit, though he had often come here when he was younger, either for some particular reason or for no reason at all, including many a time with his wife before they were married. He now walked on the park's grass, dotted with fountains and rose beds, and sat down on one of the benches arrayed in a row.

His view unobstructed, he looked out beyond the white balustrade to the sea spreading out before him. To his immediate right was moored an old passenger-cargo ship, now decommissioned; further out a suspension bridge cut across the pale blue sky, leading to reclaimed land on the far shore. Turning his gaze to the left, he saw a modern architectural pier protruding from the harbor as though a small island were gently rising from the water. Behind it lay high-rises, sketching a futuristic skyline.

He heard the faint sound of waves striking the quay and in the breeze caught the scent of the water. Thin clouds, seemingly brush-painted, were drifting across the sky.

Gazing out at the sea, bathed in soft sunlight, he had quite lost track of time when his phone rang. On the screen he saw Nagai's name. The vibrations continued off and on and then, as he was still looking at the screen, ceased. Intending to return the device to his pocket, he hesitated. He had not been back to see Nagai since bringing him dumplings, and although they had exchanged emails, they had not been in touch by phone.

After hemming and hawing, he traced his thumb over the display and returned the call.

"Sorry. I was in the toilet."

"About the mail you sent," a tone of surprise in his voice … "Is it really all right to donate it all to that research institute in Kyoto?"

"Yes, just as I said in my message."

"Eh? After all you went through to get it … "

Takumi imagined a look of perplexity in the face of the other.

"Well, with the advance in research, maybe they can do something to fix up your face."

The offhand reply seemed to have an effect. Despite expressing reluctance, Nagai now promised to carry through with the request.

Takumi was about to end the call when a further word from Nagai held him back:

"Uh," Nagai began. He sounded hesitant. "I met her … "

"The girl from the online game?"

Taken aback by the unexpected news, he had posed a foolish question. Nagai then told him that the two had recently met in person late at night in a park near Nagai's apartment. Even seeing him face to face, she was unchanged in the attitude she had conveyed on the phone. They had decided to start dating.

"We're talking about getting married next year."

As Takumi remained sitting on the bench, a group of tourists, apparently foreigners, passed from his right, clearly much enjoying the sunny weather and the view of the harbor. And now a young family with a child was coming from the opposite direction. They were chatting, the parents holding the hands of their young daughter walking between them, and occasionally picking her up as they listened to her innocent squeals. He watched them, as they disappeared from view.

"So we're thinking of having a simple ceremony with just

family members. Would you come, Takumi-kun?" There was a hint of suppressed anxiety in his voice.

"Of course I'll be there … It wouldn't do to have the groom there looking friendless, now would it?"

Nagai laughed merrily.

"I'll be getting in touch with you when we get the details sorted out."

With the call now ended, Takumi felt his tension eased. Leaning back against the bench he closed his eyes and for some time did not move. Finally, resolving to sit up, he turned his attention again to the phone in his hand. If, he thought, he needed to contact anyone, he could always use the brand-new burner phone he had obtained. Then, after first glancing casually about, he gave the phone a mighty toss. As it left his fingertips, the aluminum body drew a gentle arc, flashed in the sunlight for a moment, and with a slight splash disappeared into the water. By doing this, he lessened the likelihood of Nagai ever being implicated, as long as he himself kept silent.

He stood up from the bench and went to a convenience store within the park, where he mailed off a letter, the address on its envelope indicating the destination: Chiba Prison. He had written the letter some time before but had then revised it.

He left the park and followed the path beyond. Lining each side was a row of ginkgo trees, lush with bright new leaves. The sunlight filtering through the branches was casting shadows on the ground beneath. He suddenly felt his entire body enveloped by the boom of a ship's horn, long and vastly reverberating across the neighborhood and silencing the buzz of the city.

He vaguely thought for a moment that he was hearing once again the sound of the waves, but he did not turn back.

■ ■ ■

The pop of a can being opened filled the break room. Aoyagi, there alone in the morning, stifled a yawn as he sipped his canned coffee.

After a deal settlement, he could not sleep, no matter how much his body craved slumber. Even spending the night drenched in sweat and grasping the naked body of a woman had no effect on his condition. Closing his eyes only led to incessant, scattered thoughts racing through his mind, leaving him in the end to resign himself to insomnia. Particularly this time, perhaps because he had been for a short time caught up in most unusual circumstances, he felt extreme fatigue, both mentally and physically. Yet on the positive side he sensed that he was gradually quieting his excited nerves and returning to a normal routine.

He walked over to the window. A soft bundle of light was pouring down, illuminating the uniformly straight-edged buildings below. As he rolled the bitterness of the coffee around in his mouth, his eyes took in the fresh and invigorating scene.

Just a few months before, when the weather had obliged him to wear a coat outside, he could only view these streets with suspicion. Now they seemed to welcome him unconditionally.

Suddenly he remembered … He looked up. The surrounding high-rises were making cutouts of the sky, clear and blue in the gaps between them. He strained his eyes but could not see any airplanes. His wife and daughter were to depart on a morning flight for New York, there to undertake a campus tour of a school. By now they might be looking out from a window at a sea of clouds over the Pacific.

His cellphone rang.

"I've heard you've just snatched victory from the fatal jaws of defeat."

Through the receiver, the lively voice of a friend was

pounding on his eardrum, as if the speaker himself had reason for triumphal joy.

"So you already know. Let me treat you to dinner the next time we meet."

Had it not been for his friend's invitation to a snack bar that night, he might not have met Sonezaki of AKUNI Holdings or stumbled on the miraculous property in front of the new Yamanote Line station.

"Let's celebrate your impending presidency," the friend said jokingly.

"Let's not be hasty."

Promising to align their schedules, Aoyagi ended the call …

Leaving the break room, he passed the Commercial Business Department head Sunaga, who at the recent emergency executive meeting had been the sole opponent of the purchase. Though aware of Aoyagi's presence, Sunaga did not so much as look at him.

"You could at least thank me for clearing out your inventory."

Aoyagi's words were met with stony silence and a face tinged with hatred.

Returning to the work area, Aoyagi immediately sensed something amiss. Development Department #4, responsible for the purchase, was in an uproar. He walked up to one of his subordinates.

"What's happened?"

"It seems that while preparing to conduct a survey of the land, we were reported for trespassing. The police are there now, inquiring about the situation."

"The police?"

Had there been some miscommunication, or was this some sort of harassment?

"What? It's ours, is it not?"

"I don't know."

Leaving his useless underling, Aoyagi rushed by taxi to the scene. Along with the company's cars, there were two police vehicles. In the middle of the parking area marked off by red pylons, uniformed officers and Aoyagi's men were arguing.

"What's going on?" he snapped at a subordinate anxiously making a call.

"The person who reported us …"

Looking over, Aoyagi saw a man in his fifties, dressed in a suit and standing apart from the crowd. Noticing Aoyagi's gaze, he walked over to him.

"I represent Kawai Natsumi," he said. A glossy lawyer's badge was pinned to his lapel.

Perhaps Kawai had later regretted letting go of the land and had confided in him. It was not uncommon for personal feelings to become entangled in land transactions. Aoyagi now formally introduced himself, even as he fought the urge to raise his voice.

"We have already purchased this land. Even if she's changed her mind, from our perspective …"

"No, no," replied the lawyer, sounding exasperated, "as I've been saying, there was no such sales contract to begin with."

"What do you mean? The contract has been sealed and the ownership transferred."

"I'm not aware of any such thing. At least Kawai-san knows nothing about it. Incidentally, when did you conclude the alleged contract?"

Aoyagi provided the date, as he tried to suppress his agitation.

"That's strange. I spoke with Kawai-san on the phone that week. She said not a word about selling the land. As I am managing her assets, she would surely have consulted with me if there had been any talk of such a transaction."

Unable to fully comprehend what the man was saying,

Aoyagi was at loss for words. The lawyer looked back at him with a puzzled expression.

With whom had the contract been made? Was the nun who had shown them the statue of the Buddha not Kawai Natsumi? Had they signed a contract with and paid money to someone other than Kawai? The very thought sent a chill down his spine.

Standing next to him, explaining matters to a policeman, was the employee who had originally been assigned the site. Aoyagi now seized him by the shirtfront:

"You said there was no problem, you fucking bastard!"

He punched him in the face and sent him sprawling over the neatly arranged pylons. He was now moving without thinking, his pace quickening. A voice called out from behind, but he ignored it as he crossed the sidewalk and stepped onto the highway. He tripped, as the screech of brakes and the blare of horns struck him from behind. Just as he thought he had crossed the road, he felt a strong blow at his waist, and his view flew upside down. Blue sky filled his eyes, and for a moment he had the sensation of floating in air. He smelled exhaust fumes and saw pebble-strewn asphalt directly beneath him. His leg was throbbing with pain. Forcing himself up, he saw that his neatly creased slacks were torn, revealing a bloodied knee.

"Are you all right?" came the panic-stricken voice of a young man who had stopped his car and run over to him. Aoyagi began to run again.

The familiar temple gate came into view. A delivery truck emblazoned with the courier's logo was parked in front; an elderly uniformed driver was unloading packages from the rear hatch. Pushing him aside, Aoyagi limped into the grounds and rang the bell at Kawai's residence. There was no response. He frantically pressed it again and again, demanding instantly to know the truth, even as he wished that he could remain forever ignorant.

After what seemed an eternity, the door cracked open. A shaven-head woman peeked out from the gap with a frightened look on her face. Aoyagi stared at her uncontrollably. The person standing before him was a complete stranger, clearly not the same person as the nun who had shown him the statue of the Buddha. Kawai was by all accounts the only resident here.

"Is Kawai … Kawai Natsumi-san here?" His own voice seemed to be that of another.

"Yes. I am Kawai … "

The world seemed to move back a pace. His vision blurred; beginning with his fingertips, his body was going numb. He could hear the rapid pounding of his heart.

The delivery man approached with a cardboard box. Aoyagi grabbed his arm.

"Tell me this isn't Kawai Natsumi!" he shouted, pointing at the bewildered woman. His hands, as though broken toys, were wildly shaking. The delivery man, the box still in his hands, was no less confused.

"What's all this about," asked the woman in a loud voice, her face now drained of color. "I'll call the police."

Aoyagi stumbled toward the old man and grabbed him by the shoulder.

"Say she's not, you fucker!"

There was a scream, but he barely heard it.

"Tell me, tell me she's not!"

Someone was thunderously whispering in his ear.

■ ■ ■

The storm-like tumult had ceased.

"Hey, are you listening?"

The executives gathered in the conference room were all sternly gazing at Aoyagi.

"What happened?"

"Explain yourself!"

"So, you were conned by land swindlers, right?"

The jeers were coming nonstop from all sides.

"Speak up, you fool!"

Sunaga, head of the Commercial Business Department, was particularly aggressive. Standing alone, he pointed at Aoyagi, a vein throbbing on his forehead, his expression unnaturally animated, as though he were a child merrily torturing an insect.

"It's all your fault. Everything!"

"Is it my fault?"

Gathering himself, Aoyagi slowly stood up. The room fell silent, with everyone staring in surprise.

"Idiots! It's obviously the fault of everyone who believed in it!"

Muttering to no one in particular, he left his seat. He felt rising within him laughter he could not suppress, and with each burst of it he sensed everything he had built since joining the company collapsing beneath him. It was as though the chains that had bound him had now fallen away. He suddenly felt oddly liberated.

Putting his hands in his pockets, without glancing at anyone, he strode out of the conference room with a spirited chortle.

■ ■ ■

With its faint scent of grass and trees, the night air was clear, caressing his neck now and again to remind him of the heat emanating from his sweat-drenched body.

"Don't go silent on me. Tell me. Where is it?"

From the phone pressed to his ear he heard the urgent, low voice on the other end. As though to quell his own inner turmoil, the speaker disclosed the location and ended the call.

He caught the sound of other voices and saw coming toward him on the walkway a young man and woman, both dressed in suits. They were affectionately exchanging words as they passed him. In their hands, illuminated by the road lights, were, alongside their briefcases, matching paper bags. They appeared to be returning from a business meeting. Their free hands suddenly became entwined, as, now a single shadow, they moved on down the street.

Their ordinary lives seemed to him to belong to a world quite apart from his own.

Might he simply disappear, he thought to himself. After all, he could still cling to a modicum of freedom. He did not require approval or acknowledgment from anyone.

Out of the corner of his eye he caught the sight of a moth lying on the ground, its grayish wing half torn apart. On closer inspection he saw it feebly struggling with its tiny legs, as thin as cast-off eyelashes. For a moment, his gaze was fixed on it. Then gently he crushed it with the sole of his shoe, rubbing it against the pavement before heading toward the neighborhood's towering high-rise.

After checking in at the entrance of the jazz restaurant, he purchased a ginger ale and headed for his assigned counter seat, where the person he was to meet had already arrived and was pouring champagne into glasses.

"Sorry to be late. After all, I was the one who asked to meet you here."

He took a seat on the high stool to the right.

"No need to apologize. I've just arrived myself, and as it is, I was hoping to see you. I'm taking off from Haneda tomorrow morning."

Harrison Yamanaka glanced at the ginger ale on the counter.

"Would you care to join me?"

A champagne glass had been poured for him. Takumi declined, citing a stomach condition. Yamanaka seemed surprised, and he stopped smiling.

"It's been difficult this time, but thanks to you, we were able to succeed. I wish once more to express my gratitude."

They raised their glasses to each other. The ginger ale tasted cloyingly sweet, as if it had been made into a concentrate.

The mid-floor restaurant spanned three stories in an open loft design. From the top tier, where they sat, they could look down on the dining guests below, a grand piano, a double bass, and two drum sets arranged on the stage. Either because it was a weekday or because the members of the band were just a bunch of fledgling instrumentalists, there was a striking number of empty seats before the show.

"When was it? The last time we were here?"

Harrison Yamanaka had his gaze fixed beyond the stage. The glass wall reflected the metropolitan backdrop, the garden below now shrouded in darkness. The lights from the surrounding buildings were dazzling.

"It was four years ago."

Takumi had first been brought here after successfully acting as the frontman for one of Harrison Yamanaka's transactions. The target property, now obscured by newly constructed buildings around it, had at the time been visible from where they were sitting. They had the fifty or so top-floor counter seats to themselves, reminiscent of last time, when Harrison Yamanaka had booked them all.

"In just four years, we've come a long way. The view from here has changed significantly ... No doubt neither of us could have reached this point alone."

Yamanaka seemed to be hinting at future work together and took a sip from his glass before setting it down again on the counter.

"As for myself, I believe I can go further. Rather than reminiscing about the past here, I want to move forward, even if it involves some risk. I believe we can reach places quite beyond all imagination."

Takumi listened in silence, staring at his ginger ale.

"Unfortunately, Gotō-san and Reiko-san have expressed their desire to make this their last project with us."

Perhaps, Takumi surmised, they had all been in contact without his knowledge.

"What do you intend to do?"

Harrison Yamanaka gave him a knowing smile.

When had he ceased to feel uneasy about that smile? It seemed that from the moment he had first met him while working as a driver for an escort service, Yamanaka had been endeavoring to draw him into the inner recesses of himself.

His heart began to race. He licked the flat ginger ale and parted his chapped lips.

"Will Gotō-san and Reiko-san wind up like Takeshita-san?"

For a brief moment, the smile vanished from Harrison Yamanaka's face.

"We shall see. It will depend on their attitude, but some sort of penalty may need to be called. Such is unavoidable. To gain something, you must lose something. Rest assured, when we act, we shall do so without blundering. In this wonderfully convenient world of ours, paying a mere million can bring in someone from overseas to do a clean job of it. In Takeshita-san's case, they injected him in one go with twice, no, perhaps four times the amount needed. I saw the footage later; it was quite something to see him sweating like a waterfall, gasping like a carp. His teeth were so white, he looked like a smiling skull."

He was speaking more rapidly, his eyes gleaming with delight, almost struggling to convey the overflowing images into words.

"Was it Sasaki-san, the elderly man who helped with the Ebisu project and went to Nagasaki? He was amazing. Knowing he was cornered, he surrendered almost without resistance when they came for him. And here's the interesting part. Listen. When they were about to strangle him, he asked to be allowed as his last wish to eat some pudding. Just ordinary pudding. Luckily, the agent understood a bit of Japanese and acceded to the request. It is all quite moving. He took the pudding from the fridge, savored it to the last, and then quite on his own put the decoy rope around his neck. His expression … How shall I describe it? It was like that of a newborn or a Buddha, as if he had grasped some divine truth. I saw it all on video and yet still regret not having been there in person. It was truly a sight to behold."

Takumi took a sip from his glass. The diluted ginger ale barely bubbled, with no sweetness remaining.

"Yes, no doubt a most satisfying dénouement."

The open curtains behind the stage began to close from each side. The night view coming in from giant glass windows was slowly being ever so slightly blotted over by the reflection of the black cloth.

"Indeed, indeed," Yamanaka replied, as he stifled the chuckling emerging from between his teeth. There was the cool crackling of ice nesting in the champagne chiller and, simultaneously, the popping sound of tiny bubbles in the glass he had filled.

"Yes, and that is also how you entrapped my family."

Takumi turned to face Yamanaka. The fear that had lingered

in his heart had vanished. He pulled out a photo from his jacket and threw it onto the counter. It showed Takeshita, Yamanaka, and the medical broker who had deceived both him and his father.

"So you knew?"

His theatrical smile did not waver, and he continued in a matter-of-fact tone.

"It's a shame your family was burned to a crisp. They weren't pigs to be roasted whole. Their deaths were all so useless, utterly for nothing."

"Shut up!"

Takumi stood up from his stool.

He had been a fool to be for so long in thrall to this demon in human form.

"Your father was the director, was he not? A responsible yet stubborn man who never opened his heart to us. Then we learned that he was interested in young girls, and when we brought him a high-school lass to snuggle with, he became as obedient as could be. He was on hands and knees, weeping, as he begged us to keep it all from his family. A truly family-oriented man … When—at some time or other after we started working together—I learned your real name, I was oddly impressed that you could be the son of that tearful Lolita lover."

"Shut up, I'm telling you!"

His heart was pounding.

"Let us return to the subject. What will you do, Takumi-san? Unlike the other traitors, you will continue to work with me, am I right?"

He returned the champagne glass to the counter. Taking from his jacket's inner pocket a familiar orange-colored phone case, he played with the grained leather, as if to be reminded of its texture.

"And you think I'll go along?"

"Of course, you will!" replied Yamanaka with a burst of laughter. "What else would you do if you gave up swindling?"

Mindful of the turmoil within him, Takumi was silent.

"Do you intend to return to the worthless world? Haven't you seen enough, in all its absurdity? Whatever advances in civilization there may be, the world is ugly and twisted, and all because human beings are the creatures they are. So prejudice, poverty, and conflicts never end. The rich get richer, and for their sake the poor must go on tasting bitterness. I see those who live honestly, playing by the rules, as fools. Just look at them: They're all the more unbearable because they see themselves as cloaked in the robes of justice. What do you wish to do in a world you believe is so bound up in lopsided rules?"

Takumi had heard this sermon many times before, back when he first learned that "Uchida" was an alias for Harrison Yamanaka and had then begun working in earnest with him. His initial skepticism regarding such talk had long since worn away, and he had ceased to doubt.

"Shut up, I said!"

"I would ask you to see the world for what it is. Do not be deceived by all the falsehoods of conventional wisdom and the spirit of the moment. Believe in yourself as the land swindler you are."

Takumi wanted to block his ears.

"Stop!" he tried to shout with all his strength, but all that emerged was a rasp.

"Overcome your fate. This is not the time to dwell on the past. Let us live in the moment."

Harrison Yamanaka's jaw relaxed, as he extended his arms, the phone case still in his right hand, an easy smile on his face.

Takumi looked back fondly on the days when he was could go about his work mindlessly. There was no need to contemplate either the past or the future; he had only to immerse himself in the turbulent currents of the present. Was he engaged in the life of a swindler in defiance of the world, as Yamanaka had said, and truly living in the moment? Could deceiving others bring him peace?

"You can always start a new family. You'll come up with a better one."

Words perhaps intended to soothe had pierced his heart.

The golden sea at which his wife, son, and he had gazed together on Senagajima in Okinawa vividly came back to him. He felt on his arms and chest the warmth radiating from the boy's breathing body and caught the scent of his wife's hair as she gently rested her head on his shoulder.

"The beautiful sea," she had murmured. "Will we ever see it again?"

He had wanted so much to spend more time together; even a little more time, idly spent, would have been enough. All that had been swept away, as though the man before him had kicked a stone off the side of the road.

"Enough, you lying bastard!"

Takumi pulled his folding knife from his back pocket, locked eyes with Yamanaka, and unwaveringly opened the blade.

"What do you intend to do with such a toy?"

Yamanaka remained seated, still playing with the phone case, as he opened himself up to Takumi.

"Stab you, then confess … everything."

Gripping the knife in his right hand, he stepped back to gauge the distance. He had the sensation of floating in air, even as he was oblivious to either the touch or the weight of the knife.

"What foolishness! What will that accomplish? Will it change anything?"

Takumi attempted to reply, straining his voice. His clenched teeth would not part; he could do no more than widen his glaring eyes.

He felt the blood rushing in reverse from the toes of his feet and filling his entire body, as sweat broke out from every pore on his scalp. His vision narrowed and blurred, with Harrison Yamanaka's face being all that he could see.

"Nothing will change, you know?" Yamanaka murmured, as though explaining the providence of nature to a child. "Neither you nor your past."

"Shut up, I'm telling you!"

As he shouted, he moved forward, holding the knife at waist level and lunging toward Yamanaka's chest. The man got up from his stool and stood motionless, without any attempt to flee, staring intently at the knife. Takumi instantly and unflinchingly attacked.

■ ■ ■

The new shoes that his wife had selected, despite their chic design, were not for running. With every step, his right ankle rubbed against the leather, the discomfort quickly turning to pain. Tatsu endured it all as he pushed through the crowd to ascend the escalator.

It had been only a brief time before that Takumi had contacted him to ask whether they might meet up. He had been picking out books at a large store in Tokyo in preparation for a cruise starting two days later when he received a call from an unknown number. With an odd premonition, he answered to hear the same voice he had heard at a cemetery in Yokohama. He struggled to remain calm, as he had held out little hope of any contact. The person mentioned no more than the name of the nearest station

248 | KO SHINJO

but then shortly thereafter called back, informing Tatsu in a sub-dued voice that he would be meeting Harrison Yamanaka at a jazz restaurant.

With his weakened muscles, Tatsu ran up the escalator, his breathing erratic, as though his heart were close to bursting. Upon reaching the top, he spotted the restaurant.

"Police!"

The young male clerk at the reception counter, taken aback by Tatsu's menacing air, made only a token attempt to restrain him. Ignoring the protest, Tatsu rushed on, opening the door from which the music was coming. Enveloped in the lively, swirling sounds, he scanned the dimly lit interior. There was a figure on the upper floor. A man paying no heed to the stage below was looking down at his feet. His was a face Tatsu had never forgotten.

■ ■ ■

The tip of the knife caught the recoiling Harrison Yamanaka in the abdomen but then stopped without penetrating further.

"Too bad," he said, bending over and looking up with a smile.

Before he could even react in surprise, Takumi was seized by the collar. With no time to resist he was violently pulled toward the other, and Yamanaka's head came crashing into his face. He reflexively closed his eyes as a sharp pain ran through his nose, accompanied by the sound of shattering bone.

The knife slipped from his hand. His face contorted, he half-opened his eyes to see Yamanaka pulling back one leg, and in the next instant a knee was in his face with skull-crushing impact. His broken front teeth gouged into his gums, and in his mouth was the taste of blood. Yamanaka's face moved away as he slammed Takumi down onto the hard floor.

"It's not that being prepared eliminates worries, but it was good I had this. It's been adopted by the United States Marines for a reason, the quality being indeed exceptional."

The now groaning Takumi looked up to see Yamanaka lifting his torn shirt to reveal what appeared to be a knife-proof vest. He was holding by its grip a metal object, his index finger placed near the center. It took only an instant to see that it was a gun disguised as a phone.

The lights of the restaurant dimmed as applause erupted, soon followed by a lively piano tune as the performance began.

"Those who live in memories might be happier remaining there."

The music filled the restaurant, drowning out his voice. Harrison Yamanaka slowly cocked the hammer of the gun. His expression, though somber, seemed strangely filled with parental affection. Takumi lay on the floor, unable to move, his gaze was fixated on the gun muzzle as though drawn to it by a powerful magnet. As he stared, the opening seemed to grow larger, at last swallowing up his entire field of vision in silent darkness.

A dry crack pierced his ears.

■ ■ ■

As he dashed up the stairs two at a time, he saw Yamanaka looking down at the floor from across the counter. His face, sparsely illuminated by the stage lighting, was nearly identical to the one he had seen so many times in the interrogation room. In a frenzy, without thinking, he charged at him. Glimpsing Tatsu, Yamanaka turned and ran toward the emergency exit.

"Yamanaka!"

As Tatsu started after him, he saw a dark form on the floor. A man was lying there spread-eagled, his face bloodied and his nose crushed. Tatsu recognized him as Takumi, who was writhing in the dim light; looking closely, he saw a black stain spreading from the gray T-shirt beneath Takumi's jacket; kneeling down, he touched the area, his fingertips turning red. The shirt was soaked as if drenched in water, an extraordinary gush forming a pool of blood.

"You all right?"

As he removed Takumi's shirt, black liquid bulged at his soaked abdomen, further inundating his side of the floor. It appeared he had suffered a deep stab wound by a sharp object or had been shot.

"Hey, anyone!!"

Tatsu pressed down on the wound, while looking around. There was no one nearby. The dimly lit seating area filled with loud music as two drums reverberated in apparent competition.

"Hang on there!"

Takumi could only groan, his broken teeth poking out from his swollen lips. Beads of sweat had formed on his forehead, and he had grown pale. Tatsu's efforts to stop the bleeding had failed; he knew he could do nothing more.

"You're going to be all right! Not to worry! Do you hear me? You're going to make it!"

There was no response. Takumi showed no sign of consciousness. Tatsu shouted into his ear, telling him that he would not let him die there.

A restaurant employee, seeming to have sensed something amiss, peeked around a pillar.

"Call an ambulance! Hurry!" Tatsu bellowed, shifting his gaze. Seeing the exit sign glowing green in the dark, he entrusted Takumi to the man and ran, opening the heavy door and descending the fluorescent-lit staircase. The stairwell was open all the way to the first floor. He looked down and saw no one below.

Holding on to the railing, he sped down two stairs at a time, his knees on the verge of buckling. On the railing, wet with white paint, and on the steps, he was leaving traces of Takumi's blood. His new shoes bit into his ankles, giving him excruciating pain, as though his flesh were being gouged out. His heart rate had become dangerously rapid and though gasping for air, his lungs remained starved for oxygen. Having come this far, he could not abandon his pursuit of the man he had now at last caught sight of.

Yet now he could only hear the stomp of his own footsteps on the metal stairs. Reaching the ground floor, he leaned against the door to the outside. Again gasping for air, he glanced around. There was not a soul to be seen. The ground lights dotted the path through the park as nocturnal stillness spread out before him.

■ ■ ■

A news report on the ship had informed him that the capital region had had several days of rain over the previous week. This morning, he left home early and boarded the train at the nearest station, headed toward the city center. In the commuter-packed car it was impossible to move. Unable so much as to grab a strap, he was jostled by his fellow passengers from all sides. He could hardly wait for arrival at the terminal station. Each time the train swayed, the human walls pressed in, forward and back, left and right. The moist heat of a plump man's back in front of him was unbearable; the music leaking from behind him was more than usually annoying. If he had heeded his wife's advice to rest another day, he might now be in quite a different mood.

They had returned from their round-Japan cruise the night before. They had embarked from Yokohama on a large passenger line and spent more than ten days visiting various ports, where they savored local delicacies while engaged in endless conversations about their daughters' latest news and future plans. Tatsu had thus experienced a richness of life that had been quite unimaginable during his working years. Yet in his heart of hearts he felt he had not fully enjoyed the excursion.

Peering between the heads of other passengers he could see sections of the windows bathed in bright sunlight. Craning his neck, he looked out at the monotonous residential landscape passing by.

After purchasing sweets at a department store there in the terminal, he transferred to the subway and walked to his destination: a university hospital. At the reception desk he announced his visit and was told where he might find the patient he had come to see. The bed in the ward on the third floor was empty.

He made inquiries at the nurses' station and then headed for the courtyard facing the ward. On the way he encountered in the lobby a young detective, who with a tense look bowed low to him.

"Keep up the good work," Tatsu said in greeting, then asked: "How's our man doing since the surgery?"

"His prognosis appears to be good. The doctors say he might be discharged next month."

The surgeon had noted that the man had been lucky, the bullet having missed his vital organs.

"Has he said anything?"

"Yes, he'll answer any question asked. He may have a hole in his gut, but he seems to have manned up, prepared for anything. If he coughs up info, we'll be able to eradicate the scammers root and branch. We might even nab the chief perp, that Harrison Yamanaka. And all thanks to you."

This the young man said with a touch of pride. Tatsu offered him further words of encouragement and took his leave, continuing on his way to the courtyard.

In the well-maintained garden lay a broad expanse of fresh green grass, towering zelkova trees creating a patchwork of shade. On benches that had been placed here and there sat patients in light-green hospital gowns, passing time as they pleased, and among them was a white-haired male patient talking to what seemed to be an attending police detective and two other men in suits. He was holding a crutch and had a bandaged nose that looked painfully sore, but overall his expression, even seen from a distance, appeared serene.

Takumi had been looking at the detective, but now he noticed Tatsu. It was their first proper encounter since that night overlooking the sea at the cemetery in Yokohama, illuminated only by outdoor lamps. Here under the sun, it was not only the light that made for the slight awkwardness between them.

Their eyes met. In Takumi's softened look, there appeared to be a gleam of determination.

What to say? Tatsu approached unhurriedly, the box of sweets in hand, looking for words to begin a conversation.

■ ■ ■

In the restaurant, with its long and straight plain-wood counter, patrons all dressed in refined attire were enjoying their customary drinks and appetizers. Most of them were Singapore locals, casually nibbling on snacks and conversing with their companions. Another noticeable group was Japanese, a likely reminder that the locale was an international financial city, with more expats from large corporations and businessmen on work-related visits than tourists. Although Makita did not recognize any acquaintances in the crowd, some among them might have moved here, drawn by a more favorable tax system compared to Japan's.

"Six more years, eh? That's a long time."

Looking over, Makita saw Ōkawara sitting next to the counter, staring into space. His voice conveyed a hint of weariness. The fairness of his skin from his days in Tokyo had been lost to the sun, and the thinning hair on his forehead highlighted the age spots typical of an elderly man. The wrinkles at the corners of his eyes were tinged with the colors of hardship.

Ōkawara, who would reach his seventieth birthday next year, was one of Makita's clients. They had met about five years ago at a seminar Makita regularly held in Japan, where Ōkawara expressed his wish to leave as much of his wealth to his family as possible. Heeding his wishes, Makita recommended moving to Singapore, where there were neither gift taxes nor inheritance taxes. After relocating, Makita had been entrusted with managing Ōkawara's assets, and they occasionally met for meals such as this to catch up.

"Six years will go by before you know it, especially when you can enjoy sushi with Japan-like scrumptiousness," Makita reassured him, pouring more sake into the other's cup.

It was not uncommon for expatriates to struggle with life abroad and return to Japan midway. Ōkawara had now been here for four years. After six more years, making it over a decade spent outside Japan, he would be able to avoid taxes on his overseas assets. All that was needed to preserve both Ōkawara's wealth and Makita's profitable commission for managing it was perseverance.

"This is nothing compared to Kyubey in Ginza. You might be satisfied with this since you're still young, Makita-san."

Makita chuckled wryly, discreetly glancing around to see if Ōkawara's voice could be overheard by anyone else.

In the center of the counter, a middle-aged Japanese chef was explaining to the young Singaporean couple sitting in front of him both the anatomical parts and the provenance of a tuna block that had been shipped directly from the Tokyo fish market in Toyosu. Despite his broken English, with its schoolboy accent, his manner of speaking eloquently conveyed his feelings.

"It's hot, the language barrier is frustrating, and everywhere

I go, I see familiar faces. Even the Japanese sitting over there live in the same condo as I do."

Ōkawara continued to express his irritation, tipping his glass cup filled with chilled sake. His face flushed from the alcohol, he seemed to bear some slight resentment toward Makita.

The air conditioning thermostat had been set low, isolating the interior from the muggy outside air. Given the traditional Japanese *sukiya*-style interior and sophisticated furnishings, one might well have supposed that the restaurant was in Ginza or Akasaka.

"And speaking of Japan ...," said Makita, attempting to improve the mood by changing the subject to one he had suddenly remembered, "it seems that there's been quite a to-do back home about all those land swindlers."

Ōkawara paused, his hand stopping midway to his cup.

"What do you mean by land swindlers?"

"Haven't you been watching the news? Real estate fraudsters. It's quite a big deal at the moment. Even Sekiyō House was tricked out of, what, 10 billion yen?"

"10 billion? That's not pocket change. Was Sekiyō House always that gullible?" asked Ōkawara, looking doubtful.

"It's a huge scandal. Just yesterday, one of the crooks, some young hospital patient, was arrested. They were all over the TV, all looking really guilty. There's even a woman among them who shaved her head to pass herself off as the nun who owns the land."

The news was being reported on a daily basis. As Makita recounted the astounding and hard-to-believe exploits of the swindlers, his voice grew spontaneously louder.

"That's quite an old-fashioned scam. Who would still fall for it?"

Ōkawara had relaxed a bit, his eyes softening with amusement.

"You have quite a bit of real estate in Japan too, don't you? How are you handling that?"

Makita was only managing Ōkawara's assets in Singapore, not those in Japan.

"There's not much to handle," Ōkawara responded dismissively. "I used to leave it to others, but I don't trust anyone anymore, so I occasionally go back to check on things myself."

"Excuse me for intruding on your enjoyment," came a sudden interjection in Japanese.

"Turning toward the voice, Makita saw a gentleman, slightly older than himself, who had been sitting across the way from Ōkawara. He was dressed in a crisp white shirt with an upright collar; what looked to be an antique watch was peeking from his sleeve cuff. A solitary diner, he had been quietly enjoying his sushi as he habitually twisted a double ring on his little finger.

"I've recently moved here, but, in fact, a friend of mine in Tokyo has been a victim of the very land fraud you were discussing."

Introducing himself by the name of Uchida, the gentleman flashed an innocent smile, as though to dispel all suspicion.